Paulina stepped o... terrace and had n... Sebastian even in the dim light.

Facing the howling storm underneath one of the brick-bordered arches, he stood unflinching as a violent wind ripped fronds from the cluster of royal palms several feet away.

A sudden flash of lightning illuminated the rippling muscles of his back, the deep indentation just above the waistband of his trousers and the pale fluttering cloth he held in a tight grip. Hungrily, she drank in the sight of his broad shoulders, set against the punishing breeze. There was something dashing about him even in relative stillness—a certain grace and strength in the way he performed even the most mundane tasks.

The white thing in his hand was a shirt. He pulled it over his broad shoulders and made short work of the buttons, then turned around—and caught Paulina staring at him.

"Did you need something else?" Sebastian asked.

"Oh, I—I need help with my buttons. And my—well, my laces." She tried to say it matter-of-factly—what room was there for blushing hesitancy after all that had happened?—but Paulina was aware of the embarrassment coloring her voice.

Author Note

Not too long ago, while perusing nineteenth-century documents in the Dominican Republic's national archives, I came across a fascinating account of a man who had been forced to sign a marriage contract under threat of imprisonment. While he lived in a different time and city than the main characters of this book, this kernel became the basis of Sebastian and Paulina's story.

I decided to set it in San Pedro de Macorís, a city in the southeast of the island only two hours from where I've lived most of my life. I had been captivated by its architectural beauty on earlier visits, and I was eager to learn more about the city whose thriving industry led to it being nicknamed Sugartown.

I hope you enjoy reading Sebastian and Paulina's story as much as I have enjoyed writing about them!

LYDIA SAN ANDRES

Compromised into a Scandalous Marriage

Recycling programs for this product may not exist in your area.

ISBN-13: 978-1-335-72334-5

Compromised into a Scandalous Marriage

Copyright © 2022 by Lydia San Andres

For questions and comments about the quality of this book, please contact us at CustomerService@Harlequin.com.

Harlequin Enterprises ULC
22 Adelaide St. West, 41st Floor
Toronto, Ontario M5H 4E3, Canada
www.Harlequin.com

Printed in U.S.A.

Lydia San Andres lives and writes in the tropics, where she can be found reading and making excuses to stay out of the sun. Lydia would love to hear from her readers, and you can visit her at lydiasanandres.com or follow her on Facebook, Twitter and TikTok @lydiaallthetime.

Harlequin Historical

Compromised into a Scandalous Marriage
is Lydia San Andres's debut for Harlequin Historical.

Look out for more books from Lydia San Andres coming soon.

Visit the Author Profile page
at Harlequin.com.

Chapter One

⸎

Sebastian Linares had always felt more at home in the sugarcane fields on the outskirts of town than among the ornate masonry houses of San Pedro de Macorís. The only thing he liked about being in the bustling port town, in fact, was the sea-fresh breeze that swept through the buildings, dispelling the heat and disporting itself with hats and hems and tree branches.

The breezes were the furthest thing from Sebastian's mind as he dismounted from his horse and tied it to the hitching post outside the red-and-white building that housed the town's fire brigade. Warm, humid air pressed against his skin, and Sebastian was in the act of reaching into his pocket for a handkerchief with which to mop the rivulets of sweat running down his temples when he noticed a coach rolling to a stop on the opposite side of the street.

The coachman jumped down from his perch and opened the shabby black door to reveal a flash of white fabric, even brighter than Sebastian's freshly laundered handkerchief. A small brown hand appeared out of the darkness of the carriage, and after it followed a wide-brimmed hat that even Sebastian could tell was not fashionable.

And then, like a budding rose unfurling its petals, a woman emerged from the carriage, unbending and straightening as the coachman helped her down. Her white skirts, full over a nipped-in waist, danced slightly in the stifling air when her heels struck the paving stones. Though she wore no beads or jewelry or anything that would catch the light, Sebastian felt as though he'd been dazzled.

He was fairly sure he hadn't made a sound, so it must have been the strength of his gaze that drew the woman's attention. She tilted her head, and when her hat brim moved to reveal her smile, it was as if the sun had broken through the clouds.

Paulina Despradel. She had been a quiet, unobtrusive figure in the background the two times Sebastian had visited the Despradel *quinta* to complete his business dealings with her brother, Antonio.

There was nothing unobtrusive about her now.

It was clear from her expression that she had recognized Sebastian. Belatedly, he doffed his hat and inclined his head in greeting. Her face brightened, and she started across the street, turning to tell her protesting maid, "Surely my brother wouldn't object to my stopping for a neighborly chat."

The hand she extended toward Sebastian was encased in a glove made out of fine netting and ringed at the wrist with a profusion of lace; resisting the urge to linger over it, he squeezed it briefly between both of his own as they both inclined to press their cheeks together.

Sebastian was far from an expert in women's fashions, but even to his untrained eye her frock seemed overly laden with frills and furbelows. A shocking quantity of lace had been employed liberally throughout, frothing each ruffle and flounce and giving the effect that she was being swallowed by fabric.

"Good morning, *vecina*," he said, making sure to use the formal *you* when he added, "It's a pleasure to see you. What brings you to town on such a stifling morning?"

The property Sebastian had bought the year before was far enough away from the Despradels' home that he rarely saw Paulina and her brother. Although he had come across Antonio in the streets of San Pedro a time or two before, this was the first time he had seen Paulina in town.

"I'm on my way to Don Enrique's store to buy some things for a little gathering my brother is hosting tonight in honor of my birthday." The brown skin of her cheeks looked a little flushed, and Sebastian would have thought it was from the heat if her eyes hadn't been shining.

He inclined his head. "My kindest regards to you."

"Thank you, Señor Linares. My apologies for not issuing a formal invitation, but I would love it dearly if you could stop by the house and celebrate with us."

"Please, call me Sebastian," he said and hesitated. Being neighborly was all well and good, but he did have a lot of work left to do at the mill. "As wonderful as that sounds, I'm afraid I won't be able to attend. I was, however, also on my way to Don Enrique's. Shall we walk together?"

"That would be lovely," Paulina said, and they fell into step along the narrow sidewalk, the maid trailing behind them. "I must say, it's so nice knowing that we've neighbors again. Particularly in Villa Consuelo, abandoned as it's been for so long. I'm glad there's finally someone to breathe life into it once again."

"I was hoping to do just that," Sebastian said. The house, at least a hundred years old and built solidly enough to withstand earthquakes and hurricanes, was still empty of furniture, the property as dilapidated as it had been when he'd purchased it almost a year before. He had big plans for it, though. And he'd get to them, soon, maybe, when he wasn't so busy at the mill…

Paulina glanced at him from under the brim of her oversize hat. "How are you liking our little town?"

It took a second for Sebastian to realize that she had taken him for one of the many Cubans who had settled in San Pedro after fleeing the war at home. When he did, he didn't bother to correct her—he *was* recently arrived from Havana, after all, and as far as he was concerned, the less the townspeople knew about his past, the easier a time he would have fitting in among them.

"There's nothing little about it," he replied. "It's grown remarkably in the last few years—or so they tell me."

"Is it anything like Havana?" she asked curiously.

"In some ways." Sebastian had given little thought to the differences between both cites, save for the fact that he'd been part of a happy family in one and of a diminished one in the other. He forced lightness into his tone. "Havana is like an old dowager countess—grand and glamorous and secure of her place in the world. San Pedro is beautiful, to be sure, and growing more prosperous by the day, but it wasn't that long ago that the town was a fishing village."

Her face lit up with a sudden smile. "Can you imagine the conversations they would have if they could meet? The venerable old countess and the little fisherman?"

Sebastian couldn't help echoing her smile at the fanciful thought. He made no response, however, as they had reached the corner.

All six of the tall, thin doors leading to Don Enrique's store were open to let in the light and breeze. Paulina paused in one of the doorways, as if to savor the sight of the neatly arranged shelves and gleaming display cases. Don Enrique dealt in imported wares, and the array of beautifully packaged goods must have captured her imagination.

Sebastian was well aware that this was where he ought to bid her a good day while he continued on about his business. He had half a dozen things to do in town, most of them more important than stopping at Don Enrique's for some candied pineapple for his business partner's widow.

It still stung, thinking of Dilia as a widow. Sebastian glanced again at Paulina's face, as if the wonder in her expression could arrest his sudden onslaught of pain.

"Will you look at those feathers?" she said suddenly, nodding at the counter that held what looked like odds and ends for trimming dresses or hats.

Taking off his Panama hat, Sebastian followed her through the store as she made her way to the counter and pointed at it. The feathers were half as long as his arm and tinted in brilliant jewel tones. "What kind of bird do you think could have produced such things?"

"Not one I'd ever like to meet," he assured her.

To the right, a laugh rose from a trio of young women as they held silk flowers up to their hats. Sebastian couldn't help but notice how Paulina's gaze flew immediately to the trio and lingered, growing wistful. One of the girls glanced over and caught Paulina's eyes; though she gave Paulina a curious smile, none of them came over to say hello. Not acquaintances, then.

"The ribbons are wonderful," Paulina said, half to him and half to the young clerk lounging against the ladder fixed to the shelves. She pointed at one of the spools under the glass of the counter. "Might I have a look at the red one?"

The clerk obliged, and Paulina wound one end of the velvet ribbon around her fingers, rubbing it lightly with her thumb. The scarlet looked festive against the golden brown of her skin.

"That color would look lovely on you." One of the young women had broken away from the rest and was regarding Paulina with a frank, open smile. "I can't wear it myself, but it suits your complexion."

"Do you really think so?" Paulina asked, looking pleased.

"If it's not too forward of me, I concur," Sebastian said. "As a matter of fact, I was just thinking that—"

A hand reached out and clamped around Paulina's wrist. "We won't be needing any ribbons today, thank you."

Antonio Despradel, Paulina's brother, was one of those men who thought their money and their standing in society conferred on them the authority they otherwise lacked. Sebastian had met the man only a handful of times while in the process of purchasing the sugar mill Antonio had inherited. Carlos, Sebastian's business partner, had once remarked that Despradel reminded him of a rooster. Not the fighting kind, but the kind that lorded over the chicken yard, pecking at the hens and puffing out its chest.

It had been an apt comparison.

Without releasing Paulina's arm, Despradel began to stride to the other side of the room, saying, "Heavens, Paulina, sometimes I wonder if you aren't twelve years old. This is why I don't like leaving you on your own, you know. You've scarcely more discipline than a child."

Sebastian was nobody's hero, but neither was he enough of a cad as to let a woman be mistreated in his presence. He reached Paulina and her brother in two long strides, reaching to tap the shorter man's shoulder.

"That's no way to touch a lady," he said when Despradel turned, thin lips parted in surprise.

Sebastian didn't want to fight. Not here, among these luxurious and fragile-looking wares. The best way to avoid that, he'd learned from experience, was to inject the promise of violence into his voice. "In fact, that's no way to touch anyone at all. I'd let go of her if I were you."

Despradel's lips spread into a genial smile, even as his gaze flickered from side to side as if to ascertain if other people were looking at them and how much he could get away with. Sebastian had spoken quietly, but sure enough, almost all of Don Enrique's patrons had stilled in anticipation of a dispute. Silence hung over the store for one long second, then Despradel released his sister's wrist and ostentatiously stepped away, his hands raised.

"No need to get upset," he said with ringing bonhomie. "Just trying to hurry my sister along—we've a lot to do before her party tonight, and she is awfully prone to distraction."

"All the same," Sebastian replied with exaggerated politeness that almost certainly did not match the look in his eyes, "that's no reason to handle a woman so roughly."

The mutual dislike crackling between the two men was broken as Paulina, now freed, swept past them. "I'd just as soon not be handled at all," she said tartly. "Come, Antonio, if you're in such a hurry."

The spectators, realizing there was to be no bloodshed, returned their attention to their shopping.

Sebastian stepped back, letting the menace in his gaze serve as warning to Despradel. The other man responded to it with a smile so insolent that Sebastian felt something inside him snap.

Despradel's eyes widened at whatever he saw in Sebastian's eyes, but all Sebastian did was brush past him on his way to his sister.

"Paulina?" he said when he reached her. "I've changed my mind—I should be pleased to attend your party."

"Tío Sebas!"

Few things in Sebastian's life were as gratifying as the enthusiasm with which the four little boys greeted him as he approached the elegant pink house at the end of the street.

They'd been tossing the ball around in front of the house, but at Sebastian's arrival the boys, whose ages ranged from twelve to a tender four, clustered around Sebastian. Experience had taught them to look in Sebastian's pockets for treats; he let out a bark of laughter as eight eager little hands dug into his pockets with more enthusiasm than finesse—to the detriment of the sturdy black fabric of the suit he usually wore into town. It took them mere seconds to extract the marbles and *pilones* he'd bought at Don Enrique's, and he knew that it would take even less time for them to finish off the red sucking candy shaped like miniature mortars and pestles.

It was a heartening—and welcome—change from the wariness with which the boys had regarded Sebastian since the day he'd ridden into town with news of their father's collapse at the mill. David, the youngest and Sebastian's godson, had acquired a most disturbing habit of bursting into tears whenever he saw Sebastian, as if he was a herald of death, come to announce the passing of another loved one.

"Tío Sebas, will you take us to look at the *corriente*?"

asked David, who already sported a red border around his mouth to match his flushed cheeks.

The current? "Erm, what?"

"He wants to go see the workmen who are putting up the posts for the electrical wiring," José, the oldest, explained. "Mamá said it's dangerous to be around the men while they're working, but she won't mind if you take us."

Sebastian must have walked past them, but he'd been so intent on Paulina that he hadn't even noticed them. He laid a hand on José's curly head. "I'm afraid I can't today—I've some business with your mother. Is she home?"

"She's inside," David piped in. "Trying not to melt from the heat because these damn people think everyone should dress like they're in Europe instead of on a damn tropical island."

That sounded like Dilia, all right.

"I see." Sebastian managed to say it gravely, though it took plenty of effort to hide his smile. "Will you go and ask if I can come in? I wouldn't want to intrude if she's, ah, not dressed as a European."

David scampered up the steps. Sebastian leaned against the slim white columns that supported the arched porch and watched the other boys as they played with their new marbles.

A peal of laughter from inside the house let him know that David had delivered his message. "Come in, compadre," Dilia called, poking her head out of an upstairs window.

It was cooler inside the house, though not by much. Dilia was sitting so close to the window, it was debatable whether she was inside the house or out. She was indeed fully and very properly dressed, in a black skirt and a high-necked shirtwaist. The painted fan in her hand was her only concession to the heat, though her gray-streaked curls were plastered to her temples.

"Hot, isn't it?" he said as he dropped a kiss on her cheek and the box of candied pineapple on her lap before taking the seat opposite hers. The mahogany armchair with its embroidered cushion had once graced the parlor of her Havana house, and the familiar sight never failed to make Sebastian feel a little wistful for old times. "Feels like it'll storm today."

"I don't doubt it," Dilia said, setting her needlework on the round table next to her. "I sent for some ice water. Will you stay for a cup of coffee?"

"Don't go to any trouble on my account." Sebastian set his Panama hat on his knee. "I've got to get back to the mill. I only came into town to make a deposit into your account. There should be enough in there to carry you through the next couple of months."

"That's right." Dilia's grin might have made her eyes sparkle, but it filled Sebastian with apprehension. "Why waste your time having coffee with old widow women when you could be strolling with pretty girls? I saw you walking with the Despradel girl earlier."

He gave a brief nod. "She invited me to a party she's having tonight."

"And you accepted? Well, well…" Dilia's right eyebrow arched.

Sebastian shrugged. "It would have been rude to decline the invitation."

"That's never stopped you before," Dilia observed. "Oh, don't get me wrong—I think it's perfectly delightful that you're finally getting acquainted with your neighbors. I'm just surprised that you consented to a party. You act as if you took a blood oath to spend all your time at the mill, you know."

Antonio Despradel had driven the mill to ruin through mismanagement. It had only been with great effort that Sebastian and Carlos had been able to turn a profit in the first year—and there was still so much to be done. He lay awake at night thinking of it more often than not. It wasn't only that Carlos had invested his entire fortune in modernizing the mill to Sebastian's exacting specifications—a fortune that would have been at Dilia's disposal if it weren't for the labor-saving but ruinously expensive cane-processing machinery Sebastian had been convinced he needed to turn the mill around. No, it was the people who weighed on Sebastian's shoulders. The workers at the mill, most of whom had mouths to feed. Carlos's family. All the people who depended on Sebastian's ability to eke out enough of a profit from a crowded market.

"I have an obligation to you and the children" was all that Sebastian said.

"Yes, and where will we be if you work yourself to death?" Dilia snapped her fan shut and struck Sebastian lightly on the arm with it. "You are barely twenty-five years old, Sebastian, with no family of your own. Talk to pretty girls. Go to parties. Heaven knows you deserve to enjoy your life."

"What I deserve is to enjoy this delightful ice water without having to fend off an arranged marriage," Sebastian said, smiling at Dilia's enthusiasm. "Save the matchmaking for someone else, my friend. The last thing *I* need is a wife."

Chapter Two

The scent of the ocean, so strong in the center of town, receded sharply as the Despradel carriage sped inland. At Paulina's feet were the numerous parcels Antonio had acquired for her party—his preferred brand of champagne, as well as the imported nuts and dried fruits that he favored. On the seat opposite hers, her brother scowled at the correspondence he had picked up at the post office while she'd been speaking with Sebastian.

Absently, Paulina rubbed her sore wrist. Her brother's grip had left a mark just above the lace that edged her detestably frilly gloves. She would have preferred much simpler ones, but Antonio purchased all her clothes, as he had since she was a child, and he insisted on as great a quantity of frills and furbelows, as if to communicate to anyone who saw her that the Despradel family's coffers were as full as they'd ever been. The more dire their financial situation became, the more lace sprouted on Paulina's clothes. It was the same twist of logic that had made him spend a ruinous amount in Don Enrique's store, though it had only added to their already massive debts.

"Have you ever thought about selling the *quinta* and buying a house in town?" she asked her brother. "Particularly now that it's being wired for electricity. Just think, not having to go to the bother of filling oil lamps and—"

Antonio glanced at her over the papers in his hand. "Trust a woman to put her petty conveniences over a centuries-long legacy," he remarked. His eyebrow quirked in the way it always did when he was about to say something sarcastic or mocking, and Paulina immediately regretted her remark. "By all means, let us abandon our ancestral home and lands just so you won't have to go to the bother of filling a lamp or two."

Paulina didn't bother to point out that Antonio hadn't bothered to hold on to the rest of their inheritance— namely, the money left behind by their parents as well as the sugar mill that had been built by their father when he converted what used to be pastureland for the family's cattle ranch into sugarcane fields. The Despradels' fierce opposition to the use of enslaved people for the hard labor required by the sugarcane industry was one part of her family's legacy she could be proud of.

She tugged again at the lace bordering her gloves and started when it tore away from the white netting. She glanced up quickly to see whether Antonio had noticed and was surprised to see that he had not gone back to his correspondence but was watching her through narrowed eyes.

"Are you carrying on with Sebastian Linares?"

Paulina blinked at the sudden change in subject. "Carrying on? Of course not. Why would you say such a thing?"

"Why wouldn't I, after seeing how you were simpering over him at Don Enrique's?"

"I was only inviting him to my party tonight. It's about time we got acquainted with our only neighbor. He's lived there for an entire year and we've never made any social overtures—I didn't want him to think we're ill-mannered recluses. In any case," she added, "he might not come."

Sebastian hadn't seemed particularly inclined to when she'd issued the invitation, and though he'd accepted it firmly enough after the altercation with Antonio, Paulina knew better than to get her hopes up. It had been months since she'd gone into town, and longer still since a handsome young man had paid her any attention. That Sebastian Linares had any interest in furthering their acquaintance beyond the strictly neighborly seemed like a schoolgirl dream.

Still, she couldn't deny that the prospect of seeing him again was making her heartbeat quicken.

Antonio's lip curled disdainfully. "I don't know if I care to associate with someone like that—and I won't have you doing it, either."

Paulina knew better than to argue with her brother when he was in one of his moods, but she couldn't help asking, "Like what?"

"Can you really be so naive? You're twenty-one years old, Paulina. It's time you learned a little about life." Carelessly crumpling the letter in his hand, Antonio leaned forward. "Sebastian Linares is not our social equal. In fact, I have every reason to believe he's been lying to conceal the fact that he's of inferior birth. None of the respectable Cubans who've come over have heard of him. Nobody knows who his people are."

It might have been naive of Paulina, but she could scarcely understand why it mattered. Even from their short acquaintance, it was clear that Sebastian Linares was a much better man than her brother, for all his proud lineage, could ever be.

Antonio had gone back to his correspondence without waiting for or likely even expecting a response from

Paulina. She turned her head to look at the sugarcane fields speeding past.

The rest of the morning passed nearly as fast, what with all the preparations for this evening's festivities. Changing out of her one good frock and into her thin, shabby everyday dress, Paulina arranged flowers in vases, nailed bunches of greenery over the missing paintings in the parlor and helped polish the few remaining pieces of silver. She'd been barely seven years old when her parents died, but she remembered clearly the bustling excitement that used to permeate the rambling old house whenever her parents held one of their frequent parties. They had plenty of servants then, almost a dozen of them, all kinder and more energetic than the pinched-face maid and sullen man-of-all-work her brother employed. Even so, her mother would always plunge elbows-deep into whatever needed to be done.

"The preparations are half the fun of a party," she would tell Paulina as she arranged Castilian roses in a cut-glass vase.

It wasn't all that long ago that the Despradels' *quinta* had rung with cheer and music, but one wouldn't know it to look at the dingy chintz on the upholstered chairs or the scuff marks on the once-polished mahogany tables. Even the wicker and rattan chairs she had lined up along the house's back veranda looked the worse for wear. Paulina was grateful for the lush green landscape beyond the veranda, which the guests would face while sitting. It was much more beautiful than any of the paintings Antonio had sold over the years.

In the parlor, through which the guests would pass on their way to the veranda, the flowered wallpaper had proven no match for the tropical humidity; great patches of it had begun to peel away from the walls. Paulina surveyed it critically and decided that it wouldn't be noticeable once the afternoon light began to fade.

The fact that she was wearing the same dress as that morning, however, *was* unfortunately noticeable. The high neckline was unfashionable for evening wear—it had been ages since Paulina had attended any parties, but she knew that much. No matter. The house was clean, there were fresh flowers in her hair and Sebastian Linares had promised to come. Paulina could hardly ask for anything more.

Except perhaps for clear skies.

Smoothing down one of the many ruffles that besieged her dress, Paulina seated herself on the veranda and peered up worriedly at the overcast sky. No one would come if it looked like it was about to storm—the roads out here weren't paved, and carriage wheels didn't take kindly to mud.

The first guests began to trickle in before Paulina could work herself into too much of a state over the inclement weather. Antonio emerged from his chamber before long, freshly bathed, his hair slicked back with oil, and set about performing his duties as host. He could be quite charming when he wanted to, and before long the elderly Garcia sisters, all spinsters, were simpering over his outrageous compliments.

Having never been to a proper school—because Antonio didn't believe in educating women—Paulina hadn't any friends her own age. Most of the guests at the party were friends of the family, acquaintances who remembered her parents fondly and wished to pay their respects. Paulina didn't care. She'd been looking forward to this party for weeks, and she didn't intend to let anything spoil her enjoyment—not even being cornered by Tío Ramon, her grandmother's second cousin, who spent a quarter of an hour describing in exacting detail the flock of parrots that seemed to have settled into the mango and cashew trees on his property.

"It's a splendid cacophony," he said. "You ought to come see them the next time you're in town."

After what had happened earlier that day, Paulina was sure it would be a long time before Antonio allowed her to leave the *quinta*. "I certainly will," she told Tío Ramon.

He wasn't appeased by her comment. "You should be going into town more often, my girl. A pretty girl like you ought to have friends and beaus and liveliness. You'll end up an old maid if Antonio continues to keep you out here all the time."

It might have been true, but Paulina couldn't help but feel a flash of irritation. Here was another relative—another man—dictating what she needed rather than taking the time to ask her what she wanted. In any case, Tío Ramon was wrong in one respect. She was not a girl. As of today, she was twenty-one years old and long past the age at which women gave up dances and beaux for housekeeping and babies.

As she had been trained to do, Paulina hid her irritation with a smile. "Oh, I couldn't possibly be married right now," she said lightly. "What would Antonio do without me to keep house for him?"

"Hire a housekeeper," Tío Ramon replied dryly.

Antonio wouldn't, even if he could afford one. Paulina's brother might not be a shrewd businessman, but even he knew the value of the free labor she provided him. She had no intention of being his unpaid housekeeper forever, but finding the means to leave had proved to be difficult enough when even Antonio could scarcely lay his hands on enough pesos to keep the household supplied with lamp oil.

Clasping a glass of champagne by its delicate stem, Paulina drifted from one sparse group to the other. The conversation around her wasn't especially thrilling, but she soaked it in just the same, feeling a curious fluttering in her stomach whenever there was a flash of motion at the corner of her eye.

It was only when she saw him standing in the doorway that she realized she'd been waiting for Sebastian Linares.

He shouldn't have come.

Sebastian stood at the open door to the Despradels' *quinta*, trying his hardest to keep from running down the long list of reasons why he should stay away from that house—the main one being that he had far too many troubles of his own to borrow someone else's.

He couldn't say what it was that finally compelled him to cross the threshold and venture inside. The expression on Paulina's face when her brother had grabbed her by the wrist, perhaps. The long sweep of her eyelashes as she'd studied the ribbon. The sensation that had crackled through his limbs like an electrical current the instant she'd lifted up her gaze to his and curved her lush lips into a smile.

It was hard to say.

Although similar in construction, the Despradels' *quinta* looked nothing like his own empty house, stuffed as it was with what looked like a hundred years' worth of furniture and pictures, all exhibiting the sort of shabby elegance that came with generations of wealth. For all they were clearly expensive, the velvet drapes and chintz-covered chairs had faded with time; against their pale tones and that of the papered walls, the large oil painting hanging from the far wall stood out in marked contrast. Seated in front of rich green draperies, a dark-haired man and a woman who shared Paulina's snapping dark eyes gazed solemnly back at Sebastian.

With no servants to show him the way, Sebastian followed the sound of voices past the parlor and into a terrace where far fewer people than he'd expected sat on chairs lined up against the wall. There was no music. Antonio and a handful of other men had gathered in a corner of the terrace in what looked like a card game, and their exclamations pierced the low buzz of conversation. All five of the men gathered around the card table looked like disreputable rogues, despite the fact that two of them were dressed in the navy blue uniforms of the civil guard. Odd though it seemed to Sebastian for those roughs to be among those invited to a party celebrating a lady, it wasn't any of his business whom Antonio Despradel chose to associate with.

It wouldn't have been difficult to pick out Paulina even if the terrace had been ten times more crowded. The sky had grown dark with clouds, and the tangled foliage beyond the terrace waved ominously in the breeze. In the white dress she had worn that morning, Paulina was a bright spot against the gloom as she bent slightly to allow an older woman to whisper something in her ear.

When she caught sight of Sebastian hovering in the doorway, her smile was so bright that he once again had the momentary impression of a shaft of sunlight breaking through the clouds.

"You came," she said, pressing his hand between both of her own. Sebastian couldn't help noticing how slender her fingers were when compared to his large, sun-darkened hand.

"I can't stay long." Sebastian slid his hand into the pocket of his trousers and clenched it, hardly knowing whether he wanted to erase or preserve the memory of her light touch. His fingers brushed against something soft. "I only came to give you this."

The ribbon, when he extracted it from his pocket, lay curled and limp on his palm. Sebastian suddenly felt foolish. Making sure that Paulina hadn't been further mistreated by her brother had seemed like a noble enough reason for coming to her party, but standing here in front of her, holding out his pitiable excuse for a birthday present, he had to admit to himself that there was nothing noble about why he'd come. He wanted to see her again, plain and simple. Firm as he was in his belief that he did not want or need a wife, it clearly did not prevent him from acting like a love-struck fool.

"Thank you," Paulina said, her fingertips brushing Sebastian's palm as she wound the ribbon around two of her slim fingers. To his surprise, she sounded genuinely happy over his paltry gift. "It really is a beautiful color."

As if on impulse, she swiftly wove the ribbon into her hair and tied it into a bow, smiling at Sebastian as she did. "Will you stay for a glass of champagne?"

Sebastian had done a lot of difficult things in his life, but saying no to a beautiful woman was not one of them. He assented and a few moments later found himself seated at the far end of the terrace and being peered at by half the guests. Having been subjected to many of those curious glances since his return—mostly from young ladies and their matchmaking mothers—Sebastian had made a point of rejecting all the overtures that followed. It wasn't only, as he'd told Dilia, that he had too many burdens weighing down his shoulders to saddle himself with a wife. Sebastian was fairly sure that his chance of being recognized by these members of San Pedro society was slim, but he couldn't risk it. Not quite yet.

Turning away from the curious gazes, he nodded toward the garden stretching beyond the terrace's balustrade. It was encircled by a stone wall and bordered with bougainvillea hedges. The red flowers stood out against the glossy dark leaves, the same shade as Paulina's ribbon. "What beautiful gardens," he said politely. "I would ask you to take a stroll down there, but it would feel a bit like being put on display."

Paulina perched on the edge of the chair next to his, as skittish as the little brown birds that sometimes ventured through his open window. "They can be awful gossips, I know. Particularly— Well, it sounds conceited to say it, but I know many of them are curious about me. I don't blame them, you know. I suppose I *am* something of a curious specimen."

"Are you?"

"I feel like it sometimes. I'm sure you've been in town long enough to hear the whispers—how the Despradel girl was allowed to grow wild out here. How I've spent most of my life roaming barefoot in the sugarcane fields instead of learning about Cervantes and how to embroider flowers with other girls."

"It doesn't sound like a terrible way to grow up."

"A trifle lonely, perhaps," she admitted. "Particularly…"

"After your parents passed?" Sebastian supplied. "I've heard about their legendary house parties."

"What I remember of them was wonderful, but most of their guests had no use for little girls such as myself. I was always told to run along and play." She captured her lower lip between her teeth for a second. "There was a little boy. His mother was a washerwoman who came to the *quinta* once a week to help with the laundry. He made a few cents running errands or performing small tasks, but mostly…mostly he played with me. He taught me how to suck the nectar from *coralillo* stems and captured the prettiest green lizards for me to pet." Her lower lip, slightly reddened from her teeth, stretched into a smile. "Very few people have taken the time to know me as he did."

Sebastian took a slow sip of champagne, careful to keep his gaze on the bubbles breaking on the surface of the liquid. "Did something happen to the boy?"

"I don't know," Paulina said, and he heard the frustration in her voice. "His mother died shortly after my parents, and he was taken away by relatives, I think. I never was able to find out much about what became of him, though I asked everyone I could."

"I'm sorry."

"So am I," she said. "Sometimes I wonder what would have become of me if he'd stayed. I have no reason to believe anything would be different, save for… Well, I did always feel braver whenever he was beside me. Stronger, too. A foolish notion, perhaps, to think that a child could have changed the course of my life, but…"

"It isn't foolish," Sebastian said, thinking that Carlos had been a child himself when he'd taken Sebastian under his wing, back in Havana. "Having someone to stand shoulder to shoulder with can make all the difference in the world. It's a shame that was taken away from you."

"I still hold out hope that I might have it someday."

Sebastian found himself wanting that for her, as well, and not only for her sake—whoever found his place beside her was sure to benefit from the quiet strength running through her like a vein of gold. He wasn't given to impulsive gestures, but if he had been, he would have surely reached over to clasp her hand in his own. Not only to offer her comfort, but because her disarming honesty felt too raw in the face of all he couldn't tell her.

Sebastian glanced away, and his gaze fell on the card table where Antonio still sat. Paulina's brother was staring at them, his thick brows knitted in speculation. There was nothing explicitly menacing about the look, but it made Sebastian's blood run cold with unease.

A distant rumble of thunder interrupted his next words. As if the sound had been a signal, Paulina's guests rose from their chairs and began to take their leave, a process that usually took hours but was accomplished in mere minutes under the threat of incipient rain. Wineglasses were set down, used napkins set aside, cigars snuffed out, and the guests began to surge around Paulina.

Sebastian hesitated, knowing he should stay and say a proper goodbye. But he had never been any good at goodbyes, and in any case, it wasn't as though he had anything more to say.

He had come to make sure she was all right. That was all.

The first drops were beginning to dot the dirt path, joining the deep ruts left behind by carriage wheels. Sebastian unhitched his horse and was swinging himself over the saddle as the partygoers started to pour out through the doors without bothering to linger over conversations. A heavy drop landed on his shoulder as if in warning, but he nonetheless paused and glanced back at the house. Paulina was still standing in front of the open door, the endless ruffles on her dress fluttering in the rising wind. Her slim brown hand was raised in a wave as her guests rushed for their respective carriages, and although they were separated by the bustle, it felt like she was looking straight at him.

Chapter Three

Antonio had had too much to drink.

The warm glow that had kindled inside Paulina's chest during her conversation with Sebastian was extinguished the second she returned to the veranda to begin cleaning up the detritus from the party. It took a single glance at the expression on her brother's face to know that she should remove herself from his presence. Antonio didn't drink often, but when he did, he didn't fly into rages—his sarcastic tones grew cold and hard, and he would start in on Paulina, taking her to task over any perceived infraction or defect of character.

In the time it had taken for Paulina to close and bolt the front door, the skies had broken open. Heavy rain battered the tiles on the terrace roof, so loudly that she almost didn't hear Antonio speak from the corner where he sat lounging on a rocking chair, a hand cupped around a snifter of his usual expensive brandy.

"I thought I warned you to keep away from that man," Antonio was saying. His tie was slightly crooked, as if he had started to loosen it. "Do you know what you looked like, panting over him?"

The maid seemed to have vanished—gone to bed,

most likely. The servants' quarters were in an outbuilding by the kitchen, cut off from the rest of the house by the curtains of rain streaming down and far enough away that she wouldn't hear if Paulina called for her help with the dishes. Not that she was likely to come out in the rain.

"It was positively indecent," Antonio said. "I was embarrassed for you, and so was everyone who noticed."

"What are you talking about?" Paulina asked, though she had an idea of whom her brother meant.

"Sebastian Linares." Their neighbor's name roiled out of Antonio's mouth, charged with loathing.

The napkins would stain if they weren't soaked overnight, but the washing up could wait until the next day. Paulina emptied wineglasses over the railing, placing them on a serving tray to be taken to the kitchen in the morning. "It was a party," she said wearily, though she knew he was in no state to be reasoned with. "I won't ask him again if you don't wish me to, but I could hardly turn him away at the door."

"You wouldn't turn him away from your bed, either."

"Antonio, what on earth has gotten into you?" Paulina recoiled in shock. "You're acting as if I—as if I—"

"Look at you, pretending to be virginal when half the town just saw you making a fool of yourself over that man. I wouldn't be surprised if you'd—"

"I'm going to bed," Paulina said loudly in an attempt to drown out her brother's vulgarity. Though he always enjoyed making sure she was aware of her faults, Antonio had never spoken to her with such ugliness. She wiped her hands with a clean napkin and, despite the apprehension shooting through her chest, did her best to sound commanding. "I hope you'll be more civil in the morning."

She was halfway to the nearest door when Antonio stepped into her path.

His bloodshot eyes glared down at her, and Paulina fought the urge to turn her head when confronted with the full impact of his breath, strong enough to overpower even the scent of rain-drenched earth. "You're a disgrace to our family," he said. "Our parents would be ashamed to see you carrying on like a common tramp. You couldn't turn him away at the door? You had better hope he feels the same about you."

Paulina's throat tightened as, for the second time that day, Antonio's fingers bit into the soft flesh of her forearm.

Was it her imagination or did she see a flicker of amusement in his eyes?

Before she could decide either way, Antonio began dragging her into the house.

"What are you doing?" she protested. "Let go of me— *Antonio!*"

He paused, and Paulina hardly had time to register relief before realizing that he had opened the front door. A moment later, Paulina felt herself being pulled into the lashing rain.

Half bewildered at this development, she stopped struggling and simply stared at her brother. Surely he didn't mean to— Surely he wouldn't—

She couldn't seem to catch her breath. Her chest strained against her corset, and the water beating against her face made her feel as though she were drowning.

One-handed, he pulled open the iron gate at the end of the path and hauled her through. It wasn't until the gate clanged shut and she saw him turn the key in the lock that she realized what her brother was doing—and by then it was too late.

"Antonio!" she screamed as he turned back toward the house, but the rain and wind swallowed the sound.

A numb sort of shock was starting to settle over her as she stared at the locked gate. There was no question of trying to walk all the way to town, not in the middle of a storm and with darkness about to blanket the fields surrounding her. Sebastian. She would go to Sebastian.

Evening was starting to fall, but the sky was white with clouds, and there was just enough light for Paulina to see the path before her. The hard-packed dirt, rutted from carriage wheels, had softened into mud. She could feel it sucking at her heeled shoes with every step she took. The tooled leather would be ruined—but then, so would she.

A flash of lightning crackled just ahead of her, lighting the path with startling clarity. Paulina had a moment to make out broken branches and fallen palm fronds before the world was plunged back into darkness.

Paulina didn't waste time screaming. Seizing handfuls of fabric, she raised her skirt as best as she could and ran the rest of the way to Sebastian's house.

Villa Consuelo was smaller and more run-down than the Despradel home. She'd explored its outbuildings as a child, and though she hadn't ventured that way in years, Paulina's feet still remembered the way.

The lantern by the door was still burning, protected from the driving rain by a rather ramshackle overhang. Though it did not illuminate much more than the weather-beaten door, its glow was a welcome sight. She stumbled up the slick, muddy steps, heaving one breath after another as she reached the relative safety of the overhang.

Briefly, she considered waiting for daylight out here, but a sudden cascade of water from the leaky wooden structure disabused her of that notion. She grasped the iron knocker and let it fall several times against the solid wood of the door, then wrapped her arms around herself, feeling the rivulets run down her ribs as she squeezed the sodden fabric of her bodice. Her voluminous skirts were too soaked to billow in the wind, but Paulina felt something cold slap against the side of her face—her new ribbon. Pulling it out of her snarled hair, she shoved it into her pocket.

A few moments passed before the door was flung open and Sebastian appeared in the doorway. It hadn't been all that long since he'd left the Despradels', but in the intervening time he had been divested of half his clothing. The upper half, Paulina couldn't help but note as the light from the swaying lantern fell on the sharply defined muscles of his arms.

"Pardon the hour," she said absurdly, as if this were a social call.

To say that Sebastian looked surprised would have been an understatement. "Paulina? Are you all right? Did you walk all the way here?"

"I— That is, my brother—" Paulina bit her lip to hold back the sob threatening to burst out. "Yours is the only house near here, and I—"

"I see," Sebastian said, though he couldn't have at all, because Paulina found herself unable to choke out any more words. His expression was inscrutable even as it was illuminated by another flash of lightning. "I would take you somewhere more suitable, but I haven't a coach, and it's not a night to be out on horseback. Why don't you come inside and get dry?"

The parlor he led her to could hardly be called that— the walls were covered in paper and a brass lamp hung from the wooden beams crisscrossing the ceiling, but that was it as far as furnishings were concerned. The pattern on the tile floor stretched unbroken from the entrance to the shuttered arches set into the far wall.

"You'll need towels and a change of clothing," Sebastian was saying. "My housekeeper has gone to visit her daughter, but I can go fetch some—"

"I'm sorry to be so much trouble," Paulina said and, to her horror, burst into tears.

She buried her face in her hands to spare him the sight. To her surprise, she felt herself being drawn against a warm, solid chest.

He smelled faintly of rum, which her brother never drank because he claimed it was common. The spicy scent was underlaid by the sweet, earthy smell of her childhood, the same one that clung to her father's lapels when he came home from a long day at the sugar mill. Paulina found it steadying. She gave a loud sniff and straightened away from the warmth of Sebastian's chest.

"It'll be all right," she said, and she was pleased to hear that her voice didn't waver too badly. Neither did her fingers tremble when she accepted the handkerchief he held out and used it to wipe her face clean of tears and rainwater. "When he sobers up in the morning, he'll realize that I've done nothing wrong and take me back in."

"Do you *want* to go back?" There was something unbalancing about his penetrating gaze. Rather than make Paulina want to shrink into herself, under his gaze she felt the need to stand up a little straighter.

"I— Well, it isn't as though I've got a choice," she said. "I haven't any money or relations, really, or...friends."

"I'm your friend," Sebastian said, so firmly that Paulina's knees felt a trifle hollow. "And I've money if you want it. Enough to get you to New York or Madrid or Paris—or even Constantinople if that's what it will take to get you away from that goddamned brother of yours. So I'll ask you again. Do you *want* to go back?"

The trembling in Paulina's knees seemed to have traveled upward. She felt almost dizzy as she contemplated the fact that, for the first time in her life, she might be able to do as she pleased. The notion felt thrilling—and slightly dangerous.

The shock was beginning to clear, and Paulina was able to remember the hardness in her brother's voice when he'd mentioned Sebastian's name. That Antonio had taken a dislike to this man was more than clear. Why was another question altogether. Surely he would have to know that she would seek refuge with Sebastian on a night when walking into town would be near impossible. Why would he cast her out if by doing so he was all but driving her into Sebastian's home?

"No." She lifted her chin. "I never want to go back there again."

"Then you won't," Sebastian said with a little shrug, as if it really would be as easy as that. He turned away, saying over his shoulder, "My apologies for the lack of furniture. I'm afraid I've been so busy at the mill I haven't been able to find the time for getting the house in order."

The parlor was not in fact as empty as it had seemed at first glance—an ancient cushion lay on the tile next to an overturned crate, which held a bottle full of water, a small cask of rum and an enamel mug. A single oil lamp sat on the floor beside the crate, its flickering light casting dancing shadows on a covered plate.

Crouching in one fluid movement, Sebastian poured some of the aromatic brown liquid into the mug and gestured at her to take a seat on the cushion. "Here," he said, handing her the mug. "You could probably use some fortification right now. Have some water, too, or your head will ache like the devil in the morning."

Paulina pressed the cool enamel to her lips and inhaled deeply before taking a tiny sip. "I'm sorry for interrupting your evening," she began, feeling the rum swirl down her chest and settle low in her belly.

"You're not interrupting anything," Sebastian replied swiftly. "I would have been at the mill right now if it weren't for the storm, and since I'm not, all I've been able to do is sit here and think about all the sugarcane that's being ruined by the rain or scorched by lightning. Nobody told me that the life of a sugar mill owner held all the worries of a farmer and a merchant put together." He gave her a crooked smile. "I welcome any distractions."

"Well, I'm happy to provide one. A most dramatic one, at that." She cocked her head. "Do you often go to the mill at night?"

The covered plate on the floor held several half circles of fried dough. Sebastian held it toward her, and though her first instinct was to demur politely, the first whiff of fried dough and beef had her almost snatching at the plate. Only the fact that Sebastian had begun to talk kept her from closing her eyes to savor the first blissful bite.

"I can't seem to stay away," he said ruefully. "The machinery we installed requires constant attention, and I'm the only one who knows how to coax it into working correctly. I studied engineering in Havana, and I find machinery easy to understand, but the bookkeeping is another matter." He shook his head. "We've half a dozen ledgers, and I've found that they're liable to get into a snarl if I don't pore over them day and night. And with my partner gone…"

"Oh, yes," she said, swallowing and wiping her greasy

fingers on her skirt. "I did hear about the passing of your partner. That must have been devastating."

"He was my brother," Sebastian said quietly. Having caught sight of her surreptitious gesture, he dug into his pocket and offered her his handkerchief again. "He believed in me like no one else ever has, and I refuse to fail him."

"You won't." Paulina wiped her fingers clean and impulsively laid a hand on his bare arm. Wiry hairs brushed against her palm as she squeezed his arm gently, the sensation as intoxicating as the rum coiling through her belly.

Several droplets fell from her sodden sleeve to join the rivulets pooling on the tile around her dirty skirts. The pool had expanded slowly, and Paulina realized that the water must have been seeping through Sebastian's trousers for a while.

"Oh, but I've made you all wet," she exclaimed as Sebastian jolted to his feet.

"I'll get you a towel," he said, "and something dry to wear."

He returned in a few minutes, his expression so calm it was almost blank, carrying a stack of linens in one hand and a basin full of water in the other. "I seem to have run out of clean shirts, but I've enough towels and sheets to drape the new fire station. I don't imagine there's anything respectable about it, but at least you'll be decently covered until we can get you a new dress."

A new dress—and a new life. Paulina let out a breath.

"I'll step into the other room while you wash."

Paulina thanked him and waited until the door had closed firmly behind him to look down at herself. The water in the basin would not be nearly enough to do away with all the mud and broken leaves coating her feet and legs, though the worst of it would probably come off with her stockings. She needed a full bath—longed for it, really—but for the moment she would settle for wiping off the muck.

She set the linens down, and as her hands rose to unfasten her clothing, she remembered that unlike the plain cotton dresses she wore for everyday, this lavishly ruffled frock was held closed at the back by a dozen minuscule mother-of-pearl buttons traveling from the nape of her neck to the small of her back, all of which had been fastened by the sour-faced maid. Her stomach sank as her fingers met the limp flounces at her chest. There was no housekeeper here, and no maid.

She would have to ask Sebastian for help.

The rest of the house was dark, but the flickering glow of a second lamp guided Paulina through an open door at the side of the house. She stepped out onto a colonnaded terrace and had no trouble locating Sebastian even in the dim light. Facing the howling storm underneath one of the brick-bordered arches, he stood unflinching as a violent wind ripped fronds from the cluster of royal palms several feet away.

A sudden flash of lightning illuminated the rippling muscles of his back, the deep indentation just above the waistband of his trousers and the pale, fluttering cloth he held in a tight grip. Hungrily, she drank in the sight of his broad shoulders, set against the punishing breeze. There was something dashing about him even in relative stillness—a certain grace and strength in the way he performed even the most mundane tasks.

The white thing in his hand was a shirt. He pulled it over his broad shoulders and made short work of the buttons, then turned around—and caught Paulina staring at him.

"Did you need something else?" Sebastian asked.

"Oh, I—I need help with my buttons. And my—well, my laces." She tried to say it matter-of-factly—what room was there for blushing hesitancy after all that had happened?—but Paulina was aware of the embarrassment coloring her voice.

Sebastian nodded, and she turned her back to him, touching the place where the lace on her dress met her neck to indicate the row of buttons. Having just seen him doing up his own, it didn't surprise her that his fingers were as nimble as they were gentle and as warm as his chest had been. His knuckles brushed her sensitive skin, and to distract herself from the sensation, she asked the first thing that popped into her head.

"Do you not hate it? Living out here alone?"

"It's peaceful enough," he said after a brief pause. "And close to the mill."

"I've always dreamed of living in town," she confessed. "In one of those houses by the square, with a great balcony from which I could look at the couples strolling in the park and businessmen hurrying to the bank."

"We lived in town in Havana. On a busy street, not far from the cathedral. Carlos and I liked to sit out on the balcony and smoke cigars and drop coins and sweets to the street urchins down below. Then Carlos convinced me to rig an elaborate pulley system with two buckets, and he and Dilia, his wife, had great fun sending down all sorts of things." His soft laugh danced like a gust of wind over her exposed shoulder blades. "Dilia had gotten it into her head that she needed to practice her embroidery before having children of her own and sent down many a fancifully decorated suit of clothes. Those must have been the most colorfully dressed urchins in all of Havana."

She could tell when he reached the end of the buttons, because his fingers grazed the linen covering her bottom. Her undergarments were worn almost through, as Antonio only cared to spend money where it would be seen. Despite the warmth of the evening, Paulina felt her flesh pebbling.

She must have made a small noise, because his fingers stilled.

"My apologies. I think the laces are too wet to untangle—the knot is proving beyond my abilities."

"You'll have to cut it, unfortunately." Paulina craned her neck. "Have you a knife handy?"

Most men of her acquaintance—what few men she knew—carried knives on their person. Sebastian was no different, though she'd interrupted him in a state of dishabille. Paulina heard his noise of assent, then felt her laces being pulled tighter.

Abruptly loosened, both corset and dress sagged around Paulina. Her hands shot up reflexively to clasp the wet fabric to her bosom. A properly brought up young lady would surely scurry away at once at this breach in modesty. If there had been anything proper about her upbringing, perhaps Paulina would have done so instead of turning to thank Sebastian.

She was close enough for her filthy skirts to swish over his bare feet and brush the knees of his trousers, close enough that she couldn't fail to see the gleam in his dark eyes. Over the sound of the rain, she heard him draw in one deep, ragged breath.

The lantern hanging from a nail by the door was swinging wildly; even the glass cover around the flame couldn't keep it from going almost horizontal in the wind. It may have been the light, but Paulina was sure that what she saw in Sebastian's eyes was desire.

The skin of Paulina's back still sang with the memory of his touch. Every fiber in her body longed desperately for more—more, Paulina suspected, than she had any right to want.

Sebastian squeezed his eyes shut. When he opened them again, it was to give her a smile, even as he stepped away from her. "There," he said lightly. "You're done. I'll wait here until you've had a chance to wash."

She'd been holding her breath. Paulina let it out slowly as she gave a nod. This was an honorable man, who would commit no improprieties while she was under his roof. It was no cause for disappointment, but nonetheless Paulina felt her loneliness follow her back into the house.

Chapter Four

Sunlight pressed against Sebastian's closed eyelids. He had never been in the habit of sleeping in, and it was the brightness of the light that alerted him to the fact that he had done just that.

His eyes blinked open, and he found himself looking not at the whitewashed ceiling of his bedroom, but at the sturdy wooden beams that held up the ceiling of his parlor. The bare tile was uncommonly comfortable. Only… the softness was all down his side, not underneath him.

All the events of the previous night flooded Sebastian's mind, and he glanced down to see the woman clasped in his arms.

Paulina's hair was still in its arrangements of braids, but it was no longer neat. Dozens of tiny ringlets had escaped from their confines to ring her head and catch the light like a halo. They brushed softly against his chin in the gentle wind coming from the open doors and windows. Her lashes, which had glistened with tears the night before, fluttered and parted. In the warm morning light, her eyes were the exact shade of the rum they had shared the night before.

"Good morning," he murmured quietly, so as not to

startle her. He must have fallen asleep without meaning to—he'd had every intention of offering her his bed while he made himself comfortable on the rocking chair on the terrace. But then she'd cried, and when he'd rubbed her back as he used to rub little David's, she had collapsed against him, her body trembling with sobs, and he had gathered her close.

And apparently hadn't let her go.

She lifted her head slightly, and Sebastian felt the breeze waft over the slightly sweaty spot on his shoulder where her cheek had rested.

"Oh," she said, and licked her lips. "I— Good morning."

"How's your head?"

"It doesn't pain me. I suppose drinking all that water worked."

"It usually does," he agreed. One of his arms still pinned by Paulina, Sebastian folded his free one beneath his head and regarded her calmly, as if it hadn't been years since he'd awoken next to a woman. "You'll be wanting to freshen up. I'll make us some breakfast, and then we'll go to my friend Dilia's. She'll see about getting you something to we—"

The door, which he'd left ajar the night before, slammed into the wall, as loud as a gunshot.

Keeping a protective arm around Paulina, Sebastian rose onto his elbow as Antonio Despradel burst into the parlor, two men in civil guard uniforms at his heels.

"I told you she'd be here," Despradel said, his heavy black boots leaving behind mud prints on the patterned tiles as he strode to where Sebastian and Paulina lay, his chest puffed out like a rooster's.

Paulina sat up, clutching the sheet around her, and let out a soft noise of protest as Despradel hauled her upright. Even from the floor, Sebastian could see the way his fingers dug into her soft brown skin.

Sebastian sprang to his feet. "What's the meaning of this?"

It wasn't unreasonable to assume that Despradel had come with the intention of making trouble for his sister, and perhaps even Sebastian, not just to fetch her home. The man seemed to delight in little cruelties, and Sebastian had surmised that getting Paulina away from him wouldn't be as easy as Sebastian had made it out to be the night before. Still, he wasn't expecting the words that came out of Despradel's mouth.

"You can see it for yourselves," Despradel told the guards. "This man is a kidnapper and a despoiler of innocent young women."

Sebastian's mouth dropped open. "Kidnapper?"

"Half the town saw you cavorting with my sister at Don Enrique's store," Despradel informed him coldly. "Trying to tempt her with cheap ribbons, as if she were a common tart. It didn't work, so you resorted to stealing her away in the dead of night—and plying her with spirits," he added, looking pointedly down at the cask of rum on the overturned crate.

Sebastian let out a bark of laughter at the ridiculous fabrication. "You don't really believe that."

"What should I believe?" Despradel said, his gaze raking over the exposed flesh above the blanket Paulina held tight against her bosom. "Your word, or the ruined dress discarded outside? These gentlemen—" he gestured at the guardsmen with his free hand "—can attest to the fact that it was ripped open and the laces on the undergarments cut. What need would there be for such brutishness if nothing untoward had taken place?"

"Nothing did," Sebastian snapped. "I provided a

neighbor with shelter during a storm. If you're quite finished with whatever it is you're trying to do, I'll thank you—all of you—to get off my property."

One of the guardsmen took a step forward. "I'm afraid you'll have to come with us, Señor Linares. On orders of the magistrate."

"The magistrate?" Sebastian echoed with a sense of dawning horror. This was more than making trouble. Getting hauled in front of the magistrate with an accusation of kidnapping…

As far as the residents of San Pedro knew, he was a stranger in these parts, with no one save Dilia, another newcomer, to attest to his character. That Paulina had spent the night under his roof and in his arms was more than evident. And now there were witnesses, one of whom was all but leering with triumph, clearly insensible to the blow to his sister's reputation.

This was more than scandal. This was ruin—for Paulina, for Sebastian and for the dozens of people who depended on him, including Carlos's widow and children.

Sebastian forced his tensed shoulders to straighten. He'd find a way out of this—if not by reason, then by bribery. Failure was not an option, and though nothing Paulina said would restore her damaged reputation, the kidnapping charges would be dropped once she gave her account.

He turned to her. "It will be all right. All you have to do is explain—" Sebastian stopped dead.

He had no way of knowing if it was her brother's cruel grip that prevented her from speaking, or the fact that she was a party to the deception. Her face had gone ashen, and tears glimmered in the morning sunshine as they dropped from her eyelashes to her cheekbones, but she remained silent as she turned her face away from him.

Her betrayal rolled over him like a wave of nausea. Without meaning to, Sebastian took a staggering step backward. The guards' hands went to the pistols at their belts, and they started to close in as if to prevent him from fleeing.

Despradel was watching him closely, and whatever he saw in Sebastian's expression made his lip curl with a smile that was slight but so gleeful it made Sebastian's hand clench into a fist.

"You will please refrain from trying to coerce my sister into lying for you," Despradel said, and Sebastian *would* have struck him if two sets of hands as unyielding as iron bands hadn't seized Sebastian by the arms.

He knew better than to struggle, but he couldn't prevent the involuntary twitch in his shoulders, his body's attempt to throw off their grip. Holding himself with rigid dignity, he crossed the room in his bare feet. He didn't turn his head once, not even when the sound of Paulina's tremulous breaths followed him out the door.

It had been less than a day since he'd stopped to say hello to Paulina outside Don Enrique's store, and already she was well on her way to ruining his life.

They weren't taking him to the magistrate at all.

In his shirtsleeves, his bare feet sliding first over drying mud and then over cool tiles, Sebastian followed the guardsmen out of the blazing sunshine and into the cramped darkness of the Palace of Justice. Only when they tugged him through the courtyard did he realize that the guardsmen meant to put him directly into one of the stinking jail cells at the back.

As if anticipating that he would run, their hands tightened on his biceps. Jeers, shouts and the pungent odor of unwashed men followed them as the guards dragged

Sebastian past a holding cell. It was too bright outside for Sebastian to get much more than a glimpse of half a dozen faces pressed up against the bars before he was shoved into a cell of his own and the cold clang of the iron lock alerted him to the fact that his day had just become infinitely more complicated.

"Wait," Sebastian said before the guardsmen could walk away. The word burst out of him with more desperation than he'd meant it to, so he took care to modulate his voice as one of them glanced at him curiously. "I have money. A great deal more of it than Antonio Despradel. I would be more than happy to make it worth your while if you should release me."

The force they'd held him with had been cold and impersonal—the smirk on the guardsman's face, however, made it clear to Sebastian that he was getting some enjoyment out of it. "Would you now?"

Sebastian didn't like the look on the guard's face. "If you were to speak to the magistrate on my behalf…"

The guard laughed. "You hear that, Pedro? He wants us to pay a call to the magistrate himself."

The other guard, Pedro, the one with the tense shoulders, gave him a hard look. "Leave off, Juan. I don't want to miss my breakfast."

He set off without another word, and his partner followed him at a more leisurely pace, hands in his pockets, leaving Sebastian with only the chickens for company.

Despite the bars that made up most of one wall, the interior of the cell was dank, dark and devilishly hot. Perspiration streamed down Sebastian's temples—it wouldn't be long until he reeked as sharply as the slop bucket in the corner.

The thought sent another wave of sweat down his back. How long *did* they mean to keep him here, if they didn't mean to take him to the magistrate? And what the devil did Despradel mean by having him locked away?

It struck him, suddenly and with some violence, that no one save Despradel and the guardsmen knew where he was. Even if someone at the mill noticed his absence—which would likely happen sooner rather than later, given Sebastian's penchant for spending the better part of his day there—no one would know where to look for him. Despradel could have him held for as long as he wanted.

An expletive exploded past Sebastian's lips. His foreman at the mill was more than capable enough to hold things down for a day or two, if it took that long for Sebastian to get out, but his employees needed to be paid at the end of the week, and the money for that was all locked away in Sebastian's safe.

He had to get a message to Dilia. Neither she nor Sebastian had any powerful connections among the townspeople, but she was the one person who could advocate on his behalf in front of the magistrate—unless he, too, was involved in whatever game Despradel was playing at.

The bars separating him from the courtyard were warm, almost the same temperature as his skin. Beyond them, all Sebastian could see was the bare dirt of the courtyard and a pair of chickens scrabbling in a patch of sunshine.

Filled with a sudden inclination to smash his fist through something, Sebastian's fingers tightened around the unyielding bars, hard enough for his knuckles to ache. Then, breathing hard, he hauled off and leaned against the grimy wall.

He'd talk to the guardsmen when they returned. Dilia would pay for news of his whereabouts, and if Sebastian couldn't bribe them into freeing him, maybe they would take a few pesos for a message.

Unfortunately for him, when the guardsmen came back—so many hours later that the patch of sunshine had traveled past the iron bars and was beginning to climb up the far wall of the cell—they brought Despradel with them.

Flanked by his henchmen, Despradel scattered the chickens as he strutted through the courtyard. He stopped when he reached Sebastian's cell and gazed down at him with the vaguely amused air most people reserved for zoo animals. "I'm grieved to say that prison doesn't suit you, Señor Linares."

Sebastian wasn't in the mood for games. "Are you ready to enlighten me as to why I'm being held captive?" he asked, not bothering to rise from his spot on the ground. The heavy rains from the previous night hadn't finished soaking into the dirt, but what was a pair of muddy trousers, under the circumstances?

"It's a matter of incentive. I've found that a little solitude makes men more amenable to cooperating with my suggestions."

"Suggestions?" Sebastian snorted at the gross misuse of the word. "What is it you want, Despradel?"

The other man leaned forward so that his face was framed between two iron bars. "I want you to marry Paulina."

It wasn't surprising, not after what Despradel had said that morning, but Sebastian couldn't help but think there was an ulterior motive—if only because there was nothing in their short acquaintance that indicated that Antonio Despradel had ever done a thing for his sister's sake.

"Go to hell."

"I don't believe I will," Despradel said after pretending to consider it. The bastard was enjoying this far too much. "Not just yet, at any rate. Look," he added, sounding almost reasonable, "I've plenty of resources, and more than enough time and patience. You can either have a nasty few days in here, or you can spare yourself the trouble and say yes now."

A memory flashed through Sebastian's mind—Dilia and Carlos, leaning against the iron railing of the balcony in the Havana house, silhouetted against a blazing sunset. On the street below, elegant carriages heading to the house on the corner had begun to pile up as a mule laden with saddlebags refused to budge from the middle of the street. "That mule has nothing on Sebastian," Carlos had said, laughing. After that, every time Sebastian was being particularly stubborn, Carlos would make a teasing remark about holding up traffic and they would all laugh.

His lips tightened at the memory. "I will not say yes," Sebastian said. "Not now, not tomorrow, not if you keep me here for five months."

"That can be arranged." The mocking tone was gone from Despradel's voice; it was hard and flat as he said, "You'd rather take the hard road? So be it." He started to turn away. "Perhaps another day or two in here will make you reconsider."

"Why are you doing this?" Sebastian asked. "What could you possibly want from me?"

Something flickered over Despradel's countenance, and for a moment, Sebastian thought he might tell the truth. The moment passed swiftly, though, and Despradel's voice was hard and cold when he said, "To keep you from besmirching my family's honor." He jerked his chin at the guardsmen. "Put him in chairs. No food until he cooperates, but be sure to give him water—the last thing I want is for this dog to perish before he makes amends with my sister."

As Despradel made his own way out of the courtyard, the guardsmen let themselves into Sebastian's cell.

The guard who had smirked at him earlier, Juan, was the one to put the irons on him. Sebastian tried to ignore the heavy bracelet being clamped around his ankle and directed his words to the second guard, the one who continued to avoid Sebastian's gaze.

"If you won't free me, will you at least get a message to someone in town for me? Dilia de Gil. She'll be more than happy to arrange some payment for any news of me."

The guard remained quiet, his eyes fixed on the manacle he was fiddling with.

Sebastian pressed on. "I will personally make sure that you're handsomely rewarded for any assistance you might be able to—"

A fist cracked against his jaw, and Sebastian reeled backward, almost tripping over the big iron links, as pain exploded over the lower half of his face. He managed to catch himself before he fell, but not without catching the back of his shoulder sharply against the bars.

The guard at his ankles was, for once, not smirking, but gaping up at his partner.

Sebastian followed his gaze. The other guard was cradling his fist in a large hand, something that looked like fear glinting in his eyes.

"Shut up about messages," he said. "Shut up about all of it."

The expression on Juan's face was quickly shifting from surprise to glee. "Want me to gag him, Pedro?"

Pedro started like a spooked horse, then jerked his head into a nod. His partner grinned and pulled a grimy handkerchief from his pocket.

Pressed against the bars, the manacle tight around

his ankle and the chain binding it to the ring on the wall pulled as taut as it went, Sebastian squared his shoulders and said, quietly but distinctly, "No."

The advantage ought to have been entirely on their side—but Sebastian had desperation on his, and that made him more reckless than he otherwise would have been.

Sebastian had dealt with his share of bullies when he lived on the streets. Loath as he had always been to get into scuffles, he knew how to handle himself.

One of his hands hadn't been bound yet. When Sebastian caught Juan eyeing it as he approached, he made a show of shuffling his feet enough to make the chains rattle, hoping it would make the other man cocky.

"I would prefer to handle this like the gentlemen we are," Sebastian said.

The guard grunted. "Listen to this one. Gentlemen. Cowards, more like."

Sebastian waited until Juan was close enough to smell his breath, then launched himself to one side and pushed the other man from behind, pinning him against the bars. The guard wrenched himself free and came at Sebastian with a snarl.

Sebastian used the momentum to twist him around. One swift kick behind the leg and Juan was kneeling in front of Sebastian while Sebastian hooked his manacled hand around the other man's head and pulled the chain taut against his unshaven throat.

Juan strained against his hold, gasping, even though Sebastian had a firm hold on the chain to prevent it from digging into his throat.

"You can finish putting the irons on me," Sebastian said as he stood over the guard, trying to keep his breaths shallow, "but I won't be gagged. Do we have that clear?"

The lout was in the act of jerking his head in a nod when something tumbled from his pocket and hit the dirt floor with the jangle of metal.

The keys.

Less than five centimeters away from Sebastian's bare toe.

For one long second, all three men in the cell held their breath.

Sebastian could have pounced for it—but with bound ankles and one bound wrist, he wouldn't have gotten far before the guardsmen overpowered him. So instead, he nudged it toward Juan with his dirty toe and unhooked the chain from around the other man's neck. "Are we agreed, then, to act like gentlemen?"

There was no need for threats. Without bothering to answer, Juan snatched the keys from the floor and stormed out, barely waiting for Pedro to exit the cell before slamming the door shut with a clang.

Chapter Five

Overhead, the sky was blazing a bright blue. Inside Paulina's chest, however, another thunderstorm was raging.

"I won't help you ruin that poor man's life," she said.

She was back in the house she'd thought she had escaped for good. Antonio had hauled her, numb with shock, there that morning before disappearing for the next several hours—just enough time for Paulina, whose sole pair of shoes aside from her house slippers had been ruined in the storm, to search through the trunk containing her mother's things in the hopes of finding a pair sturdy enough to withstand the long walk to town.

She *would* talk to the magistrate. It didn't matter how hard Antonio's fingers had dug into her arm that morning—the abject disappointment on Sebastian's face had made her chest seize with shame at her cowardice.

Antonio had found her before she'd even reached the gate, and now here she was, gripping the back of a chair while he pulled a steaming plate of rice, beans and pork toward him, paying her as much mind as he would have a bothersome mosquito. There was a plate for Paulina, too, but she couldn't countenance eating. Her stomach was still roiling, both from the rum she'd had the night before and from the cruel trick her brother had played on Sebastian.

"I won't help you ruin his life," Paulina said again.

Antonio glanced up briefly. "You'll do as you're told for once in your life."

She lifted her chin. "I'll go to the magistrate and tell him you're lying—"

Antonio gave a bark of laughter. "And just what do you think that would accomplish? The magistrate and every other guardsman in this town are indebted to me in one way or another. If I were in fact plotting to ruin Sebastian Linares's life, there's nothing *you* could do to stop me."

While Paulina often felt powerless when it came to her brother, she had never until that moment felt helpless. As much as she hated to admit it, she recognized the truth in Antonio's words—there *was* nothing she could do to stop him, no matter what he tried to do.

"It just so happens," Antonio continued, cutting a sliver of pork from the chop on his plate, "I have other plans for Linares. I mean to make him marry you."

"Is that why you drove me out yesterday?" Paulina asked grimly. "Why you cast me out during a storm?"

He raised a shoulder into a shrug. "I have it on good authority that Linares can never resist playing the savior. I knew it was more than likely that he would take you in."

"I could have been killed."

"Don't be dramatic," Antonio said coldly.

"Did you not notice the lightning? The falling branches?" Paulina could hear her voice growing higher as she recalled her panicked run through the gale.

Antonio forked up a mound of rice and beans and

looked up at her again. "Have you realized that you've never thanked me?"

"Thanked you?" Paulina echoed, her mouth dropping open.

"For everything I've done for you. I've kept a roof over your head for almost fifteen years. You've been fed, clothed in the latest fashions. You've wanted for nothing. And now I've even found you a husband."

Being urged, or even forced, into marriage to a near stranger was nothing unusual for a woman. It was, however, more than Paulina could countenance.

"But it's all right. I forgive your lack of gratitude, painful though I find it." His plate mostly empty, Antonio stood and chucked her under the chin. Though the gesture was casual, his eyes were dark with warning. "As long as you behave."

Paulina met his gaze steadily, though her stomach was still pitching. Behaving was precisely the last thing she intended to do.

Perhaps it was true that the magistrate wouldn't help her, but there had to be someone who would. And she knew just the place to find that person—the mill. It would mean avoiding the walk to town, too, for which she was grateful. It was barely past one in the afternoon, and the sun was hot enough to sear a person's skin.

Antonio always took his siesta out in the veranda, sprawled on a rocking chair with his booted feet up on the railing. It wouldn't be difficult to sneak past him and cut through the sugarcane fields to reach the mill without taking the main road, where she might be spotted.

For most of her life, Antonio had warned her away from playing in the fields lest she be snatched by an outlaw or a cane cutter, but she had only ever found friends there. Today would be no different.

It might have been, if she'd stepped directly out into the veranda and through the gardens. Instead, she went into her bedroom to fetch her hat.

Paulina thought later that despite all that her brother had revealed of his character and his intentions in the past day, a small part of her must have still believed that he couldn't be all that bad. That part was extinguished when Paulina, her hat in her hands, heard the soft *snick* of her bedroom door being pulled shut.

She dropped the hat and flew across the room to rattle the doorknob. Locked. Antonio had locked her in.

"Let me out," Paulina called through the thick wood, trying to keep her voice sounding steady and reasonable.

It wasn't her brother who answered.

"I'm sorry, miss," said the maid—not the sour-faced woman who had trailed her in town the day before, but the frightfully young girl who had been sweeping the steps when Paulina had been dragged home that morning wearing nothing but a bedsheet. Paulina had never seen the girl before, but that was no surprise, as Antonio fired and hired household staff at the slightest transgression. "I'm under orders from your brother not to open the door without his say-so."

"I understand," Paulina said, her mind churning. "What's your name?"

"Berenice, miss. I—I don't want to get into trouble."

Could she somehow persuade the girl into releasing her? Bribe her? There was a laughable idea—Paulina hadn't even a decent pair of shoes, much less anything that would suit as a bribe.

Turning, she leaned against the closed door...and found herself gazing at the shuttered windows of her first-floor bedroom. Here was a better idea.

The windows were far shorter in the bedrooms than in

the rest of the house, and they were set high into the wall
to discourage petty thieves. Paulina dragged her bureau
underneath one and cleared everything from its surface,
then climbed atop it without too much difficulty, despite
the fact that the leather soles on her mother's old shoes
were worn almost to slickness. Unlatching the shutter,
she peered out through the opening.

The sugarcane fields were bathed with sunlight. Beyond them, she could see the mill's thick smokestack.
The sky above it was a deep blue, unmarred by the steam
it belched whenever the machinery was in use.

Paulina, who had spent most of her childhood climb-
ing trees, hefted herself onto the windowsill. It wasn't
until she was preparing to swing both legs over the side
that she saw the coachman lounging beneath her window, no doubt posted there by her brother.

Antonio had thought of everything.

She was trapped.

There was no help for it.

That was what Paulina told herself as she stood just
beside her bedroom door, clutching the heavy water jug
from her washstand.

Her temples were damp with perspiration, a product
of her nerves and of the heat that had been collecting in
her bedroom over the past two days. With both door and
windows shut tight for the past couple of days to prevent
her from escaping, there was no hope for a breeze to relieve the oppressive atmosphere.

The cheerful yellow flowers painted around the jug's
border were so at odds with what she was about to do that
Paulina almost burst into nervous laughter.

She swallowed it back and called through the door,

"Berenice? Would you mind refilling my water jug? I accidentally overturned it and I'm *so* thirsty."

Pressed against the door frame, she could hear the maid's muffled assent and the jangle of keys. Paulina hefted the jug and braced herself as the door started to slowly swing open. Paulina made as if to hand Berenice the jug but instead flung the water at the startled maid with all her force.

It was a few seconds before the maid gathered her wits and gave chase, and by then Paulina had pelted into the dining room and was pulling down chairs behind her to make it more difficult for Berenice to follow.

The four arched doors leading to the terrace were all open. Through them, Paulina could see a blur of blue and green—the cloudless midday sky and the garden below it, through which she could escape.

There was a crash behind her, and though it was likely Berenice stumbling over the overturned chairs, instinct made Paulina glance over her shoulder.

It was only for a second, but when she turned back, there was a dark figure blocking the doorway.

Antonio.

Paulina tried to whirl toward the other archway, but the soles of her mother's old shoes had been worn smooth. Skidding, she slammed into Antonio. He let out a grunt as the impact knocked the breath out of him, but he kept both his footing and his presence of mind—before she had time to peel herself away, he had trapped her against him with one viselike arm.

Paulina hadn't brawled a day in her life, but at some point she had stumbled across the notion that the only surefire way of stopping someone was to strike them between the legs. She tried to jerk up her knee, but her skirts tangled around her legs, so instead she dipped her head and sank her teeth into Antonio's forearm.

With an undignified yelp, he flung her into one of the rocking chairs on the veranda.

"You provoking little…" He rubbed the indentation on his forearm and gave her a baleful glare. "Just where do you think you're going?"

"Anywhere but here," she snapped. "What do you mean by keeping me locked in for days on end?"

"I wouldn't have to if you didn't keep trying to run away," he said, sounding aggrieved.

Berenice appeared in the doorway, soaked and flushed, and Antonio dismissed her with a flick of his fingers, scowling as he considered Paulina. "I thought you had more sense than to go against my wishes, Paulina, but clearly I have a habit of overestimating you. Here I am, doing my best to salvage your honor and that of our family, and all you want is to be left free to run after a man you've met twice. That's where you were going, isn't it? To find Linares?"

"It's none of your concern where I was going."

She lunged to her feet and he caught her by the arm.

"You want to go to him? Well, then, let's go."

He had been drinking the night he cast her out into the storm, but today he was sharply sober. His fingers were like iron against her arm as he pulled her toward the carriage, pausing only to say a word to the coachman, who grunted in response.

Refusing his help, Paulina scrambled onto a seat. "I won't marry him."

Her voice was firm but low, and for a moment, Paulina wasn't sure if Antonio had heard her over the rattle of the carriage wheels.

"It will be worse for him if you don't," Antonio said.

"You'll cost him his reputation. Is that what you want? To have Linares disgraced for life because you were flighty enough to spend the night under his roof?"

After the events of the previous day, Paulina had begun to think that nothing her brother did, however vile, could shock her. His words, however, made her mouth drop open. "You would really try to blame me?"

The grave expression he put on might have fooled anyone save for Paulina, who had never seen true sincerity on her brother's face. "If anyone's to blame for this situation, it's me. I have done my best to raise you to be an upright young lady, but it's clear I have failed you, Paulina. Even my maid and coachman would attest to the fact that I had to keep you locked in your bedroom to prevent you from running after Linares for a second attempt to compromise your virtue."

"You're reprehensible," Paulina told him, and she wasn't surprised when he laughed at the emotion in her voice. "How can you play with people's lives so cavalierly? Haven't you a conscience?"

Antonio shrugged. "Haven't found much need for one. Money's a far more useful thing to have. Here's some free advice for you, little sister—the world rewards money and those who have it, not scruples." He chucked her under the chin with another laugh, and she turned away, disgusted and a little shaken.

He had never really mentioned marriage before, at least not in regard to her. She'd always assumed he meant to keep her at the *quinta* as some sort of unpaid housekeeper. For him to be so insistent about marrying her off to Sebastian…he must have figured out a way to wring profit out of it.

It certainly wasn't for her benefit.

The carriage rolled to a stop, and she and Antonio alighted in front of the Palace of Justice.

"What have you done?" she whispered, but Antonio wasn't paying her any attention. He was speaking to a group of guardsmen in uniform who were smoking by the entrance. One of them came forward, and, giving her brother a respectful greeting, he led them inside.

The jail cells at the back of the Palace of Justice were a wretched sight. Most were crowded with prisoners, foul-smelling and dark, and the dirt yard that formed a sort of courtyard before them was smeared with chicken droppings.

The guardsman stopped in front of a cell, and Paulina let out a cry when she saw Sebastian through the bars. Clad in a shirt that looked like it had been used as a cleaning rag for months, his face streaked with grime, he was chained to the bricks at his back.

Bitterness welled up inside her. He wouldn't have been here, looking like this, if it weren't for her.

The guardsman unlocked the cell, and Antonio hauled her in through the open door, saying with disgusting cheerfulness, "Good morning, Linares. Have you given any thought to my offer?"

Sebastian's eyes flicked toward Paulina, but there was no acknowledgment in them. "Go to the devil," he said through parched lips.

"Must we really go through all this again?" Antonio let out an exasperated sigh. "I didn't want to do this, but as everyone here can see, your lack of cooperation forces me to take extreme measures." Stepping closer—though Paulina noticed he remained just out of reach of the latter man's powerful arms—Antonio spoke down to Sebastian. "You will either marry my sister to make up for your dishonorable actions, or—"

"What?" Sebastian croaked out. "You'll starve me? Withhold water? Whatever it is you want, Despradel, you won't be able to get it if I die."

"I'm grieved at such an accusation," Antonio said, though he only looked annoyed. "I don't mean you any harm, Linares. All I want is restitution. And since we all know that a woman's virtue, once taken, cannot be put back…"

Without conscious thought, Paulina had been edging back, away from Antonio and Sebastian. The warm, damp bricks at her back, filthy though they were, were much preferable to Antonio's punishing grip.

"Men never have to face the consequences for such things," Antonio remarked, hauling her forward. "It's always up to women to deal with society's shame and condemnation. Would you really allow Paulina to be ruined when a single word from you could save her from being repudiated by every respectable person in San Pedro? She'd be out on the street—a man of virtue such as myself can't be expected to countenance such goings-on under his own roof. And what will happen to her then? Do you really want that on your conscience?"

"Don't believe anything that comes out of his mouth," Paulina said furiously, struggling against his grip.

Antonio smirked. "Something tells me that Linares is not likely to trust either one of us. As well he should— we all know how treacherous females can be, and especially when it comes to snaring themselves a husband."

"Sebastian…" Paulina began, but her words were lost in her own cry when Antonio dug his fingers into the soft flesh of her upper arm.

"You'll both be disgraced," Antonio said. "Tell me why I shouldn't shove her into a group cell and let the prisoners do with her what they would?"

Paulina couldn't see Sebastian's face—his head was bowed, and he was silent as well as motionless. Her stomach clenched. Part of her wanted him to continue refusing Antonio, who had surely been lying when he said he would cast her out into the street. Or worse, into another jail cell.

But part of her wanted Sebastian to be the honorable man she believed him to be—the honorable, upstanding, heroic man she had built him up to be in her mind.

Paulina forced herself to keep her gaze on that bowed head, almost holding her breath as she waited for his response, though she didn't know whether she was willing him to say yes or no. Her stomach was pitching as if she were on a ship about to wreck—which, in a way, she was. Whatever Sebastian's response, her life was about to change.

She couldn't help thinking about the night of the storm and how he'd given her strength when her emotion had worn through what she'd believed to be the end of her resilience. When she'd awoken in his arms, even knowing the upheaval she was facing, she'd been almost...happy.

And while it was probable that he hadn't felt the same way, surely she hadn't imagined the gentleness in the way he'd held her. There was something between her and Sebastian, some unspoken sense of possibility. Maybe marriage, a treacherous part of her insisted, would give her the opportunity to find out for sure.

Antonio's fingers were digging painfully into her arm, and Paulina's own were clenched around folds of her skirt.

And still, Sebastian's silence grew around them.

"So be it," Antonio said finally. He nodded to the guardsman, who moved at once to open the cell.

Paulina wrenched her arm out of Antonio's grip. "Let go of me. I can walk under my own power."

"Stop," Sebastian rasped, lifting his head. He swallowed. Even from where she stood, her knees loosening with relief, Paulina could see what it cost him to say what he said next. "Stop. I'll marry her."

It was over in minutes.

Sebastian and Paulina's wedding was as brief as it was joyless. One of his manacles was removed so that he could sign the marriage act. His hand left streaks of dirt on the thin, grayish paper of the clerk's ledger. The man had been summoned from the civil registry and presented with the suitable papers—how Despradel had acquired them, Sebastian did not wish to know.

Paulina was ashen, her face a pale brown smudge in the gloom of the cell.

A handful of nights before, she had cried on his shoulder, and like absolute fool, he'd believed every damned word that had fallen from those pretty lips. This wasn't the first time that Sebastian had been taken in by a beautiful woman pretending to be in trouble—but he would make damn sure it was the last.

Even the clerk looked troubled as he oversaw the proceedings. "This is most irregular," he had muttered as he'd entered the cell and caught his first glimpse of the bride and groom. Any protest on his part was quelled by a warning sound from Juan, who had begun wearing a pistol that he stroked ostentatiously whenever he was around Sebastian.

As for Sebastian himself, he kept a tight rein on his emotions. There was no need for any of them to see the dread curdling in his stomach. It didn't seem right that his entire life should be destroyed by something as inconsequential as two signatures on a piece of paper.

The only person who seemed jubilant was Despradel. As soon as the ink was dry on the marriage certificate, he folded it and slid it into his pocket. "I'll keep this safe, if that's all right with the happy couple," he said with a leer.

He left the cell first, a companionable arm slung firmly around the clerk, who looked as if he were about to lose his breakfast. Only when they had been gone for a while did the two guardsmen release Sebastian from the wall, though they kept him in shackles until they had shoved both him and Paulina into a waiting coach.

As the iron around his wrists was yanked free, one of the guardsmen slapped the side of the carriage to signal the coachman. The horses set off at once, halfway down the street before Sebastian could so much as think to swing a fist toward either guard.

Paulina had pressed herself into a corner of the carriage, as far from Sebastian as she could get in the enclosed space. Whatever her role in this godforsaken mess, she was clearly planning on playing the innocent until the bitter end.

Sebastian had had plenty of experience with that kind of playacting, and if there was one thing he knew, it was that he'd rather take up residence in that filthy jail cell than fall again for such tricks.

"Thank you for what you did back there. I should have been in dire straits if you hadn't—"

"Don't touch me," he snarled, and the slender hand that had been reaching toward him was instantly jerked away.

He felt like a wounded animal that had just been released from an iron trap—raw and broken and more than willing to snap his teeth at anyone in his sight. "I don't know what it is you two want from me. I don't know what made you target me in this way, and I certainly don't pretend to know what else you have in store for me. Your brother wanted you respectably married? Congratulations. You are now my lawfully wedded wife. You will live in my house and eat at my table. But make no mistake—I want no part in this sham of a marriage. You will not touch me again."

She reared back against her seat, as if struck by the force of his words. Everything inside Sebastian burned with the urge to apologize, but he forced himself to keep still.

Silence pressed in around them, and it went unbroken as the carriage rattled its way out of town.

Chapter Six

When Paulina was six years old, her parents had hosted a wedding at the *quinta*. The party had been one of their largest and most extravagant—close to a dozen house-guests had arrived the week before the wedding, and still more people streamed in from nearby towns on the day itself. The bride had been a distant cousin of her mother's, and she had worn white gardenias in her hair.

Paulina had pictured her own wedding countless times since then. But what she had never imagined was arriving to the end of it, perspiring and ragged and miserable, next to a husband who could barely bring himself to look at her.

Damn Antonio for robbing her of yet another dream.

The carriage came to a stop in front of Villa Consuelo. Wearily and slightly awkwardly, Paulina hopped down from the high perch without waiting for Sebastian. After what he'd said, and the heavy silence that had settled between them, she was certain he would have no inter-est in helping her down. And yet here he was, coming around the side of the carriage, grasping her arm when she stumbled as the fabric of her skirt snagged on a splin-ter. It was true that he released her arm like he'd been burned the very instant she was steady on her feet, but the small kindness heartened Paulina.

"Sebastian! There you are!"

The cry was uttered by one of the two women who stood in front of the steps and was quickly followed by a muttered, "*Santísimo!*" when Sebastian walked into the pool of light cast by the hanging lantern.

"What happened to you?"

"We were so sure you'd had an accident, but your horse is in the paddock—"

Paulina hung back. Both women wore black and were older than her, one by a handful of years and the second one by two or three decades, judging by the gray in her hair. They reached out for Sebastian like a mother and a sister would, though there was no resemblance between them.

He allowed them to fuss over him, murmuring something that made them smile despite the worry furrowing their brows. It made Paulina think about the way he'd looked at her in Don Enrique's store, and later when he'd handed her the red ribbon. She could have basked in his quiet warmth all day, and her chest tightened at the thought that she might never get to. Whoever these women were to him, they were lucky that they had no cause to worry about losing his regard.

With a start, Paulina realized that their gazes had turned to her.

Sebastian, who had just patted the older woman's shoulder, stepped away and gestured toward Paulina. "This is…" His eyes flashed. "This is Paulina Despradel. My wife."

Paulina could hardly miss the stress he laid on the word, nor the way the women's mouths fell slightly open when they heard it.

Half expecting their shocked expressions to turn into hostility, she was taken aback when the younger of the two women brushed past Sebastian and came to Paulina's side, leaning in to kiss her cheek.

"I'm Dilia, a good friend of Sebastian's." Her dark brown eyes were quick and curious but also kind as they swept over Paulina. "It's a pleasure to meet you. A pleasure and a surprise, if you'll forgive my saying so."

"For us both," Paulina said, and she was gratified when Dilia laughed.

Sebastian made a low noise at the back of his throat. "She'll need a bedroom."

"And a good meal and a bath, I imagine," the older woman said briskly. "Come with me, my dear. I'm Josefa, the housekeeper. I'll get you settled in."

Paulina murmured the requisite pleasantries as she was guided into the house. She couldn't help but sneak a glance backward. Sebastian's shoulders were slumped beneath Dilia's hand, and the two stood close together, speaking in low voices.

When she turned back toward the house, Doña Josefa was waiting at the far end of the front room, something like pity and suspicion mingled in her expression.

Paulina couldn't blame her.

"Will your belongings be brought later?" Doña Josefa asked. "We've a boy that can help with any luggage, but he'll be on his way home soon."

"I haven't any," Paulina said, surprised to realize this was true. "No luggage, I mean, and no belongings."

And nothing she wanted out of her family's *quinta*, save for the few things of her mother's inconsequential enough to have escaped Antonio's notice when he was scouring the house for things to sell.

Doña Josefa didn't seem perturbed by this admission.

"Your husband isn't much for having too many things, either, and let me tell you something—it makes housework a sight easier. Less polishing and dusting, you know."

"I would imagine so," Paulina said, having seen what passed for furnishings in Villa Consuelo.

She wouldn't have minded if their path through the house had included a detour to the overturned crate and Sebastian's rum cask, but the housekeeper didn't slow down as they passed several closed doors.

When they reached their destination, Paulina waited by the doorway as Doña Josefa bustled in, unlatching the louvered doors at the far end and pulling them open to reveal a dim chamber furnished with a bed and a table that looked too rickety to hold more than a water jug. It was scrupulously clean, though, as was the rest of the room—not a single dust mote drifted in the shaft of light coming in through the open shutters.

A mosquito net hung limp from one of the bedposts. The bed itself was surprisingly luxurious, considering the bareness of the rest of the house, its crocheted coverlet heaped with silk and embroidered pillows.

It was also large enough for two. Of course, Paulina would not be sharing it with anyone.

She bit her lip, trying not to show how disappointed she was by the prospect.

A large chest in the corner contained bedsheets, all bleached a bright white by the sun. The ones Doña Josefa pulled out smelled fresh, as if they had been laundered only days previously. "I'm sure you'll want to have nicer ones made, but these will do for now."

Paulina hastened to help her make the bed. "I don't need fancy blankets."

"Hmm." Doña Josefa's iron-gray brows drew together in obvious skepticism. "I expect you'll want to make changes around here, regardless. It's only natural for a new bride." Easily lifting a corner of the heavy feather mattress Paulina was struggling with, Doña Josefa tucked a fold of the bedsheet under it.

Paulina made a noncommittal noise in response.

"I'll bring you something to eat while the water for your bath warms up," Doña Josefa said, adding, as she caught Paulina glancing toward the door, "I expect he'll want to clean up, too. He'll come to you when he does."

Would he? Paulina had a feeling that Sebastian had said all he meant to back in the carriage.

Still, the tiniest spark of hope flared to life inside her chest. Sebastian was her husband now. Certainly he didn't mean to ignore her for the rest of their lives. That would be impossible, not to mention impractical.

Yes—he would definitely come to her. And then she would have the opportunity to convince him of her innocence, and perhaps even convince him that being married to her might actually be a good thing.

"What the devil happened?" Dilia asked the moment they had stepped into the front room. "You look like you've been through a war or two."

Sebastian closed the door behind her and scrubbed a hand over the bristles covering his jaw. "I feel as though I have. Nothing's broken, though, I don't think," he added, feeling that the assurance should have eased at least some of the creases on Dilia's forehead, not deepened them.

The overturned crate with his rum was still in the middle of the room, though the guardsmen's muddy footprints had been wiped off the tiles. If it weren't for the fact that he was now saddled with a wife, Sebastian could almost pretend they had never been there.

Sebastian poured a hefty slug into the enamel mug and offered it to Dilia, who declined with a moue of distaste.

That small attempt at hospitality was all Sebastian had in him. Raising the mug to his lips, he drained every last drop of rum in it and cast it aside before sinking to the floor, his head in his hands. "I'm married," he said to Dilia.

"Legally?" she asked.

"I think so." Briefly, Sebastian outlined the events of the previous three days.

In response, Dilia grew thoughtful. "I wonder why you." At his raised eyebrow, she elaborated. "Not that I don't believe you wouldn't make a good match for anyone short of a royal princess—half the matchmaking mothers in town have tried to claim you for their daughters, after all. But it isn't as though wealthy, handsome men are scarce around here. There must be a reason why Despradel targeted you specifically."

"I've been wondering the same thing myself. Wealth and devastating good looks aside—" Sebastian scrounged up a smile for Dilia and was relieved to see the crease on her forehead soften. "I can't help but think it had something to do with what happened at Don Enrique's store. Whether because I embarrassed him by challenging his treatment of Paulina, or because half the town having witnessed it would have made it easier to convince them of an entanglement between us. Or maybe it's just that he knows I haven't any well-connected relations to intervene on my behalf." He sighed. "But speculating isn't going to do me any good. What I need is to figure out what to do now."

"Get an annulment, for one," Dilia said briskly. "There's not a judge in his right mind who wouldn't grant you one."

Sebastian wasn't so sure about that—not after seeing

how readily Despradel had persuaded the guardsmen and the clerk to do his bidding, but he didn't say so out loud. There was no need to alarm Dilia any further. It had been bad enough seeing the consternation on her face when he had come into the house. He rubbed his face again, glad for the stubble that covered the bruise on his jaw.

Dilia had paused, clearly wishing to say something and just as clearly hesitant to offend him. From experience, Sebastian knew he had to wait for her to speak in her own time.

Her question came a handful of seconds later. "Do you think this is anything like what happened with that woman, back in Havana?"

Sebastian tried to make his shrug look careless. "It wouldn't be the first time a beautiful woman has tried to swindle me. At least she didn't go so far as to marry me."

"Fortunately," Dilia muttered. She fetched the mug from where it had rolled, halfway to the door, and poured him some more rum. "You'll need a lawyer. We'll go into town as soon as you get cleaned up."

"I have to get to the mill first."

"You're in no condition to be going to work," Dilia told him, and Sebastian had to admit—to himself—that she wasn't wrong.

"I've never been away this long," Sebastian said, but he made no effort to stand. He was already light-headed from the rum, and he would have been hard-pressed to pull himself up on the saddle, never mind stay upright all the way to the mill.

"And yet the mill is still standing."

"As far as you know," Sebastian muttered mulishly.

Dilia shook her head in fond exasperation. "This may come as a shock to you, but the walls of the mill will not in fact tumble to the ground without you to prop them up."

Perhaps not, but the mill had held up Sebastian when he'd needed it the most. For weeks after Carlos's death, he had taken refuge among the machinery and the paperwork, infernally dull though the latter was. Each entry into the ledgers had been a small reassurance that dozens of people would be taken care of, at least for another month.

"A cool bath and a hot meal," Dilia told him, in a tone that brooked no argument and that Sebastian had often heard her employ on her unruly boys. "That's my condition for letting you out of the house."

"That doesn't seem entirely unreasonable," Sebastian agreed grudgingly.

"Good boy. Wait here while I go help Josefa heat up the water and rustle up something to eat. And Sebas?"

He softened at the sound of his old nickname.

"It will all be all right—as long as you refrain from sharing a bed with her. It would invalidate an annulment, and if she were to get with child…"

The notion, or perhaps it was the rum's fiery fingers, made Sebastian feel suddenly flushed. "Don't you worry about that," he said, as firmly as he could manage when the world around him was wobbling like warm *majarete*. "I have no intention of sleeping with my wife."

The word tasted bitter. Sebastian took another sip of rum.

He must have fallen asleep right there on the floor, because he awoke some time later, his head reeling. There was still some light streaming in through the shutters, but he couldn't tell if it was evening or very early in the morning.

He staggered out in search of the promised sustenance.

The kitchen was out back, and rather than walk through the house and risk encountering Paulina, he made his way through the length of the terrace.

Sebastian was so used to being alone in the house, save for his housekeeper, that when he caught a flash of motion through one of the shutters out of the corner of his eye, he paused on instinct and peered through the wooden slats.

Josefa must have settled Paulina in the room next to his, because there she was, stepping out of the tin bathtub, droplets of water catching the light like beads as she stretched languidly and reached for a towel to wrap around herself. Her hair was wet and swept over her shoulder, revealing the slender nape of her neck and the cluster of tight ringlets plastered to her dark skin.

Sebastian hadn't thought about women—not in this way—in…his aching head couldn't remember how long. He hadn't *wanted* to.

This sudden arousal flaring in him at the merest glimpse of Paulina's back was as unexpected as it was unwelcome. He'd meant it when he'd told Dilia that he had no plans to sleep with his wife. He sure as hell wasn't about to lust after her, either.

Even if the sight of her dark skin gleaming as beads of moisture rolled into the deep indentation at the small of her back was sure to follow him into his dreams.

Damn, but she was beautiful. Maddeningly so. Inconveniently so.

Intolerably so.

Mostly because it reminded him of being a scrap of a child, trudging alone through the streets of Havana, craning his neck for a glimpse into windows full of things he thought could never be his.

Of being even younger and being instructed to play

with the young lady of the house while his mother worked, the girl with satin bows and crisply starched pinafores that showed every mark of his muddy hands so clearly, he didn't dare touch her.

Abruptly, Sebastian turned away. If his heart was racing, it was only a product of the rum, and of having been startled.

He bounded down the steps and found himself striding to the outdoor kitchen as if there were wild boars after him.

The tantalizing smells wafting from the large pot on the *anafe* almost made him stumble. Josefa liked to cook over wood instead of coal, and the pleasantly smoky scent billowed out past the three wooden walls surrounding the cook fire. The other side was open to the yard and held the collection of rickety stools and upturned buckets that served as the dining room—Sebastian had been meaning to get himself a table, but he hadn't gotten around to it yet.

Thank heavens he'd enough beds and mattresses.

The three-legged stool Sebastian sank onto rocked alarmingly—or perhaps that was just him, still reeling with exhaustion and hunger and the remains of the rum.

"You look like something chased you here," Josefa observed as she heaped a large serving of rice and pigeon peas onto a tin plate.

"You put her in the room next to mine."

"Should I not have?" She raised an eyebrow as she handed him the plate. "Would you rather your wife slept in the horse paddock?"

Sebastian winced at the word *wife*.

"Like that, is it?" she remarked, but she refrained from questioning him. Josefa had many fine qualities, among them her excellent cooking skills, but by far the one Sebastian appreciated the most was her discretion.

The slice of avocado on the side of his rice glittered in the evening light as if it had been dusted with moonlight and magic instead of salt. Sebastian dug his fork into its tender side, pausing with it halfway to his mouth. "Has she eaten?"

"She ate, all right," Josefa grumbled. "She may be a slip of a girl, but she's likely to eat you out of hearth and home if her dinner was any indication. You might want to talk to Leo about planting some more yuca and plantain if we're to keep up with her appetite."

Sebastian muttered something incomprehensible through the spoonful of rice and avocado he had just shoved into his mouth, then followed it with a change of subject that was guaranteed to make Josefa forget all about Paulina's appetite. "Did your daughter have her baby?"

Josefa brightened and began to tell him all about her newest grandson.

The shadows cast by the outbuildings were beginning to lengthen. Sebastian shoved heaping spoonsful of rice into his mouth, Josefa requiring little of him in the way of conversation save the occasional grunt to indicate he was still listening.

"And the others?" he said when he had cleared his second plate. "Is everyone all right?"

"As fine as Candida's goat. He got out of his pen again and went romping through the fields. Ate up half the *auyamas* Leo's mother had planted, too. That animal is going to end up in someone's pot before long." Taking his plate, she tossed him a clean, damp rag that he used to wipe some of the grime from his face and neck.

Slowly, some of the tension in his shoulders started

to ease. They were all fine. Either Despradel was more honorable than Sebastian had given him credit for—doubtful—or he hadn't known to target them.

"The water's almost ready for your bath," Josefa told him.

Sebastian nodded. "I'll bring in the buckets so you don't have to carry them."

"Leo can do it. You look tired enough to fall over, but I put freshly laundered sheets on your bed and you're not getting any of that filth all over them."

Sebastian glanced down at the rag on his lap. It was streaked with dirt, as were his hands and forearms. "Filth?" he repeated. "You call this filth? It's just a little dust."

He lunged after Josefa with his hands in the air, as if he meant to wipe them on her spotless black dress. She snapped her apron at him with an indignant, *"Mira, muchacho!"*

Before long, the two of them were howling with laughter. Josefa lowered herself onto an overturned bucket and wheezed, waving a corner of her apron in dismissal when Sebastian offered her a glass of water.

"You'll be the death of me yet, mark my words." She dabbed her apron on her corner of her eyes as her wheezing subsided and her gaze grew serious. "We were worried about you."

"I know." Sebastian said, giving her a firm pat on the back. "But I'm here now. And I'm all right."

He cast a look back at the house. Villa Consuelo wasn't much to look at, not yet. Leo didn't usually come at night, but there he was, quietly going around lighting lanterns and hanging them from the hooks outside the doors. He must have given Paulina a lamp as well, because a warm glow spilled through the louvered shutters of her bedroom.

Her temporary bedroom, he amended silently. First thing tomorrow, he would go into town and pay a call to the lawyer who'd assisted him and Carlos in the purchase of the mill. With any luck, by this time next week, Sebastian would no longer have a wife.

Chapter Seven

The birds were singing at the top of their voices when Paulina awoke in an unfamiliar bed the following morning. Before she had even wrenched her eyelids open, she was reaching across the mattress…and finding nothing but a cotton-covered expanse of bed.

She propped herself up on her elbow and regarded the empty space beside her.

Something more bitter than disappointment welled in her chest. Pressing a hand just below her collarbone, Paulina willed the pain winding around her heart to recede. She was not going to give in to the tears gathering just behind her eyes, not after all she'd been through. And certainly not because of her misguided expectation that Sebastian would relent.

The chances that he would were slim, of course. Still, knowing that hadn't stopped her from arranging her curls enticingly on the pillow, wishing she had pearls or diamonds to wink at him in the darkness. She had even fiddled with the shoulder of her nightdress, leaving its satin ribbon undone so that it slipped invitingly off her shoulder.

She'd been as foolish as a schoolgirl.

Flinging the thin blanket aside, she sat up. What did it matter that Sebastian hadn't come to her bed the previous night? He'd been tired and hurt and so had she. Maybe he hadn't wanted to disturb her. After all, they'd both had a long, hard day, and heaven knew they'd needed some rest. He might even be outside her door now, waiting for her to awaken.

With that encouraging thought, she sprang out of bed and rushed through her ablutions, using the last of the lukewarm water in the clay jug.

The clothes she had worn the day before had been taken by Doña Josefa to be laundered, but she had washed her undergarments in last night's bathwater and laid the shabby linen on the cane-backed chair by the door. To her surprise, there were two clean blouses and a cotton skirt folded over her combinations—Doña Josefa must have brought them while Paulina was still asleep. Both blouses were a trifle plain, but well-made, much finer than the frilly white monstrosities Antonio had purchased for Paulina. She chose the plainer one of the two, enjoying the sensation of the soft fabric slipping over her skin.

There was no mirror in the washstand—in fact, there was no washstand at all, only a chipped enamel basin on a rickety table, next to the jug—so she gathered her hair into a twist and pinned it up as best she could, hoping that it looked presentable.

And then, her stomach fluttering with nerves, Paulina walked out into her new home.

Which was as empty of people as it had been of furniture.

It wasn't until she ventured outside that she found Doña Josefa standing over a cauldron the size of a bathing tub, muscular arms submerged to the elbow as she scoured an enamel bowl.

"Good morning," Paulina said. "Did—? Is—?"

Doña Josefa gave her a shrewd look as she wiped her hands dry on her apron. "He's gone to the mill. He'll be there most of the day, I expect, so you needn't be on the lookout for him."

With a start, Paulina realized she had instinctively glanced in the direction of the mill. "Oh."

The short word didn't come close to conveying the depths of her dismay. So he did mean to stay away. He did mean to pretend that she wasn't his wife—that she didn't exist.

Her hand clenched into a fist. He had the right to be angry with their current circumstances, she would give him that. It wasn't like she herself wouldn't have preferred for things to have happened differently. But they hadn't, and ignoring her wasn't going to change the fact that they were now married.

Doña Josefa didn't remark on Paulina's lackluster response. She bustled to the table and began to pile food onto a plate. "You'll be wanting breakfast, I expect. Would you like me to bring a tray to your bedroom? I can have Leo bring it to the terrace if you'd rather take your coffee there."

"There's no need to trouble yourself on my account," Paulina said, perching on a three-legged stool. "I can see you've plenty to do without having to tote trays in and out of the house."

The housekeeper's eyebrows rose, but she handed Paulina a tin mug without comment. Though tepid, the coffee was excellent, and Paulina had downed half of it by the time a plate of eggs and sliced avocado was placed on her lap. There were hot roasted *batatas*, too, and another mug full of milk so fresh it was still warm. A far cry from the linen tablecloths, bakery buns and hot choc-olate Antonio insisted on, but all the better for it.

The kitchen itself was similar to the one at her old home, with its three wooden walls surrounding a cen-tral brick-ringed cook fire—aromatic wood, she noted, rather than sooty coal or even the dry sugarcane pulp often used in the region. The scarred worktable stand-ing against one of the walls was piled with reed baskets full of eggs and *víveres*, some with dirt still clinging to their tough exteriors.

As Paulina ate, Doña Josefa pulled down a bulb of garlic from the bunches hanging from a large iron nail. Breakfast may have been over, but the next meal would be soon in coming.

Paulina took one last sip of her now-cool coffee. "Does he always work through lunchtime?"

Doña Josefa frowned as her large thumbs worked off the garlic's papery skin. "A dreadful habit, mark my words, and one I haven't been able to break him out of. I was hoping that would no longer be the case, now that there's a fetching young lady waiting for him at home."

"He won't want to see me." Paulina touched the tines of her fork to the smear of yolk that was all that remained of her breakfast. She glanced up to see that Doña Josefa was giving her another one of her incisive looks, her eyes sharp beneath her wrinkled lids. Paulina returned it with a steady one of her own.

But all Doña Josefa said was "I wouldn't be too sure about that." She dropped the denuded cloves into a large wooden mortar before adding, "Your husband has a heavy load on his shoulders that he thinks he has to carry all by himself. He'd spend entire days up in that office of his if we let him."

"We?"

"His foreman, myself and most everyone who works in the mill or thereabouts. His foreman once threatened to throw him over his shoulder and haul him home when he caught him sleeping at his desk for the second time in a row."

Paulina couldn't help a smile at the image of broad-shouldered Sebastian being carried home like a tired child. "It sounds like he has a lot of people looking after him."

"He does his share of looking after us, so it's only fair," Doña Josefa said. The glance she cast at Paulina over the rim of her mortar felt like a warning, and Paulina answered it the only way she knew how.

"I won't hurt him," she told the housekeeper. "Not intentionally, in any case. He did me a kindness and has paid horribly for it. I would hate for him to suffer any more on my account."

Doña Josefa nodded in what looked like approval, but all she said was "I can't imagine you'll have much of a choice in the matter. There never is when it comes to love."

There were a lot of things between Sebastian and Paulina, but love was definitely not one of them.

A sharp intake of breath from Doña Josefa made Paulina glance up from her empty plate.

"Sebastian?" Paulina blurted out. Her heart was fluttering, and not just at having been startled—from the way Sebastian was frowning at them, she had the uncomfortable feeling that he might have heard what the housekeeper had just said. "But I thought… Doña Josefa said that you never come home for lunch."

"I'm not here for lunch," he returned immediately. "I came to make sure my house was still standing."

The knot that had been tightening her stomach had

all but dissolved at the sight of him. Still, she rose and set her plate next to the basin, then made a show of putting her hands on her hips. "What exactly did you think I would do? Dismantle it stone by stone the minute you had your back turned?"

Behind her, the housekeeper excused herself and slipped away.

"I wouldn't put it past you," Sebastian said.

It was such a ridiculous accusation that Paulina couldn't help but scoff. "Should I be flattered that you think me capable of all sorts of villainy?"

He raised an eyebrow. "Is that the sort of thing that pleases you?"

"No, Sebastian!" Good heavens, this man could certainly try her patience. "What in the world do you think I'd have to gain by destroying your home?"

"Far be it for me to know what goes on in that scheming mind of yours."

"I am not the unscrupulous scoundrel you think I am."

"And I am no fool."

To make up for the difference in their heights, he had unconsciously leaned forward, and he was now so close that the angular slope of his nose was in danger of brushing hers.

So close he could have kissed her without having to do much but tilt his head down.

A most inconvenient frisson down her spine made her take half a step back.

"No, not a fool," she told him, adding in a rush, "but it is foolish to insist on putting a wall between us when we should—"

"A wall is all there will ever be between us," he snapped. "And don't you forget it."

With that, he turned on his heel and stalked out of the kitchen yard, leaving her once again.

Sebastian didn't come home until late in the evening. Paulina had gone into her bedroom to bathe before dinner, and when she stepped out, it was with a jolt of surprise to see him sitting on the floor of the terrace.

His back was turned to her, and it was bare.

Paulina stopped abruptly, her foot coming down hard on the tile beneath it. The breadth of his shoulders was outlined in flickering lamplight, in echo of the way he had been highlighted by lightning on the night of the storm, when he had stood in the same place, gazing out into the lashing rain.

The sky behind him was mild tonight, but Paulina was filled with the same longing to spread her palms on that sweat-slick expanse of skin and feel the flex of his muscles. Had their circumstances been different, she would have knelt behind him and pressed her body against his, her hands on his bulging arms and her lips following the drop of perspiration making its way down the back of his neck…

A shudder slid over her.

As if he could feel the waves of heat radiating from her skin, Sebastian glanced backward. "Is anything the matter?"

Paulina grasped at the fraying threads of her composure. "I know you don't want me around, and I'll stay out of your way if that's what you wish. But before I do, there's something I wanted to tell you."

All she wanted was to finish giving voice to the thought that had been circling her mind since the day before. She'd tried it that morning, before he had stalked away, and she was going to give it one more try, if only to show Sebastian that she didn't intend to be put off that easily.

His shirt had been flung over the railing, and Paulina was almost overcome with the impulse to press it to her face and see if it still smelled warm and spicy. Or better yet—bury her head in the crook of his neck.

He must have noticed her looking at the shirt, because he yanked it off the railing and pulled it on, shrugging the white cotton over his shoulders. It wasn't until his head popped out through the neck hole and his eyes met Paulina's, eyebrows raised in inquiry, that she realized she was staring.

Tearing her gaze away, she said the first thing that came to mind. "I— What are you doing?"

"Carpentry."

"In the dark?"

She saw his chiseled shoulders move into a shrug. "I rarely have the opportunity to work on it in the daytime. Besides, I've a lamp."

Paulina studied the back of his head. "The mill does seem to take up much of your time."

Neither Antonio nor her father, when he still lived, had spent such long hours at the mill. Then again, neither of them had contrived to eke much of a profit from it, either.

"A great deal of people depend on it remaining a profitable enterprise," he answered flatly and turned back to his work.

Using the back of a hammer, he pried off the remains of a broken baluster. Instead of casting it aside, he fit one splintered end against another piece he must have dislodged earlier, as if in preparation for joining the two. As Paulina watched with growing fascination, he set one piece down and clamped the other one between his powerful thighs before using both hands to run a small tool over the ruined edge.

Wood shavings tumbled from his trousers to the floor in pale curls as the broken end of the baluster grew smoother.

Paulina couldn't help but contrast Sebastian's pains-taking restoration to the careless way her brother hauled his boots onto his railing, not noticing or even caring that it was starting to come apart from the wall.

"Was it damaged by the storm?" she asked, perching on the edge of the rocking chair.

"It's been broken for years." Sebastian's hands swept over the wood as if he were caressing it, and Paulina tried not to imagine that same hand running over her bare leg. "It's a beautiful old house—or it was, once. I had grand plans to restore it to its former glory, but all I seem to have repaired is part of the roof and half a meter of this balustrade."

His voice drifted off, then he seemed to shake him-self, as if recalling that he had no interest in having a conversation with Paulina. He cleared his throat. "What was it you wanted to tell me?"

He reached for the jar of nails next to the hammer as Paulina started to answer. The cuff on his shirt pulled back slightly, showing the deep violet bruises around his wrist that must have been left by the manacles. Even in the dim, unsteady light of the lantern, the brutal discol-oration looked painful.

Paulina stifled a gasp.

He caught her look and, scowling, yanked his cuff over the bruise. "What?" he demanded again, in harsher tones.

"Oh, I—just wondered if you were ready for dinner."

"I already ate," he replied in clipped tones, turning back to his work.

Paulina nodded and started toward the kitchen in silence. She was on the top step when she paused and studied the top of Sebastian's head. His tight curls had been cut short, leaving his ears and nape looking oddly vulnerable. What she wouldn't give for the freedom to graze them with her fingertips as she passed and have her gesture met with a smile.

"I had nothing to do with it, you know," she murmured.

"I know nothing of the sort," he said coldly.

She nodded. "You've no cause to trust me. I know that. And I know you mean to dissolve this marriage—"

He snorted as if finding offense in the very word.

"—as soon as the law will allow. But if I'm to live in your house and eat at your table—"

He started at hearing his own words said back to him.

"I will do my best to gain what little trust you can afford me. Not because we've been forced into a marriage, but because I'm as much a victim of my brother as you are, and fighting each other will do neither of us any good."

He gave her an irritated glance. "Didn't you *just* say you meant to stay out of my way?"

"I changed my mind," she said, lifting her shoulders into a shrug. "I've spent far too long making myself small to appease my brother. If that's what *you* want, you'll have to find yourself a different wife. I won't make a pest of myself, but neither will I cower in a corner. I'm tired of feeling like I ought to tiptoe around everyone."

She said it quietly enough, but Paulina surprised herself with the force behind her words. She cocked her head. "Who knows? I might even try my hand at being contrary, just for the fun of it."

She had gone down the steps and was halfway to the kitchen before Sebastian spoke again, so she didn't quite hear what he said, but it sounded awfully like, "Good for you."

Sebastian set down his spokeshave and yawned so hard his jaw cracked. He'd woken before dawn in order to ride into town and borrow some clothes from Dilia, as Josefa had pointed out that her own dresses would swamp Paulina's shorter frame. Josefa had been busy frying eggs when he arrived, and rather than drop the clean frocks into the basket with the dirty laundry, he had taken them into Paulina's bedroom himself, holding his breath as he folded them on the chair by the door.

In the dim light of dawn, Paulina was a series of curves under the thin blanket. The hinges had let out a soft whine of protest when he eased the door open, and she had stirred, the long column of her bare arm moving over the pale cotton.

He hadn't taken so much as a step into the room, but the sweet floral scent that seemed to cling to her had followed him all the way back to his horse and down the well-worn path leading to the scattered handful of wooden houses between Villa Consuelo and the mill.

He had stopped in to see Doña Candida first. The elderly woman's intrepid goat had broken out of its pen again, and Sebastian took the time to mend the enclosure with some sturdier wood before hauling the bleating beast back into its confines. Before leaving, he slipped a handful of coins into the half-rusted can where she kept her life's savings and tucked several bills into the bottom, in case he should run afoul of anyone else—though he hoped there weren't many people in San Pedro who would resort to kidnapping.

Sixteen-year-old Leo's widowed mother was next. He'd taken her a tonic for her debilitating headaches and another book for Leo, who consumed them as voraciously as Sebastian did the crisp *cazabe* he was offered. Sebastian had offered to pay for Leo's schooling, as well as a small house in town for him and his mother, and with only a few months until the school year began, the pair were in a flurry of preparations for their upcoming move.

There were several other houses on the way to the mill, and Sebastian visited them all, eager to reassure himself that their inhabitants were as well as Josefa had claimed they were.

If anyone had noticed his absence, none remarked on it, and Sebastian breathed a sigh of relief at not having to explain the events of the past several days.

As much as it pained him to admit it, the mill had indeed fared well in Sebastian's absence. His foreman was more than competent, the workers all well trained by Carlos. In their care, the mill ran as smoothly as the still-shining machinery into which Carlos had invested most of his fortune.

Nothing seemed to have caught fire, at any rate, and the cane itself had gone unharmed in the storm.

"I was beginning to worry," his foreman remarked when Sebastian swung down from his horse outside the large wooden structure. He grinned at Sebastian from under the brim of his woven reed hat. "Finally decided to take in the sights in San Pedro?"

"Something like that," Sebastian replied, half amused at the foreman's suggestion that he'd been carousing in brothels. It saved him having to explain what had happened, though, and for that he was grateful.

A note from Dilia had been waiting on his desk when he reached it. Knowing that Sebastian would never agree to be so far from the mill, she had offered to put up Paulina at her house in town. Sebastian had meant to tell Paulina when he got home—he would have, if she hadn't utterly disarmed him with her remark about not cowering in corners. It had made him recall, in painful detail, all he'd said to her in the carriage on their way home from the Palace of Justice.

Sebastian cast a glance at Paulina's door. Her light was still glowing through the narrow slats. He hesitated, nudging his spokeshave aside, then suddenly recalled the way those beads of water had cascaded over the pronounced dip of her lower back and thought better of risking those treacherous slats. He'd tell her tomorrow after he returned from town.

But when he arrived the following evening, after a disappointing visit to a lawyer who claimed to be too busy to take his case, he found her clambered up a stool on the terrace, her braid swinging slightly as she twisted one of his turnscrews into the hinge of her bedroom doors.

The plain frocks he had borrowed from Dilia on her behalf suited her far better than the ridiculous white dress had. Without the overabundance of ruffles and flounces to obscure her figure, she looked lithe and shapely as she stretched onto her tiptoes to reach the top hinge.

It wasn't only her braid that was swinging.

"I've been meaning to do that," Sebastian said, rubbing the back of his head as he watched her deftly remove the old iron fittings. The new ones he had purchased were lined up neatly on the floor. "I would have gotten to it, eventually."

"You've enough to do. I thought you might appreciate some help."

"I don't need your help."

"The words you're looking for are *thank you*," she said a little tartly, twisting to look at him. "And I didn't say you needed my help, only that you might appreciate having one less chore waiting for you in the evenings. Will you hand me the chisel?"

He obliged, feeling bemused as he took the turnscrew she passed him.

"Where did you learn to do all this?"

She gave a slight shrug. "I lived in an old house, too, you know, and I've a brother who hates parting with his money unless it's for something he believes other people will admire. I had to either learn how to do household repairs myself or live in a permanent state of dilapidation."

Sebastian absorbed the news of Despradel's miserliness with little surprise. A glance at their *quinta* had told him as much, and even if that hadn't been the case, Antonio's decision to sell the mill could have only come from deep financial need.

If Despradel had found himself unable or unwilling to bear the cost of his sister's upkeep, marrying her off would have certainly seemed like a reasonable course of action. That he had chosen Sebastian for it was likely convenience.

The way he had done it, however…was it merely some sort of innate cruelty, or perhaps just repayment for having felt slighted by Sebastian that day in town?

The dislodged hinge clattered to the stone floor. Paulina hopped down lightly from the stool and turned to face him.

Her eyes were astonishing. Not only because of their rich brown color, or the way they seemed to catch and hold all the light around them until they were as luminous as lanterns. It was the expressiveness of them that made Sebastian catch his breath.

He must have been staring. She cocked her head at him.

"I assure you, I know how to put it back together," she told him. "You needn't wait to make sure I do it— heaven knows you could use some rest."

Vaguely disconcerted, though he couldn't say exactly why, Sebastian picked up the spokeshave he had been using to smooth down the broken baluster. "I'm not tired," he lied. There was no need to admit that his thighs ached from the long ride into town and his shoulders still felt cramped from the irons. "And that door's too heavy for you to manage on your own. I'll hold it up while you get the last hinge."

She looked briefly startled, as she did every time anyone showed her the slightest kindness—as if she was unused to even the most basic courtesies.

Unsurprising, considering that damn brother of hers.

Working together, they made short work out of swapping the old, rusted hinges. Sebastian held the shutter in position, trying not to let on that his muscles were screaming in protest, while she leaped up onto the stool once more and screwed in the new hinges.

"These doors really ought to be painted," she was saying from above him. "The old paint is coming off in my hands. Would it be all right if I asked Leo to help me sand them down tomorrow? I saw some cans of paint behind the kitchen that might do, though you might want to purchase some the next time you're in town—how do you feel about a bright, cheery yellow?"

As a matter of fact, Sebastian was partial to bright, cheery yellows. What he didn't like was the desperate panic beating at his ribs as she smiled down at him, for all the world as though she and her brother hadn't conspired to keep him bound in a stinking cell for days.

"This isn't your home," he said abruptly, releasing the secured door.

"I know that," she told him from above, flint in her eyes. "I know it better than you possibly could. I'm reminded of it at every minute of the day—that I live in a house that will never be my home, and that I'm wed to a man who despises me. Forgive me for trying to make the best out of a wretched situation."

As she stepped down from the stool, it gave an alarming wobble and sent her flying.

Sebastian caught her reflexively, his aching arms wrapping around her slender waist and pulling her against his chest as if his body remembered the last time they had stood that way and was eager to repeat the experience.

And like the last time they had stood that way, his body felt seared from the inside out, though he hadn't had so much as a sip of rum.

It was made even worse by the image that flashed into his mind. He didn't have to close his eyes to see again Paulina stepping out of the bath, the pronounced curve of her lower back glistening with beads of water right where Sebastian's hands were now placed.

Her lips pouted in an approximation—or perhaps anticipation—of a kiss. Her front tooth was ever so slightly crooked—endearingly so, he would have called it, had it been anyone else's. He couldn't let himself find anything endearing in Paulina Despradel.

"I don't despise you," he said softly. Too softly. He forced ice into his voice. "I don't…feel anything for you. As a matter of fact, I don't think about you at all."

He was protesting too much. She ought to have been

able to see right through him. If she did, she didn't show it. Her only response was to stiffen in his arms.

He'd hurt her feelings. Yes, well, he'd meant to. He didn't need her getting any ideas about what her being in Villa Consuelo meant.

It would do him well to keep that in mind, as well.

"And I would appreciate it if you could manage to remember that you're a guest here. It's not up to you to paint my doors or repair my shutters, and it's definitely not your place to order my staff about."

Gently, he set her on her feet. And then, feeling as though her touch had scalded him and needing to put enough distance between them to keep himself from burning, he walked off into the night.

Her eyes were as luminous as they were expressive, and the image of them followed him all the way to the darkened mill.

Chapter Eight

A fallen log wasn't the most comfortable place for Sebastian to have his morning coffee, but peaceful spots were in perilously short supply these days and sitting at the edge of the cane field with only a flock of birds for company was the closest thing he could get to peace.

He couldn't really see the house from here, save a glimpse or two when the wind parted the leaves in the right way. It was just as well.

Setting down his enamel mug, he snapped open his newspaper and stared at the sun-dappled page. He had paid visits to almost all of the lawyers advertising there and had been turned down by all of them. Their reasons for doing so were varied, mostly inconsequential...and utterly fabricated.

Sebastian was on fairly good terms with the few townspeople in his acquaintance, and he knew he was considered a respectable businessman, if a trifle distant from society. He hadn't any debts, and he paid his bills on time.

Why, then, would every lawyer in San Pedro, prominent and disreputable alike, decline to take his case?

Sebastian had thought that plunging into action would

go a long way toward restoring at least some measure of peace, but this entire situation only continued to make him feel desperately helpless. It wasn't a sensation he was accustomed to, or one that sat well on his shoulders.

With no one around to see it, he didn't bother to stifle a yawn. He'd stayed late at the mill the night before, creeping into his bedroom a scant few hours before dawn. It had made him irritable—not just the lack of sleep, but the indignity of having to sneak into his own home like a common patio thief.

He'd ride into town again today, after a brief stop at the mill, and see about the rest of the lawyers in the directory. First, however, he needed at least five seconds' worth of quiet while he finished his coffee.

Evidently, that was too much to ask.

A flock of tiny black birds detached itself from the branches above Sebastian and set off across the sky, chattering. As if in response, the tangle of vegetation separating Sebastian from the fields gave a violent tremble. Sebastian had an instant to hope for a wild beast, or even Candida's confounded goat, before something much less desirable emerged through the parted leaves—Paulina.

"What are *you* doing here?" he asked ungraciously as he lowered his newspaper.

She looked surprised, and tired, and Sebastian felt a pang of something that felt uncomfortably like guilt even as he reminded himself that he was doing this not for his own sake, but for those of everyone who depended on him. Then she seemed to draw up, as if she could pull strength around her like a cloak.

As if she could tower over him in spite of the considerable difference in height between them.

"I was going for a walk," she returned. Her hair had been woven into braids and wound around the top of her head, an arrangement that made her cheekbones look more prominent and her gaze more intense. "That is, if I am in fact allowed to go for walks and not expected to wait somewhere convenient for the next time you feel like telling me how unwelcome I am in your home."

Defiance suited her. Her hands were on her hips, her hair was half-unbound and blowing in the breeze, and she was glaring at Sebastian with enough heat that he could almost feel it curl around him and settle low in his belly.

It was damned unwelcome.

"I'm not the kind of person who holds people prisoner until they do his bidding," Sebastian pointed out, the words coming out more harshly than he intended as he tried to cover up the frisson of desire.

"One can only hope there aren't many of those around here," she muttered and started to turn away.

"In a hurry to go conspire with your brother?"

Her hesitation made his shoulders tense. "You don't have to look at me as though you've caught me with my hands on the dough. I *was* on my way home, as it happens. Not because I'm in league with Antonio, but because there's something I want to fetch."

"A set of irons?" he said sarcastically.

"My mother's portrait." Her sharp reply made him feel slightly chastened.

He tried to cover it up by raising an eyebrow. "Do you really think your brother will let you stroll out of the house with a painting under your arm?"

"It's not a painting." She let out a breath. "A few months before she died, my father had a miniature of hers painted by an acquaintance who attended one of their parties. It was set into a locket." She lifted her chin in the half-defensive, half-defiant manner he was beginning to recognize. "I took the locket from her jewelry box because I was angry that they were leaving again, to attend a cousin's wedding in Puerto Plata, and they didn't mean to take me along. I took it and hid it in my bedroom, and it was still there when they died. Antonio doesn't know I have it, or he'd likely try to sell it, though it isn't all that valuable."

Sebastian nodded. He didn't have anything of his own parents' save for a few faint memories, and he'd often wished that the adults who'd taken over his care when his mother died had thought to save something—anything—for him to remember them by. He couldn't fault them for not doing so, however—they'd had no choice but to be ruthless about their practicality.

Setting the newspaper next to the remains of his coffee and the jacket and hat he had cast off, he stood from the log. "I'll take you."

"Take me?" she asked warily.

"Surely you don't think I would let you go to your brother's house unescorted. If he's the villain you say he is, capable of forcing you to do just about anything—"

"Oh, you—" With a low sound that might have come from anger or just plain frustration, Paulina turned away from Sebastian and began walking in the direction of the Despradels' *quinta*.

She had a right to be angry. He knew he was being insufferable. More than that—he was being outright mean.

Women's clothes not being conducive to moving with any sort of speed, it took only a few long strides for Sebastian to catch up with Paulina.

"Why don't you just send me away?" She was looking straight ahead, as if navigating the overgrown path required all her attention. "Take me to the harbor and put me in a boat and send me to New York, or Madrid, or Paris, or even Constantinople, like you offered on the night of the storm. I would do it myself if I had any money."

"Don't think I won't do it," he said grimly. He'd thought of nothing else since Dilia had suggested that Paulina stay with her, and he had ultimately discarded the idea. He needed her here, if only to ensure that she signed whatever document was drawn up to dissolve the marriage.

"Trust me," she said, pushing a palm frond out of her way. "I would far prefer it if you did."

"We don't all get what we want."

"I'm aware of that." She could have said it bitterly, but there was only weariness in her tone.

"Yes," he said after a long pause. "I suppose you are."

The words were hardly out of his mouth when a breathless Leo popped into the path in front of them, having come through the brush. "Don Sebastian? Will you come to Doña Candida's? There's…a situation." He looked desperately apologetic, though Sebastian could have told him he wasn't interrupting anything of consequence.

"The damned goat got out again?" Sebastian said, sighing in resignation, already turning to follow Leo to the elderly woman's house.

"Not exa—"

"Did you hear that?" Paulina asked suddenly. "It sounded like a scream."

Sebastian cast a sharp glance in the direction she was looking at, but all he could see was the tangle of vegetation that surrounded them. "The goat, I expect. The determined little ba—beast keeps breaking out of its pen and chewing through his ropes. I've half a mind to put *him* in irons."

"It was a human scream," she said and darted down the path.

Swearing under his breath, Sebastian pelted after her, Leo at his heels.

Vines and branches whipped at Paulina's face as they raced toward what, yes, did sound like a woman's shrieks.

Sebastian began to run in earnest, overtaking her in a couple of bounds of his long legs. Paulina kept pace with him easily enough, though her long skirts were swirling around her ankles.

The screams subsided, and by the time they reached a clearing by a steep embankment, it had been replaced with something that sounded distinctly like scolding.

It was coming from a girl, whose bare feet were planted firmly in the packed dirt of the clearing as she yanked a rope out of a young man's hands. Looming threateningly over her, the young man raised a hand as if to slap her. Rather than cower, the girl stood her ground.

"Berenice?" Paulina was startled into saying out loud.

"You know her?" Sebastian asked, sparing Paulina a glance.

"She works at my brother's house." The last time Paulina had seen her, the girl had been acting as his assistant jailer, keeping Paulina locked in her bedroom. Warily, she followed Sebastian toward the group that had gathered around her and the young man.

Sebastian seemed to be something of a local hero—or, if not hero, at least enough of an authority figure that Paulina caught the expressions of relief as the group parted respectfully to let him through.

"What seems to be the problem?" he asked mildly.

Berenice spoke up first. "I was on my way to work when I caught this boy trying to steal Candida's goat!"

"I wasn't stealing anything," the young man said immediately, and he was promptly backed by one of the bystanders.

"That's Candida's grandson," said a man with a graying beard, spitting out a stream of tobacco into the ground. "And if you ask me, he's got more of a right to dispose of her property than the little busybody."

Berenice's brow rose. "*Busybody?* How dare you?" she said furiously, but was forestalled by Sebastian.

"Candida's grandson?" Sebastian directed an agreeable smile at the boy. "I've never met you before, have I?"

"I've been in Moca, trying to find work," the youth explained reluctantly.

"Ah, you must be Alfonso, then. I'm Sebastian Linares. I'm a friend of your grandmother's."

From the look on the boy's face, Paulina could tell he doubted Sebastian's claim to friendship.

"I'm no great friends with her goat," Sebastian added, though his attempt at humor wasn't well received by Alfonso, "but I do know that your grandmother's awfully fond of him. She wouldn't happen to be here, by any chance?"

"She went to visit a friend in town," Berenice put in. "And he was taking advantage of her being gone to sell it without her consent."

"I don't see how it's any of your business what I do with my grandmother's livestock," Alfonso told her. Paulina, looking at the scraggly specimen at the end of the rope, wasn't sure she would have used that word herself. "Don't you have anything better to do than to meddle in something that clearly doesn't concern you?"

Berenice's brows drew together. Before she could say anything in her own defense, Paulina stepped in. "That's no way to speak to a young woman," she said sharply.

"Particularly when she's looking out for your own grandmother's interests."

The young man turned to Paulina as if noticing her presence for the first time. His expression morphed into a sullen scowl. "I'm only trying to do right by the old lady. She needs money more than she needs a useless old goat that's always causing trouble."

"I see," Sebastian said, flicking a glance at Paulina. "And does Candida agree?"

Alfonso's scowl deepened. "She doesn't know what's good for her. I found a man who's willing to take the goat off my hands for twelve pesos. It's a good deal. And this one—" he jerked his chin toward Berenice "—probably just wants it for herself."

A murmur from the people gathered made him cocky, though Paulina wasn't sure they were in agreement with his pronouncement.

Alfonso gave a sudden lunge for the rope Berenice was still holding. The goat, which this far into the proceedings had been content to gnaw on it, suddenly saw an opportunity to escape. He wasted no time—snapping the frayed rope with a single bound, he leaped away, but not without first kicking Berenice aside.

The spectators scattered as the goat went right through the crowd, heading straight toward the low branches of a nearby tree. Dodging the goat's horns, Paulina threw herself after Berenice, who had crashed to the ground right at the edge of the embankment behind them. Her fingers grazed the girl's dress, but she couldn't reach her in time before Berenice went tumbling down.

Only Sebastian's arms around Paulina's waist prevented her from following Berenice down.

He gripped her against him, hard enough to make Paulina's pulse roar in her ears.

"For heaven's sake, Paulina," he said irritably, though she had noticed the hitch in his breath, "have some care for yourself."

She pulled away. "I'm perfectly fine."

The incline was only about twice Paulina's height, but it was damnably steep, and she could see no clear path down. Some distance below Berenice, a narrow stream tumbled over a series of rocks.

"Don't worry," Paulina called down. "We'll find a way to get you up. Are you hurt?"

"My ankle," Berenice called back. "I think I broke my ankle."

Behind her, Sebastian was telling the men to fetch a longer rope with which to haul the girl up. Paulina was the only one who saw Berenice sit down suddenly, like a marionette whose strings had been abruptly cut.

"*Santísimo*, she's going to faint," Paulina exclaimed. She didn't think twice about it. Seizing one of the long vines dangling down from a tree growing right at the edge of the embankment, she tested it with her weight. It would hold her, but not any of the men clustered behind her.

"Paulina?" Sebastian sounded bemused. "What—?"

She didn't waste time to hear his protests but used the vine to let herself down onto the ledge where Berenice had fallen. Paulina had spent much of her childhood shimmying up trees and swinging from vines, but it had been a while since she'd last done such a thing, and her descent was not as smooth as it should be—the vine scraped the skin of her palms as Paulina slid down a little too suddenly, forcing her to let go and leap down lightly onto the wide ledge.

Berenice was conscious, but her breathing was ragged

and her face screwed with pain. Paulina put an arm around her. "You'll be all right."

Sebastian's head appeared over the edge, brows knit together into a thunderous frown. "Leo went to fetch a longer rope. You could have waited."

"Berenice was feeling a little faint," Paulina said up to him. "I thought she'd appreciate some company down here."

"By all means. Would you like a pot of coffee and a cake for your visit? Or perhaps a bottle of port?"

Was it her imagination, or did he look slightly admiring under the disapproving frown?

Not that it mattered.

"Sarcasm doesn't suit you," Paulina called, and she was rewarded with a smile before he withdrew.

Heedless of the mud and broken leaves, she sat herself beside Berenice. "It won't be long before they find a rope long enough to pull us up."

The girl nodded. "Thank you for coming down here. That was…brave."

"Or foolhardy, as I'm sure Sebastian will waste no time in telling me." Nonetheless, Paulina offered the girl a smile. "It was brave of *you* to try to keep Alfonso from making off with his grandmother's, er, livestock."

"Doña Candida has been good to me since my parents died," Berenice said softly. "And she loves that wretched beast. I didn't think she'd appreciate coming home to find the goat gone."

"And she won't, thanks to you. You did right to stand up to that grandson of hers."

Berenice pressed her lips together, but a smile managed to find its way past them. "Just wait until Doña Candida gets back. *She'll* have a lot more to say to him. She doesn't have a lot of patience for Alfonso's schemes for getting rich quick—I know she was hoping that he would find enough work in Moca to keep him occupied for some time."

"Maybe Sebastian will be able to help in that regard," Paulina said, though it wasn't Alfonso she was concerned with. "Are you still in my brother's employ?"

Berenice gave Paulina a sudden glance, then hung her head before saying softly, as if admitting to something wretched, "I am."

They had no opportunity for further conversation just then. A good length of rope having been secured, Sebastian and the other men above prepared to haul them both up. Paulina made sure Berenice went first.

Once the girl was safely over the edge of the embankment, Sebastian cast down the rope again for Paulina to tie around her own waist. Seizing the rope in her scraped hands, she scrambled up the embankment as quickly as she could—and almost cried out when her foot slid on a patch of slick vegetation and she found herself facedown in the mud, her arm scraping painfully over a protruding root.

Only the rope squeezing her midsection kept her from plummeting all the way down to the rocks poking out of the water below.

"Paulina!" Sebastian shouted. His face came into view, and he looked ready to vault over the edge himself. "Hold on tight. I'm coming down."

"No." She couldn't have explained the sudden panic that gripped her at the prospect of him rescuing her again, but it was enough to make her lift herself out of the mud, a trifle shakily, her fingers tight around the rope. "I can pull myself the rest of the way."

"Are you—"

"I can do it," she said grimly, half to herself.

Sebastian was waiting for her at the edge, his powerful arms clasping her tightly as he pulled her up. She was not ashamed to admit that she clung to one of those arms for the second it took for the hollowness in her stomach to dissolve—thick and hard as branches, they felt reassuringly solid.

He made no move to dislodge her, and Paulina wondered if he could feel the hammering of her heart against his arm. "Are you all right?"

"Fine," she said shakily, then essayed another, firmer, "Fine."

She stepped away from Sebastian to find Alfonso looking at Berenice's ashen face with a troubled frown. "I didn't mean... My grandmother, she— I really didn't think she would mind me selling the goat."

"Maybe it would be better if we let Doña Candida be the judge of that," Sebastian said gently. "In the meantime, if it's work you want, why don't you stop by the mill tomorrow? I'm sure we can find something for you to do."

Paulina could see the gears grinding in the boy's mind. On the one hand, whatever deal he had struck for the goat must have been profitable enough that he seemed reluctant to abandon it.

On the other, it was clearly not the best idea to rebuff Sebastian outright. One had only to look at him to know he was prosperous as well as respected, and even if the young man had no interest in a job at the mill, anyone with a little foresight would try to keep in Sebastian's good graces.

He gave a grudging nod.

"Why don't you and Leo take the goat back to its pen while I see to Berenice?" Sebastian suggested, clearly not trusting the young man to go on his own.

Another nod, and both young men departed.

Paulina, who had crouched next to Berenice, was probing at her ankle. "It *is* broken," Paulina said. "I'm not expert, clearly, but it looks like a bad break."

"Oh, your poor hands," Berenice cried, grasping the objects in question, and Paulina realized she had left smears of blood on Berenice's leg. "Your palms are torn to shreds."

The cuts were fairly nasty, Paulina saw, but it was Berenice's ankle that worried her. It was puffed and swollen, the dark skin around it badly discolored. They would need a doctor. She lifted her head to tell Sebastian, but he was already crouching beside her.

"We had better get that seen by someone at the Municipal Hospital," Sebastian told Berenice, but the girl wasn't paying him any attention. Her lips were trembling as she looked at Paulina, and it didn't seem to be from pain.

"I'm sorry about helping your brother lock you up." Berenice's voice broke, and she buried her face in her grimy hands, though not before Paulina saw, with considerable surprise, the tears running down her cheeks. "He said he would hurt my little sister if I didn't follow his orders."

"I won't let him do anything to either of you," Sebastian said fiercely. "I'll find a place for you to stay until your ankle heals. In the meantime, I'm taking you to the hospital."

"Don Antonio will be waiting," Berenice said, looking apprehensive.

"Let him wait," Sebastian said grimly, adding softly, when he saw the girl's brows knit together, "You won't be able to work in this state. We'll send word that you'll be indisposed for a while."

Paulina put her arm around the young woman's shoulders to help her up. Sebastian put a stop to that by scooping up Berenice. "I can manage."

It wasn't until they had returned to Villa Consuelo, much later that morning, that Sebastian turned again to Paulina to voice what he had clearly been turning in his mind for the past several hours. "He locked you up?"

"Only so that I wouldn't go to you," she said, as matter-of-factly as she could.

Sebastian gave her a hard nod, more an acknowledgment than an expression of gratitude. Still, she couldn't help but notice the slight shift in the way he was looking at her—less like a thorn that had gotten wedged into his side, and more like someone he was trying to figure out.

Paulina stepped out of her muddy clothes, all too aware that in the next room, Sebastian was doing the same. She tried to summon up some of the irritation that had propelled her on her walk earlier that morning, but all she felt was tired.

And curious about the look he had given her when he'd asked about Antonio locking her up. It was as if he had still believed that she'd been Antonio's conspirator, and Berenice's testimony had begun to disabuse him of that notion.

It was as if he was seeing her in a different light.

Paulina unbuttoned her mud-caked blouse and pulled it over her shoulders, the abused muscles in her arms aching from the effort. The cotton garment whispered to the floor to join the skirt she had already discarded.

Mud had seeped through to her undergarments, staining them faintly with brown. She wiped them as best as she could with a clean rag, then began dressing in her spare frock. It couldn't be helped—Paulina had the one chemise and pair of drawers, which she laundered each night and hung by the louvered doors to dry, and in the pale yellow dress their lack would be noticeable.

She would have to stay in the sun until she'd dried out, that was all.

Once more presentable, and with her clothes bundled in her arms to be soaked before the stains could set, she strode into the kitchen yard. Several large tamarind trees shaded the area, though here and there sunlight filtered down through the protective canopy. Paulina paused in one such patch, soaking in the brightness and the heat.

She closed her eyes and tipped her head back. The morning sun was always warm, rarely as searing as it became as the day wore on.

When she opened them again, it was to see that Sebastian, not Doña Josefa as she had expected, was standing in the kitchen.

And he was looking at her.

Unaccountably flustered, Paulina shifted her light bundle of clothes to her front to hide the way her chemise and dress were molded damply to her chest, and hurried the rest of the way to the kitchen.

Sebastian had also changed clothes. His pristine shirt was buttoned at the cuffs and the neck, though he wore no necktie, and the droplets of water glinting in his close-cropped curls attested to his own ablutions. Trying to pretend that she was not flooded with awareness—of the faint scent of soap wafting from him, or the fabric clinging to her hardened nipples—made her clumsy.

They reached at the same time for the blouse she had dropped.

Their fingers tangled on the muddy cotton, hers slim, his broad and blunt. There was absolutely no reason for the simple contact to make her heart race—no sensible reason, at any rate.

Paulina yanked her hand back, remembering to keep her hold on the blouse. "I'll thank you not to manhandle my clothes."

He lifted an eyebrow. "You're welcome."

The sardonic tinge in his voice sent prickles up and down her spine. She turned her back to him. She could hardly ask him what he was doing in the kitchen, it being his property and all, so she settled for asking about Doña Josefa, who was nowhere in sight.

"She went to the Municipal Hospital to make sure the doctor knew what sort of poultice to apply to Berenice's foot. She'll have the entire hospital following her orders before nightfall."

Paulina couldn't hold back a smile. "That sounds like her."

The tub they used for laundry was too large for just her skirt and blouse, so she looked for the enamel basin—and found it in Sebastian's hands.

"I needed that," she said.

"This will only take a moment. Give me your arm."

She narrowed her eyes at him. "Why?"

"Because it's badly scraped, and I've something that will make it feel better."

"Why should you care?" Paulina said.

It came out more forcefully than she'd intended; rather than look taken aback or annoyed, Sebastian merely met her eyes.

"I care," he said, so seriously that Paulina had to look away.

She shifted her gaze from him to the basin, which was filled with clear water.

Her skepticism must have been written all over her face, because he gave an impatient sigh and set the basin down on the table, then showed her the contents of a covered mug next to a clean rag. "I'll clean out the dirt, then put some *remedio* on the scrapes. Josefa brewed it, if it makes you feel any better. Will you give me your arm now?"

Mildly discomfited, she complied, extending her right hand in his direction, palm upturned as if she were offering him something. The sleeve of her dress ended just below her elbow, very close to one edge of the scrape. Very gently, he folded up the fabric so that it wouldn't get in the way, then dipped the rag into the clean water and began to bathe her wound.

He did it confidently, and Paulina would have thought he were used to this sort of thing were it not for the fact that she knew that was how he did everything.

Paulina was no stranger to longing. In fact, she was acquainted well enough with it to know that the sensation twining around her limbs was something…different. Something deeper.

Something that made her wonder what it would be like if he were to trail the backs of his fingers over the soft, unmarred skin on the inside of her arm. If he were to lower his head and press his lips to the tracery of veins on her wrist. And perhaps venture farther, following the line of her arm all the way to her neck and the hollow beneath her ear.

It was just as well that Sebastian had no idea how his touch affected her—or the thoughts currently searing their way through her mind.

In order to distract herself from his confident hands, she looked straight ahead and found herself staring at his chest instead, which didn't help matters any. The wide expanse of his shirt was bisected by light brown suspenders, which were daubed with spots of mud.

"There's mud on your suspenders."

Sebastian glanced down. "Yes, well, I only have the one pair."

"They'll get your clean shirt all dirty. Here." She plucked the damp rag by a clean corner and briskly began to brush off the worst of the dirt.

"Paulina." His large, warm hand rose to cover hers, pressing it lightly against the center of his chest. It felt so natural that, for a moment, Paulina's world tilted and rearranged itself and she had to remember that they had never, in fact, stood together in that way.

She didn't want to look up into his eyes—not for fear of what she might see there, but for fear of what she might not. "That's a little better, but you'll have to soak your suspenders overnight," she said, concentrating very hard on a spot near his left shoulder.

"Paulina," he said again. "You...ah... What's that in your arms?"

"My clothes," she said after a brief pause. He had clearly changed tracks in the middle of speaking, and even though she had been ready to bolt a moment before, she felt a burst of disappointed curiosity. "I only have the one change of clothes, so I need to wash the mud right away if they're going to dry by tomorrow."

He frowned. "I should have sent you to the dressmaker to have more clothes made. My apologies. I know I've been remiss in—"

"It's fine," Paulina said, cutting him off. "I don't need more clothes, not really. And I wouldn't want to take advantage of your hospitality."

"You haven't. Also, you never did get your mother's portrait," he said gruffly.

"I suppose I didn't."

"Would you like me to go fetch it for you?"

She shook her head. "I don't think it would be a good

idea for you to go there on your own. Antonio is sure to get into one of his moods when Berenice fails to arrive, and we both know what that can lead to." She lifted an eyebrow and finally looked up into his eyes, confident that there was nothing but a dark sort of humor in hers. "It's just as well. Going to the *quinta* was probably a bad idea. Even for the portrait—it's probably more trouble than it's worth."

"I doubt that," he said with the gaze of a man who was intimately acquainted not only with grief, but with loss.

It made Paulina wonder if he was also an orphan. He'd told her a little about Carlos, and there was Dilia, the woman who had been waiting for him when they'd returned from the Palace of Justice, but Paulina was reasonably sure he hadn't mentioned any relations, at least in her presence.

He hadn't released her hand. Looking down at the scraped skin, the furrow between his brows deepened. "I haven't any bandages, but I can have someone fetch a doctor—"

"That's all right," Paulina said. "I'm fine."

"Paulina, I—"

His thumb grazed the back of her hand. If he had done it intentionally, it would have been a shockingly intimate touch—but of course, Paulina thought wildly, trying her hardest to keep her face from betraying her, it had probably been involuntary. A mere jerk of the muscles. Not a caress.

Definitely not a caress.

"I didn't know he'd locked you up. If I had…"

"You'd have believed me when I told you I had nothing to do with his plans? Doubtful."

His eyebrow quirked. "That morning when he burst in on us. You didn't say anything. I thought…"

Paulina gave a little sigh. "I should have come to your defense, I know. I was numb with shock. And embarrassed. And not wearing any clothes, if you might remember."

"Oh, I remember," he murmured.

"That puts one at a disadvantage. Honestly, I think I'd grown a little too used to giving Antonio his own way. It was…easier." She shrugged, looking down at their joined hands. "Maybe I'm as weak as he thinks I am."

"There's nothing weak about you, Paulina," he said, and her gaze skipped up to his. He gave her fingers an absent squeeze and released them, sliding his hands into his pockets. "I think I was perhaps a bit hasty in putting any blame on you for…all this. I should apologize."

"Yes, you should," she said tartly.

"I misjudged you."

"You certainly did."

To her surprise, he smiled down at her. "You aren't going to go easy on me, are you?"

She found herself smiling back. "Not in the slightest." A tiny sigh escaped her. "At first I was hurt that you could think me capable of such duplicity. But then I realized—you don't know me. Not truly. Otherwise, you'd have realized that this kind of marriage is the last thing I would want. I had always thought that if I did ever marry, I would marry for love. Like my parents did. They found such joy in each other. I couldn't help but want the same."

"I don't know if I can give you that. But I do owe you an explanation." Sebastian stepped away then, but only far enough to lean against the worktable, his solid hands gripping its wooden edge tightly enough for Paulina to see that whatever he was about to say wouldn't come easily.

"Before we left Havana—before I convinced Carlos and Dilia to leave, that is—I became entangled with someone. I—don't think it's necessary to go into the details. Suffice it to say, she told me everything I'd ever wanted to hear. She made me believe…"

He made a dismissive gesture, but Paulina saw the ghost of an old wound flickering in his eyes. "That isn't important," he continued. "The point of this story is that I was very young and very foolish and fancied myself some sort of chivalrous knight or something equally as ridiculous, and she did not hesitate in taking advantage of my romantic notions. It was little things at first—minor domestic disasters that I could avert with a handful of pesos, earnest pleas for small loans for her ailing father… Before I knew it, she and her father had swindled me out of what little I had."

He didn't seem to hear the low noise of distress that escaped Paulina's lips. She should have suspected that Antonio was not the first person to take advantage of Sebastian's giving nature. That Sebastian had been justified in his suspicion of her… Paulina didn't know why that made her chest feel so tight.

"And then, the moment she realized that I was not Carlos's true brother, and therefore not about to inherit half of his parents' estate, she left. Literally left the island, without so much as a note to let me know that she'd gone." His lips lifted into a humorless smile. "I don't want to say that she left me with nothing, though she stripped my bank account almost bare, and for months afterward I felt like she'd stripped my heart right out of my chest, too. I know I've been suspicious of you—"

"You had a good reason to be." Paulina was still holding her bundle of clothes in the crook of her right elbow. She laid it down on the table and began to empty the water from the basin. Something was simmering in her chest, some strong emotion she couldn't quite name. "I'm not her, you know. I wouldn't— I didn't want any of this to happen."

"I know that now," Sebastian said quietly.

He was close enough that his breath grazed her ear. Paulina looked up at him, and her breath caught at the emotion in his eyes.

Unbidden, her hand rose to land lightly on his jaw. She breathed in sharply and would have snatched her hand away at once had he not trapped it with his own much larger one.

His touch was electrifying.

Tingles zinged down Paulina's arm, collecting somewhere just beneath her breastbone and speeding up her pulse.

Sebastian's head inclined toward hers.

"We shouldn't," she murmured.

"I know," he answered.

With those words hanging over them, their lips met in something that was surely more than a kiss. Something more vital than an exchange of breath. Something more intimate than an exchange of souls.

Paulina's heart was racing when she pulled away, gasping. Sebastian looked as stunned as she felt.

Unfortunately—or perhaps fortunately—before either of them could say a word, a voice came from behind them.

"Don Sebastian? You're needed at the mill again. One of the men had an accident."

Letting out a sharp breath, Sebastian dropped his hand from Paulina's and turned to face the messenger boy who was standing at the edge of the kitchen yard, looking apologetic at the intrusion.

Paulina took advantage of Sebastian's distraction to slip away with the basin, the soap and her dirty clothes. The splotches of mud had begun to dry. It would take a great deal of scrubbing to get them all out, but that was for the best.

Maybe the exertion would make her forget just how good his touch had felt.

Chapter Nine

After sleeping in for three days in a row, Paulina finally managed to awaken before the sun had brightened enough to send bars of light through her shutters.

She hurried into her clothes, making a perfunctory attempt to tidy her hair, and rushed out so fast she nearly collided into a tree. No—not a tree. Sebastian, who had just emerged from his own chamber, the faint aroma of soap wafting from his person. In his shirtsleeves, framed by the dark lines of his now-clean suspenders, his arms were as thick—and as hard—as branches.

He had vanished for much of the previous afternoon and had returned after dinner looking out of temper and smelling distinctly like goat. When questioned, he had muttered something about having ruined two shirts in a single day and dragged the tub into his bedroom. He hadn't emerged by the time she had retired, but Paulina, awake and restless with memories of the kiss they had shared, had heard him fussing with the railing long into the night.

"You don't sleep much, do you?" she said in lieu of a good morning, hefting the bundle of fabric she had tucked under her arm.

Sebastian shrugged. "I don't need to," he said, but he belied his own words with a yawn so wide his jaw made an audible popping sound.

Paulina limited her remarks to a skeptical, "I see," as they began the walk to the kitchen.

He let out a breath that sounded like a laugh. "Dilia makes me take naps," he confessed. "Orders me, in fact, as if I were one of her boys."

"I can see why," Paulina replied. In the time she had known Sebastian, the crinkle of exhaustion hadn't left his eyes. "Have you ever thought about taking some initiative and *not* waiting for someone to bully you into napping?"

"I've a lot to do," he said simply.

He didn't seem inclined to mention what had happened between them the day before, and Paulina thought it was probably for the best. It wasn't likely to happen again, after all. Sebastian was probably already regretting that it had happened at all. Both the kiss and his confession.

Through the tamarind trees that canopied the yard, Paulina could see the sky beginning to lighten with pale bands of light. Below the sprawling branches, however, it was still fairly dark. Paulina could barely see the hulking shape in the middle of the kitchen yard—and judging by the way Sebastian almost walked into it, neither could he.

"What's this?" he asked warily, eyeing the shape as though it were one of the wild boars that lurked in the mountains rather than a harmless old door laid out on trestles.

"Our new dining table." Paulina shook out the clean bedsheet she had tucked under her arm and laid it over the peeling wood. "Doña Josefa helped me set it up before we went to sleep last night."

"It was about time, too," the housekeeper remarked

from behind the cook fire, which was already roaring beneath a pan of frying eggs and onions.

"I hope you don't mind," Paulina said, glancing up at Sebastian. "We thought it would be fun, and the door didn't appear to be in use…"

"It's a ridiculous idea," Sebastian replied as Leo came up behind them with the milk pail, saying a soft good morning.

Paulina's heart sank. "Oh, all right, I—"

Stuffing a hand into the pocket of his trousers, Sebastian pulled out a wad of bills, two of which he handed Leo. "Go to Ronaldo's workshop and buy the biggest and finest table he has." He scowled down at the overturned bucket at the head of the table. "And chairs. At least eight of them."

Leo nodded and made as if to leave right then, but Sebastian caught him by the back of his shirt. "After you've eaten."

Paulina, who had opened her mouth to say the same thing, snapped it shut.

Sebastian turned to Paulina with a glower, which she met with the sunniest smile she could muster.

"Are you trying to look forbidding?" she asked, fetching the jar of flowers she had left by the water barrel and placing it squarely on the center of the table. "Maybe you ought to furrow your brow a little more. Or growl. That'll do it."

He shook his head, clearly trying not to laugh. "I've got to get to the mill."

Coming up behind him with the coffeepot and two mugs hanging from her little finger, Doña Josefa pressed him down onto the three-legged stool. "You have time to eat breakfast before you go."

"And you are as bossy as a general," Sebastian said

with a good-natured grumble, but he submitted to Doña Josefa's orders.

Briefly, Doña Josefa laid a hand on top of his head before heading back to the cook fire.

It was a curiously familiar gesture for a housekeeper to make to her employer. Paulina tilted her head and looked at the pair more closely. They looked nothing alike, though they were both large and broad in their own ways. Doña Josefa had soft, blunt features, while Sebastian's looked like they were chiseled out of stone. Was there a similar cast to their shoulders? Did they hold their heads the same way?

The kitchen yard began to lighten as she and Leo helped Doña Josefa carry the rest of the breakfast things to the table. Through the branches, the sky looked freshly laundered, a bright blue with clouds like frothed soap. It reminded Paulina of the lather she had worked up the day before, trying to erase her memory of Sebastian's touch. The scrubbing hadn't helped, and even if it had, it would have been for nothing—Paulina could count at least half a dozen times their fingers tangled over the eggs.

Perhaps the table had been a bad idea.

Sebastian reached across the table for the pitcher of milk Paulina had just taken hold of, and when his fingertips brushed the tender skin on the inside of her wrist, she gave up on breakfast and lifted the folded newspaper by Sebastian's plate. It wasn't recent, but Paulina didn't care. Humming under her breath, she discarded the first half until she came to the advertisements, which she perused with quiet contentment.

There were three houses for sale in town and two for rent. Not for the first time, Paulina wished they came with pictures, though the short descriptions were satisfying in their own way.

"Has there been a murder?" Sebastian asked.

Paulina cocked her head. "A murder?"

"It must be a shocking one, the way you're poring over the paper."

"Oh! No, I'm just looking at the houses for rent."

Raising an eyebrow, Sebastian said, "Houses for rent? I hope our hospitality hasn't been lacking."

"Doña Josefa has been wonderful to me," she said pointedly. "Leo, too. This is just a habit I have. I suppose it amuses me to pretend like I'm looking for a house. I've always dreamed of living in town."

"Why is that?" he asked, looking at her as if he really were interested in the answer.

Paulina gave a little shrug. "It's so lonely out here in the country. I'd much rather be close to other people and be able to go to frolics at a moment's notice and strolling on Sundays. It's a silly notion," she added firmly, folding the newspaper back into a tidy rectangle.

"There's nothing silly about not wanting to be lonely," Sebastian said, frowning down at the tin mug cradled in his long, strong fingers. "I enjoyed living in town back in Havana, though it did get a trifle hot and noisy sometimes. There were plenty of afternoon strolls and all sort of frolics, too." He nodded at the newspaper. "Which one would you choose?"

With the advertisements hidden inside the fold, the only words visible were the name of the paper and the banner unspooling beneath it reading *Noticias, Variedades y Anuncios*.

Even without a visible reminder of what she had just read, Paulina didn't have to think long to make a decision. "The masonry house on the corner of Calle El Retiro. Or—no. I'd buy an empty lot and have a house built to suit my tastes. Large, airy rooms with high ceilings and whitewashed walls and boxes full of white bougainvillea in every window. And two long galleries, one upstairs and one down, with plenty of room for guests and dancing."

Paulina made herself stop, suddenly aware that she had gotten carried away. "It sounds overly grand, I know. The truth is, I'd be just as happy with a shack if it was mine and mine alone."

Sebastian's brow was furrowed. "Sounds like you've given it a lot of thought."

"Yes, well. I've never been able to make any decisions for myself. Not about where to live or what to wear or who to befriend. Thinking about those things was just the only thing I *could* do, so I was apt to do plenty of it." She spread her hands. "Dreaming is free, after all."

He gave her an odd look. "You've never chosen your own clothing?"

She shook her head. "Antonio picked out every scrap of lace on those awful frocks he made me wear. My hair ribbons, too."

Paulina didn't know what to make of the sudden stillness that came over Sebastian. "Did he…mistreat you?"

"He wasn't violent, if that's what you mean. He just made himself so disagreeable to be around that it was always easier to let him have his way." Paulina shrugged. "His main complaint seemed to be that I was too much of an expense for him. Maybe he thought I would ruin him if I was allowed free rein at the dressmaker."

Over the years, Paulina had grown used to answering every flare of Antonio's temper with a turn of her head. She had looked away or left the room or otherwise found a way to keep from confronting the fact that her brother had grown up to be hard and mean and greedy.

There had always been a part of her that had been

uncomfortably aware of just how much she depended on Antonio. When her parents died, and none of their friends or relations had offered to take her in, Antonio had been quick to make her understand that as the new head of the family he held not only the purse strings— he held the reins of her life. Not only was he going to make all the decisions from now on, she had no right to question him, or to even offer her opinion.

The only thing that had gotten Paulina through those stifling years was dreaming about how one day she would be free. And now she was, in a way. No closer to that house in town, perhaps, but free nonetheless.

"Seems to me he's done a better job of emptying out his coffers himself," Sebastian remarked. He took a swig of his coffee. "I asked around town, and word is your brother's mired in countless debts. Losing at cards being much more of an expense than a few hair ribbons."

She felt her lips tugging upward as she recalled the red length Sebastian had given her for her birthday. What a pity it had been ruined in the storm. "I wouldn't be so sure about that. Do you know how many hundreds of pesos I could spend just on the ribbons Don Enrique carries in his store? I'd buy yards and yards of every color and hang them from my dressing table like streamers." She laughed at herself, tracing the rim of her mug with her fingertip. "A silly aspiration, perhaps, but a tad more attainable than purchasing an entire house."

Sebastian looked thoughtful—even a little forbidding—and Paulina wished she hadn't said quite so much. She began to gather the empty plates from her side of the table.

She had gotten so used to the way her sharp longing for companionship had lodged inside her chest like a particularly prickly burr that it hadn't occurred to her until now that her dreams would sound pitiful to someone else. It had been that way for as long as she could remember, even when her parents had been alive. She had never been able to find a place among the grown-up guests that crowded into their *quinta*, or among the girls of their set that she rarely saw. The little boy who had played with her among the sugarcane had been her one true friend—until he, too, went away.

At some point, she had come to believe that heart-wrenching loneliness was all life had to offer her. Save for the scant handful of hours when she had waited in bed for Sebastian that first night, when she had allowed herself to picture something different, for once.

"It isn't the worst hardship anyone's had to bear," she said as she piled the plates together.

"Don't make light of what you went through," Sebastian said with sudden heat, reaching for her wrist. His shirt cuff pulled away again, but this time he hardly seemed to notice the flash of discolored skin it revealed, or to care that she saw it. "You may not have worn manacles, but your brother kept you captive as surely as he did me, and for much longer. Denying you even the scant freedom due to you as a woman? It's nothing short of villainous."

Paulina stood as if frozen, captivated by his vehemence.

"You were locked up for only a few days. But Paulina, you've been trapped for most of your life."

Sebastian rose and, seizing the dirty crockery from her arms, carried it to the washtub where the housekeeper was already beginning to warm up water. "I should be on my way," he said. He started to add something else, then seemed to change his mind. "I won't be back until late."

She nodded her acquiescence, offering him a faltering parting smile.

* * *

There was a vase on his chest of drawers.

And there were *flowers* in it.

Sebastian eyed it as warily as he would have a snake.

He had come directly into his bedroom after a long, hot morning at the mill, intending to rest for a few minutes before lunchtime, and the little pitcher crowded with fiery red hibiscus blossoms was the first thing he'd seen.

He ought to resent this evidence of her intrusion into his home, his *life*. Maybe he would have, if he hadn't been filled with a grudging respect for the way she was managing to make Villa Consuelo into more of a home than it had been in the time he'd owned it. The business with the table, earlier that morning, had filled him with embarrassment at how thoughtless he'd been toward both Paulina and Josefa, who'd uncomplainingly made do with the little he'd provided them in the way of accommodations.

Well, he was about to change all that.

Quickly splashing some water onto his face and wiping off the excess moisture, he went in search of Paulina.

She, too, deserved better, and not only in the way of furniture.

Her brother had treated her abominably. That had been more than evident from the moment he'd met her. But every time Sebastian thought he knew the extent of that ill treatment, it turned out that he'd only scratched the surface.

Sebastian had known his share of tightfisted men who enjoyed a little begging and pleading from the people who depended on them. The ones who needed to be flattered before they'd part with a single *chele*. Antonio Despradel, Sebastian suspected, wouldn't relinquish so much as a dust mote for his sister's sake if it somehow didn't benefit him.

It wasn't begging he wanted, or flattery—it was control.

A few days ago, nothing could have persuaded Sebastian that he had anything in common with the youngest daughter of a wealthy household—a woman who kept to her home and only emerged swathed in yards of lace and finery, delicate as the rose he had compared her to when he'd first met her in town. A pampered woman, he would have called her.

He couldn't have been more wrong. She'd endured privations, just as he had. Only Sebastian had had two things she hadn't—family and freedom. In his darkest days, when getting a crust of bread to soothe his growling stomach seemed like an impossible dream, he'd still had more than her.

Anyone might have pitied her for it, but Sebastian was filled only with admiration at her resilience.

Paulina was fetching water from the barrel when he found her. The barrel was almost as tall as he was, and the water must have been low, even after all the rain that had fallen the night of the storm, because she had clambered onto the damn stool with the wobbly leg and was leaning so far into the barrel that all he could see was the roundness of her bottom above the rim.

The sight of it reminded Sebastian of how Carlos used to tease him for his single-mindedness when it came to the business. Sebastian hadn't only eschewed the company of the fine young ladies of the town, he'd kept mostly to himself for the better part of two years.

"You've got to have someone to come home to," Carlos had told him one evening as they pored over figures, teasing having given way to the serious tones Carlos adopted whenever he gave Sebastian some much-needed brotherly advice. "Knowing you, that's the only way you'll ever leave this confounded office."

"I've got all I need right here," Sebastian had told him, gesturing at the ledgers and diagrams scattered over his desk. "What woman could compete with all these beauties?"

No distractions until the mill was a success. That was what he'd told himself whenever he awoke in a panic in the middle of the night, sweating over the way Carlos had risked his family's future on Sebastian's word. No distractions. He needed them still less now.

And yet he was having a hard time remembering why as he watched Paulina's full bottom swaying beneath her plain brown skirt. He wasn't in the habit of ogling women's backsides, but there was nowhere else for him to look as he neared her.

She went on her tiptoes, apparently straining to reach the water. It had the effect of lifting her bottom even higher, for all the world as if she were trying to show it to its best advantage. Another man might have pressed up against her, taking it for the offer it wasn't, but Sebastian had been taught better.

He cleared his throat to warn her of his presence. From the depths of the barrel, he heard an exclamation, followed quickly by a splash, and the next thing he knew, she had kicked the stool out from under her own feet and was clinging to the lip of the barrel.

Even flailing inside a barrel, she managed to be graceful.

There was no help for it—and there was no avoiding her bottom as he seized her by the thighs and helped her down.

"Let me guess," she said when she emerged, drenched

and sputtering slightly. "You've been meaning to put in a spout?"

"I will eventually," he said defensively. He'd bought it, at any rate, though it was getting rusty as it lay unused among his tools.

"Hopefully before someone drowns in there." Paulina smoothed back her wet ringlets. Water clung to her long eyelashes like tiny diamonds, making them shimmer in the midday light and making Sebastian wonder what she would say if he asked her to close her eyes so he could kiss the drops away. "I'd do it myself, but as a guest here, I wouldn't want to presume."

"I deserved that," he told her ruefully as he dug into his pocket for the square of linen he had tucked in there earlier. "I'm sorry for startling you."

He handed her his clean handkerchief, which she waved away, along with his apology.

"It was that dratted stool. I was going to try and fix the wobble, but Doña Josefa needed water to finish mopping the house. I've half a mind to throw it into the cook fire instead, before anyone else becomes its victim—that's the second time you've had to rescue me from falling off the wretched thing."

"Lucky I came home when I did, then."

"Why *are* you here? I didn't expect you home for lunch," she said, and damn if she didn't sound exactly like a wife would have. She must have realized it, because she blinked and added, "I mean, I thought you spent all day at the mill."

"I had something to tell you."

"Oh?"

Striving for nonchalance, Sebastian said, "I sent word into town and set up an account for you at Don Enrique's store, should you need to procure anything for yourself or the house."

"Why would you do that?"

He shrugged, feeling slightly embarrassed. "I haven't the time to see about buying drapes or furniture, and Josefa has far too much to do for me to pile yet another thing on her plate. Of course, you needn't do anything if you'd rather not. I just thought…"

"Oh, no, I would like to."

"I would like for you to be comfortable while you're in my care. Don't stint on anything, no matter how much it costs. I should hate for any of you to want for anything. And Paulina?"

"Yes?" she asked softly.

"Get yourself a length of ribbon in every color that strikes your fancy."

Her answering smile filled the hollowness in the pit of his stomach. Sebastian cleared his throat and nodded at the water barrel. "Would you like me to fetch you the water you needed? My arms are longer."

"I can do it myself if you tilt the barrel. It's half-empty, so it shouldn't be too heavy."

"Oh? You don't think I'm strong enough to move a water barrel myself?"

She raised an eyebrow. "My apologies—I didn't know I was in the presence of Hercules. By all means, go ahead and shock me with your feats of strength."

Even as he laughed, Sebastian was struck with a sudden pang. Carlos would have liked her. He would have been aghast at the situation Sebastian had found himself in, but Carlos definitely would have liked Paulina.

Sebastian was about to reply with something equally—and recklessly—flirtatious. He managed to stop himself just in time—but the words that popped out of his mouth instead were no better. "Will you come into town with me? I've somewhere I want to take you."

Surprise lifted her brows. "Right now?"

"Unless you're too busy taking impromptu baths in the water barrel," he said, flicking away a drop of water dangling from one of her ringlets, for all the world like an infatuated schoolboy.

The slight widening of her eyes stopped Sebastian short.

He was aware that he shouldn't get too friendly with Paulina, or give her the wrong impression. Not because he still harbored any suspicions when it came to her character, but because it had taken him only a couple of days to find out how closely to the edge he was skirting. Another kiss, another invitation from that intoxicating mouth, and he would find himself in a most uncomfortable position.

Sebastian may have been a lot of things, but he wasn't the sort of cad who took advantage of women under his protection. And for better or for worse, Paulina was now someone else he had to take care of—at least until he found a way to annul the marriage.

Making her his wife in more than name would not only ruin his chances of doing so, it would bind them together in ways he couldn't allow himself to be bound, given his responsibilities toward so many others. The very thought made his pulse roar in his ears.

Giving in to the attraction tugging at them both, however tempting, would only end in certain heartbreak.

Then again, he couldn't bring himself to push her away, as he'd tried only a few days before. Particularly not after having glimpsed that haunting loneliness in her eyes when she'd spoken about longing to live closer to town. It would have been too cruel, and Paulina had been the recipient of enough unkindness.

Sebastian was no longer a schoolboy—and neither was he the naive youngster who had let himself be used for the sake of a pretty smile. The lesson he had learned then was a hard, bitter one, and it was still so raw, Sebastian doubted he was likely to fall for such machinations again. No matter how beautiful Paulina's smile might be or how luminous her eyes, he knew better than to let himself be seduced again.

As impossible as the prospect would have seemed even days earlier, there really was no reason why Sebastian couldn't be friends with his wife.

He examined her face. The trace of wariness was gone from her eyes, though he could still sense some sort of reserve. No doubt she was making the same sort of calculations he just had.

"We can go another time if you'd rather," he offered, in case she had come to a different conclusion.

"I'd like to go." Paulina pushed back a strand of wet hair. "But I should freshen up first. I'm sure I look an absolute mess."

He wiped her face dry with the handkerchief she had declined, then tucked two of her curls behind her ears, trying not to linger on their delicate curves. "You look beautiful," he said firmly and took her hand to tug her to where his horse was hobbled. After a moment, her fingers curled around his own, and she consented to be led.

Sebastian had never seen the need to purchase a carriage when the saddlebags on his horse were capacious enough for anything he needed from town. He didn't realize his mistake until he had helped Paulina up onto the saddle and swung himself behind her and found his thighs nestling into hers.

And then, when he reached over her shoulders for the reins, effectively wrapping her in his embrace...well.

She kept her back very straight, which was effective in keeping their upper bodies from touching but would prove painful by the time they arrived in town.

"It'll be more comfortable if you settle back against me," Sebastian suggested. "Just...pretend I'm a chair."

"I wouldn't want to incommode you."

"You won't," he told her firmly. "If you sit like that all the way into town, your back will be stiff for days."

There was no need to think of anything else that might grow stiff on the ride, particularly not when her bottom was pressed so firmly against him.

More distracting than that was the little sigh she let out when she leaned back against Sebastian, her head resting on his left shoulder and the loose strands of hair around her temple tickling the side of his neck.

Realizing he was holding the reins in a grip so tight his knuckles were turning white, Sebastian forced himself to relax as he clicked his tongue and urged his horse toward the road to San Pedro.

Chapter Ten

"Are you going to tell me where we're going?" Paulina asked. They could have ridden all the way to the other end of the island for all she cared—seated in the saddle in front of Sebastian, his arms loose around her, she was in no hurry to get to their destination, whatever it was.

"It's a surprise," he said, speaking almost directly into her ear. Paulina suppressed a shiver of delight. "A token of friendship, if you will."

"Friendship?" She twisted as best she could to look at Sebastian's face. His eyes were shaded by the brim of his Panama hat, but his shapely mouth was forming what to Paulina looked like a cautious smile.

"If you're willing."

"To accept your friendship?" Turning back around, Paulina tried to smother some of the hunger in her voice. At least he couldn't see the sudden tears stinging her eyes. That wasn't the only thing she wanted from Sebastian, but it was a start. "I wouldn't object to that."

There was a pause behind her, and it went on long enough that she could feel his stillness at her back. "But would you like to have it?" he said finally.

"Yes. I would like it very much."

The sun was at its most potent when they arrived at a fairly nondescript house, a handful of streets away from the church at the center of town. Paulina blinked the brightness out of her eyes as a girl in an apron led her and Sebastian to a wide, bright terrace at the back. It was furnished with a worktable piled with bolts of fabric and a gleaming sewing machine set into a wooden stand. The woman sitting before it rose gracefully from her seat the moment she spotted them, a hand extended in greeting.

"This is Blanca," Sebastian said after he had introduced Paulina, "the finest modiste in San Pedro, or so I'm told. She's going to make you an entire wardrobe."

Sheer delight leaped into her chest, and Paulina couldn't help but show it, even as she protested, "Oh, but I couldn't possibly accept such extravagance."

"Not even for my sake?" Sebastian asked. At her questioning glance, he elaborated. "You're my wife now, and for better or worse, you represent me and my household. I'd rather not have it whispered around that I haven't done well by you. Or that my business is so unprofitable that I can't afford to clothe my bride. Really, you'd be doing me a favor."

"Oh." Paulina looked at the dressmaker, who had discreetly turned to sort through the fashion magazines on the table. "Well, I suppose, in that case…"

Sebastian smiled in satisfaction. "Thank you for being so agreeable." He inclined his head toward Blanca. "I'll leave you to your work, Señora. I'll return in an hour or so."

The moment he disappeared through the doorway, Blanca and her assistant fell upon Paulina, exclaiming over her shapely hips and long legs. Paulina submitted to their attentions and found herself growing absorbed in sorting through the scraps of fabric and lace on display.

Blanca laid out fashion plates on the table, picking out the ones she thought would be most flattering to Paulina's figure, and together the three women assembled combinations of fabric and trimmings to go with each.

It was overwhelming, in an entirely blissful way. Until that moment, Paulina hadn't quite realized how stifling it had been to sit idly by while someone else made all her decisions for her, large and small. Choosing her own clothes might have been inconsequential for anyone else, but going through the process of determining what she liked and what she didn't made Paulina feel like she had control over more than just her clothes—like maybe she could have control over her own life.

As well as the magazines and samples, Blanca had an array of finished garments that she pulled out for Paulina to inspect. Before long, one end of the table was heaped with silk petticoats, combinations made out of linen so fine it felt like gossamer against her skin, two night-dresses with satin ribbons and breathtakingly intricate lace bordering their immodestly plunging necklines and an assortment of crisp white blouses with eyelet embroidery and tucks in the sleeves.

Her attention drawn by an intriguing glimpse of yellow, Paulina extracted another blouse from the pile. The whisper-thin fabric was embellished with bands of creamy yellow embroidery on the bodice and the full sleeves.

"Bishop sleeves," Blanca explained. "It's the latest thing."

"They look very elegant," Paulina said. "And I love the embroidery."

"It would suit you splendidly. With a few tucks, here and here…" The dressmaker pinched a fold of fabric in illustration. "I could have this ready for you in minutes. I also took the liberty of selecting a skirt for it."

Gesturing for Paulina to follow, she pulled a dress form from behind a painted screen. The cambric-covered figure was wearing a day skirt the color of the late-morning sky.

Gently, Paulina touched the fabric with her fingertips. "It's beautiful. I don't think I've ever worn such a color."

"It's very becoming," Blanca said. "I've only to put in a dart or two for it to fit properly. Here's a bow for the neck."

The bow was made out of the same fabric as the skirt, and it made for a pleasing contrast against the crisp white of the shirtwaist and the twining butter-colored vines on its sleeves.

"Why don't you try them on so that I can make the adjustments right away?"

How could she have said no? Paulina stepped behind the screen and shucked off her pale yellow dress, which suddenly looked shabby and frumpy in comparison with Blanca's exquisite garments. The blouse felt like silk as she pulled it over her threadbare chemise, and the skirt fit as if it had been made for her.

"I don't think you'll have to make any alterations," Paulina called through the screen as she fastened the buttons at the waist.

The other women were so absorbed in their discussion of hat trimmings that they didn't realize Paulina had emerged until she cleared her throat. They turned and beamed immediately.

"I was right about that shade of blue," Blanca said, looking satisfied as she reached up to adjust the bow around the neck of the blouse. "It looks wonderful against your skin."

"I'll have to take your word for it," Paulina said, craning her neck for a glimpse of herself in the long oval mirror that was partially obscured with discarded clothes.

"Maybe not," the assistant said under her breath, and Paulina felt her pulse stutter to a stop as she followed her gaze to the far side of the terrace.

Sebastian was standing in the doorway, and he looked stunned.

Looking self-conscious, Paulina smoothed a hand over the sky-blue fabric hugging her hips. "What do you think? Do I do you credit?"

Sebastian started at her question, as if he'd been gazing at a painting that had suddenly burst into song. When he managed to formulate words, they came out softly. "It would take a far more eloquent man than me to answer that question."

He still would have tried, if he hadn't recalled that they were not alone. The dressmaker and her assistant, ever discreet, had retreated to the far side of the room to confer over a dress form, making a point of looking absorbed in pinning some sort of garment around it.

Sebastian cleared his throat. "Are you ready to go? I can come back later if you need more time."

"I think I've got everything I needed," she said. "And far more, besides. Are you really sure—"

"I'm sure," Sebastian told her, and he asked the dressmaker to prepare the bill.

Blanca jotted down some notes in a miniature notebook. "That's three day dresses, one tea gown for Sundays, two plain skirts and five shirtwaists. In addition to the blue-and-yellow ensemble."

Paulina frowned. "I have no need of so many clothes."

"Nonsense," Sebastian said firmly. "Dilia owns twice

as many, and she's been in mourning for a year. Blanca, how soon can these be ready?"

"Two weeks, I should say."

Paying Blanca and making arrangements for the clothes to be delivered to Villa Consuelo was the work of a few moments. Through it, Sebastian could feel his gaze darting toward Paulina, who was chatting with the assistant as the apron-clad girl folded a pile of delicate underthings into a satin-covered box. It wasn't the frilly garments that held his attention, but the light that had come into her eyes at his pale excuse for a compliment.

Privately, he resolved to offer her many more, if only because he liked watching her bloom under the attention, like a wilting plant that had been aching for sunlight.

From the way her fingers fluttered to the bow at her neck and continually smoothed down the fabric of her skirt, he could tell that she was enamored of her new ensemble. It was that more than anything that prompted him to say, as they emerged onto the scorching sidewalk, "I was going to take you home, but you deserve to be seen by all of San Pedro. Would you care for a stroll around the park? Later, I mean, when the sun goes down a bit."

"That would be lovely." Her eyes were shining. "What do you propose to do in the meantime?"

"You need hats and jewelry and handbags and any number of things that haven't occurred to me," Sebastian said, adding, as he spotted a woman in the distance who was shading herself with something pale and lacy, "Like a parasol. And neither of us have eaten. I'd say we have plenty to occupy us for the rest of the day."

"You don't need to return to the mill?"

"Not today," he lied, offering her his arm. It was the polite thing to do, but his body had quite a different idea about the hand innocently grasping his inner elbow.

Every brush of her knuckles against his rib cage, covered in layers of fabric as it was, sent ribbons of unexpected desire running through him.

He took her to La Belleza, José Oliva's hotel, café and restaurant. Sebastian wasn't personally acquainted with Oliva, but it was in his establishment that he, Carlos and Dilia had stayed upon their arrival from Havana. The restaurant on its ground floor had to be the most elegant in all of San Pedro, with its starched linens and crystal chandeliers that tinkled lightly in the breeze. Sweeping murals covered the high walls, and potted palms set at intervals in front of the floor-to-ceiling drapes highlighted their intense color.

San Pedro society was on full display in the crowded main dining room—ladies in white dresses frothy with pearls, men in fashionably cut suits that showed off their gleaming watch chains.

They made no attempt to hide their curiosity as Sebastian, Paulina on his arm, followed the maître d'hôtel to a table right in the center of the room.

Sebastian laid the immaculate linen napkin over his lap, watching with amusement the awe in Paulina's expression as she took in the entirety of the room. She wasn't quite gawking, but it was more than clear that her damned brother had never brought her to this kind of place.

There was a bustle around them as what seemed like a small army of waiters in black bow ties descended upon their table to fill their water glasses, hand them leather-bound menus and recite the day's specials. Paulina listened with endearing seriousness, concentration etching a fine line between her gently arching brows.

"It all sounds so good," she said. "I couldn't possibly decide."

Sebastian narrowed his eyes at her. "Oh, yes, you will. What's more, you'll order for me, too."

Her gaze flicked toward him, and she sat up a little straighter, as if to signal that she accepted his challenge. She perused the menu again. "For myself," she told the waiter, "I'd like the red snapper."

"A wonderful choice," the waiter said. "The fillet comes in a light cream sauce, which partners well with our Spanish Albariño, which we keep chilled—perfect for such a warm day. What will the gentleman like?"

An impish look came into Paulina's face. "Oh, I don't think he's very hungry. Perhaps some bread and butter?"

Sebastian growled, making Paulina laugh. "I'll take a bite out of you if you don't get me some proper food, you scamp."

"All right, all right. Let's see. San Pedro is known for its cattle, so why not *filete a la pimienta*?"

"That does sound good," Sebastian said, though she hadn't so much as glanced at him in confirmation. It did his heart proud.

The waiters retreated almost as suddenly as they had come, and Sebastian found himself, once again, sitting across the table from Paulina. Had it only been that morning that she'd confessed to never having selected her own hair ribbons? Was it too much to hope that a single shopping experience had helped her break free from those years of deprivation?

With her uncanny knack for divining his thoughts, Paulina leaned forward. "I wanted to thank you, Sebastian. For the clothes and—and all this," she said, gesturing around her. "It's all so grand and beautiful and…"

"And?" He raised an expectant eyebrow.

"And I could really get used to it," she said, her smile turning so wicked at the edges, it was all he could do to keep from knocking aside the carnations in their silver vase and lunging across the table to devour that curl with his own mouth.

Not exactly the sort of thing a friend would do.

"I hope you do," he told her, swallowing back the urge. "It's only a fraction of what you should have had growing up. I know that restaurants and new clothes can't come close to making up for all you've lost…"

"Having your friendship does." She looked at him with those clear eyes of hers. "I appreciate that as well, Sebastian. I hope you know I don't take it lightly."

"Neither do I," he said, and the arrival of the breadbasket prevented him from saying anything more.

The fish was followed by port and demitasses of strong, sweet coffee. At Paulina's request, there was even ice cream, served in delicate etched dishes and topped with sliced almonds. She kept Sebastian so distracted with her enthusiasm and curiosity for every item on the menu that when he finally glanced around, it was to find that the restaurant had emptied and the waiters were close to dozing as they leaned against the far wall.

By then, the shops had reopened for the afternoon. Fueled by wine and port and the sparkles in Paulina's eyes, Sebastian swept her into every one they passed— Manuel Lebron's shoe store, where he insisted she try on several pairs of fine leather pumps; El Lente de Oro, where he talked her into a painted fan and two parasols, one silk and dripping with lace and the other one sprigged with little flowers…

Lacking a carriage to haul their purchases home, Sebastian paid an additional fee for them to be delivered to Villa Consuelo the following day.

A startlingly colorful sunset was starting to blaze in

the horizon when Paulina laughingly begged off going into yet another store.

"You did promise me a stroll in the park," she said.

"So I did."

The park was only a few streets away. It wasn't Sunday, when afternoon concerts were traditionally held, but a handful of musicians were practicing in the gazebo set into the center of the park. The low notes wafted in their direction, borne along on the warm, fragrant breeze.

Paulina tilted her face up to the last of the sunlight. The sudden change in angle made her lashes cast feathery shadows on the lustrous brown skin over her cheekbones.

Sebastian tore his gaze away, making himself admire the freshly painted iron fencing around the flower beds.

Then she spoke, and he was obliged to turn back to her.

"If it's not too bold an observation to make…you don't seem to mind spending enormous quantities of money on providing me with a wardrobe. It makes me wonder…"

He made an encouraging noise, though he wasn't sure where she was going.

"Why haven't you done the same for Villa Consuelo? You've lived there a year, haven't you? Why," she said, and Sebastian braced himself, "are you depriving yourself the comfort of a decently furnished home?"

The breath he let out felt as gusty as cyclone winds. He would have been tempted to make light of his answer if he wasn't certain that Paulina wouldn't let him get away with that.

"I really was busy, in the beginning. Carlos and I had a devil of a time getting the mill to run smoothly after the state it was left in by your brother. But then…"

"Then he died?" Paulina supplied gently.

Sebastian dipped his head into a nod. "And suddenly

I was responsible not just for his wife and children, but for the mill and everyone who works there. If the cane caught fire or the machinery broke down and we didn't make enough in profits to cover everyone's salary... The prospect of spending money on drapes and chairs when doing so might have taken the food out of someone's mouth made my stomach curdle."

"I see." She walked in thoughtful silence for a few minutes. "Last year's *zafra* was unusually profitable for everyone, wasn't it? I remember reading in the newspaper that sugar prices rose worldwide."

"Your memory's impressive," Sebastian said. "And yes, the mill made almost double what Carlos and I had projected."

"And with there being no export tax, it stands to reason that this year's will be similarly profitable. After all, we're well past hurricane season, and the cane is ready to be harvested. Barring some sort of sudden catastrophe..." She bit her lip for a moment. "Would it make you feel any better if you were to establish some sort of trust that the mill and cane workers could draw from in case of an emergency? You could contribute whatever you needed to it and that would free up the rest of your funds—and your mental energy—for frivolous things like buying furniture for your home."

It shouldn't have surprised Sebastian that she had solved, in a matter of minutes, something that had been plaguing him for over a year. It was as Carlos used to say—Sebastian had a bad habit of getting so bogged down with worries that it often rendered him unable to notice the solutions that were right in front of his face.

"I'll speak to my bank manager about it first thing tomorrow."

"And in the meantime," she said, "I'll take you up on

your suggestion to procure some furniture for the house."
In the late-afternoon sunlight, the smile she flashed him
looked golden. "I'll be glad for a project to occupy my
time."

Chapter Eleven

The following day found Sebastian riding into town again, this time to speak with his bank manager about Paulina's suggestion and to put in another order for the metal tracks he was having laid through the sugarcane fields to more easily transport the cane to the mill once it had been cut. It was an expensive proposition but one that would relieve the cane cutters of a great deal of labor.

He had never shared his saddle before riding to and from town with Paulina the day before, but he found himself missing the space she'd occupied on the leather seat. On the way back to Villa Consuelo in the falling dark the day before, she had drowsily relaxed against his chest, her head pleasantly heavy on his shoulder. What was it she had said at the restaurant? That she could get used to it?

Well, so could he.

The notion wasn't nearly as alarming as it should have been, and Sebastian paused to consider why. He'd enjoyed her company more than he'd expected. Maybe he had also been lonely. Maybe he, too, had needed a friend. Secure in his control of himself, and in no danger of letting himself be seduced, he had allowed himself to see her for who she truly was—a remarkably interesting woman.

And a damn desirable one.

Nor for the first time, Sebastian thought about Antonio Despradel's reasons for forcing them into marriage. It wasn't like it would have been so difficult to find Paulina a husband by conventional means. She was everything a man could want—everything Sebastian would have wanted, if his circumstances had been different.

Who wouldn't want to wake up every morning to the sight of those luminous eyes?

Or that round bottom pressed against—

Sebastian swore out loud, to the consternation of the two sparrows perched on a fence post, which took immediate flight.

Paulina had far more to offer than her beauty, of course. She was brave and intelligent and more skillful with a hammer than he could have imagined.

Sebastian had awoken that morning with every intention of fixing the shaky stool, only to find that the leg that had wobbled like a loose tooth was now perfectly solid. On it was a note, pinned down by a rock. It read, *My apologies for taking liberties, but I couldn't let the stool claim another victim.*

Then he'd gone to find the spout for the water barrel, and of course Paulina had taken care of that as well. She'd even managed to scrub away some of the rust that had accumulated on the metal in the months the spout had been lying among Sebastian's tools.

And damn if it hadn't felt like a weight off his shoulders. A weight he hadn't realized he was carrying until it had been lifted.

Sebastian sighed. He didn't like intrigue, and he wasn't particularly good at it—not just that; it made his head ache. He said as much to Dilia when he stopped by the pink house after his errands, a heat-induced headache pounding behind his eyes. She all but ordered him to take a nap on her stiffly upholstered settee, as if he were another one of her boys.

As pieces of furniture went, it wasn't the most comfortable, or even particularly beautiful. The only thing it had to recommend it was the fact that it had been placed close enough to the louvered doors that opened out into the front gallery that a most agreeable breeze wafted over his overheated body.

Dilia must have sent the boys out to play in the street, because the house was utterly quiet. Or perhaps Sebastian was just that tired. He fell asleep almost instantly, and when he dreamed, it was of a woman in a pale yellow dress, dancing in the sunlight.

Whereas Paulina's bedroom was overcrowded with all the previous day's purchases, the rest of Villa Consuelo was awfully bare. There were no lace curtains or oil paintings or fine silver candlesticks gleaming from a sideboard—there weren't even any sideboards, or much in the way of furniture.

Even Sebastian's bedroom, Paulina discovered when she ventured inside alone to sweep its floors, had only a bed and a chest of drawers. A small mirror hung from a single nail; below it a set of shaving implements had been lined up on a clean towel. Another glance around the room revealed a neat pile of clothing atop a crate.

She had seen a different side to him the day before, and not just because he'd been so extravagantly generous toward her. He was so devoted to everyone in his care, to his own detriment. When was the last time someone had taken care of him?

Trying for briskness, but falling short, Paulina tied the mosquito net to the side and began denuding Sebastian's bed of its linen. The light cotton blanket, folded and tucked underneath the single pillow, smelled faintly of him—laundry soap underlaid with the earthier scents of sugarcane and sunbaked skin. Paulina tucked the pillow under her chin as she stripped off its plain cover and caught a whiff of the spice she had smelled when she'd pressed her face against his chest on the night of the storm.

A sudden urge insisted that she do the same with his pillow. Paulina would never know if she'd have overcome it or not as, at that moment, a shout came from the parted doors.

"The new table's here! Oh, Paulina! Come see the new table!"

Abandoning the pillow with alacrity, Paulina snatched the sheets off the mattress and added them to the basket on the terrace, then hurried down the steps to see a pair of burly men with their shirtsleeves pushed up to their elbows carefully unloading the table from a large cart. The dining table in her family's *quinta* had been a massive hulk of dark, carved wood; this one was beautiful in the simplicity of its well-turned legs. She ran a hand over the smoothly polished top.

"Centenary mahogany," said one of the workmen.

The man beside him made an impatient noise, clearly straining under the weight. "Where do you want it, Doña?"

"The terrace, I think," Paulina said with a gesture. "To keep it out of the sun and rain."

In the space of several minutes, the men had finished unloading the new dining set and the cart was rumbling its way down the path while Leo and Doña Josefa clustered around the table. The chairs were wood and rush, but to look at their faces, anyone would have thought they'd been made of gilded wood.

It was a start, Paulina thought, recalling that she had thought those very words the day before in regard to the friendship Sebastian had offered her. A start—but why should any of them settle for just a start?

"We should have a feast," Paulina said suddenly. "To celebrate the new table."

Doña Josefa gave a swift nod. "I know just what to make."

"Stewed goat?" Paulina offered, and they all laughed.

"Leo, go to Candida's and see if she'll sell you one of her guinea hens." Finding several coins in her pocket, Doña Josefa pressed them into the boy's hand.

"We ought to have a proper tablecloth. I'll go into town to buy one—and a new vase and candlesticks," Paulina added, recklessly adding to the list in her mind. "We'll make an elegant occasion of it."

And so it was that less than an hour later, Paulina was arriving in town, freshly bathed and clad in one of her new shirtwaists, her hair wound into an intricate coronet of braids. Her modish straw hat cast a decent enough shade over the bridge of Paulina's nose; even so, she was feeling like a roasted chicken by the time she arrived in town. This late in the morning, the sun was blazing mercilessly overhead, without the merest scrap of a cloud to soften its potency.

She was passing a pretty, sherbet-pink house when a voice rose from the elegantly columned gallery shading its front door. "Paulina? Paulina Despradel?"

Glancing up, she spotted a familiar-looking woman on a rocking chair, wearing the same black dress she had worn the last time Paulina had seen her, on the day of her marriage. Paulina raised a hand as she bid Dilia a polite good afternoon.

The other woman set down her needlework and went quickly to the railing. "*Santísimo!* Did you walk all the way here?"

"I caught a ride part of the way on a vegetable cart," Paulina said, then wondered if she should have admitted to such unladylike behavior.

Dilia didn't look disapproving, merely friendly. "Won't you come sit with me for a spell and get out of the sun? It's scorching out there."

Paulina hesitated. "I would love to, but I came to town on an errand, you see…"

"I promise not to take up too much of your time—I would never forgive myself if I let you get on in such a state. Please, come up and have something to drink with me. I've some tamarind juice, or lime if you prefer."

Before she knew it, Paulina found herself ensconced in one of the rocking chairs set deep into the shade of the porch, a set of louvered white doors at her back and a cool glass of juice dripping condensation onto her lap.

Dilia hadn't resumed the seat next to Paulina's yet, having been called to the aid of a little boy with a badly scraped knee. As she waited for Sebastian's friend, Paulina gratefully sipped the juice, feeling slivers of ice slip past her lips.

A faint snore behind her made Paulina crane her neck in search of the person it had come from. The louvered doors, which had been ajar earlier, were pushed farther open by a stray breeze, revealing a sleeping Sebastian.

She'd assumed he'd gone to the mill, and so to find him here, asleep, in the middle of the day, should have been surprising. Anyone who had been paying attention to the shadows under his eyes, however, would have known how badly he needed the rest.

He hadn't attempted to fold his body onto the cramped settee but lay with his long legs flung over the spindly carved arm, a roll-shaped cushion under his neck. One of his powerful arms trailed to the floor, where it brushed the patterned tiles; the other was thrown over his forehead, as though shielding his eyes from the light pouring in from the gallery.

Poised and contained during his waking hours, in sleep Sebastian allowed himself the abandon he eschewed in the daytime. It was a glimpse at a side of Sebastian Paulina had never seen—and one that made her feel oddly flushed as she summoned up the memory of the one night she had spent in his arms.

If they were to share a bed again, would he let himself fall into a sprawl next to her? Fling his arm over her as a smile of contentment softened his lips?

She wanted the chance to find out.

The startling strength of her desire almost made her gasp out loud. As if he could feel it, Sebastian stirred.

Quickly, Paulina averted her eyes to find that Dilia had returned and was watching her.

"I try to make him sleep when I can, but I'm afraid one of these days he'll figure out that I can't actually force him to do anything." Dilia smiled briefly. "My boys have, at any rate."

"Your boys? You've four of them, right?" Paulina said in a blatant attempt to distract both Dilia and herself.

"Four little terrors that keep me in plenty of mending," Dilia said, smiling at Paulina as she reached for the needlework she had abandoned.

"Tell me about them," Paulina said, and Dilia obliged with enthusiasm.

Stopping just short of breathing a sigh of relief, Paulina sat back and allowed the sweet tartness of the tamarind juice to cool her down. All the while, though, she was aware of the certainty blooming larger and larger inside her chest—she was uncomfortably, inconveniently, irrevocably in love with her husband.

When Sebastian drifted back into consciousness, it was to the sound of Paulina's voice.

"I suppose we're getting used to each other," she was saying.

"He deserves more than someone getting used to him—he deserves love. From someone who means it."

"I hope he finds it," Paulina replied.

"But not with you?" Dilia's disembodied voice may have sounded cool, but Sebastian was sure it was accompanied by one of her probing looks.

It was an odd subject for a dream, even taking into account the fact that lately Sebastian's thoughts seemed consumed with Paulina. Which was only to be expected, he told himself hazily, seeing as she was always *there*—putting vases in his bedroom, standing in patches of sunshine and trailing that slight floral scent wherever she went so that his entire home seemed to be filled with her.

Opening his eyes and gazing straight up, Sebastian considered whether he was still dreaming or whether he had somehow been transported back to Villa Consuelo. But the white ceiling was dappled with light refracted from the small chandelier Dilia had brought from the Havana house, and he could hear the faint but unmistakable sound of little David wailing at his brothers.

Then he realized that the sound had come from the gallery, which meant that Paulina was sitting on one of the rocking chairs on the other side of the louvered doors—and that her conversation with Dilia was not one he should overhear.

In one swift movement, he had swung his legs to the floor and was pulling the doors open the rest of the way. Even though the lace-edged blouse she wore was bright white, he observed as he leaned against the door frame, there *was* something reminiscent of sunshine about her.

Even Dilia, clad as always in her mourning clothes, looked brighter for being beside Paulina. She glanced up at the sound of the hinges, and Sebastian was forced to step out into the gallery.

"Paulina?" he asked as if he had just noticed her. "I wasn't expecting you here. Did something happen at the house?"

Glancing up at him, Paulina set down the glass she'd been holding and wiped her hands on her skirt. "The new table arrived this morning, and I decided to go to Don Enrique's store for a new tablecloth."

He raised an eyebrow. "So you walked all the way from Villa Consuelo?"

"I caught a ride on a farmer's cart."

"I see. Well, we can't let your industriousness go to waste. I'll go with you to Don Enrique's and then I'll take you home. Dilia, my dear, I'm grateful as ever for your hospitality."

"Oh, but why don't you both stay for lunch?" Dilia said. "The cook is making *moro de guandules* and those *yuca arepitas* you love…"

"Another day."

Bending to kiss her on the cheek, he rescued his hat from a corner of the porch, where it was being employed as a receptacle for rocks by one of her little scamps, and set off down the street, Paulina at his side.

The streets were markedly quiet this close to noon, the

scents of garlic and *sazón* filtering through open doors and windows—so quiet that Sebastian was able to hear the growl of Paulina's stomach. She murmured an embarrassed excuse, pressing her hand to her midsection.

Sebastian glanced down at her. "We can go back to Dilia's if you're hungry," he offered. "Her cook's *arepitas* really are truly excellent."

"Oh, no," Paulina said hurriedly. "Doña Josefa is making a special meal for us. I wouldn't want to spoil my appetite or be late."

"Then maybe an *empanada*?" Sebastian nodded at one of the houses they were walking past. Half-hidden behind an overgrown hibiscus bush was a handwritten sign listing the foodstuffs for sale. "The Alvarez sisters make the best *lambí empanadas* in town."

Interest sparked in her eyes. "*Lambí?* I don't think I've ever tried it in an *empanada*."

"That really needs to be remedied," Sebastian said firmly. "They make *dulces*, too—we could get some *dulce de coco* for the others."

They went inside, and Sebastian watched her gravely consider all the options before selecting a jar of *dulce de coco* and one of stewed papaya to bring back home. Like he had the day before, Sebastian found himself egging her into getting more things, to the delight of the elderly sisters who were adding up the purchases with gleeful smiles.

Finally, they came out onto the front yard with a basket laden with jars hanging from the crook of his elbow and the last two *empanadas* of the day in each of their hands.

Sebastian had hardly raised the *empanada* to his mouth when he stumbled over a bootblack's box. Its proprietor, who couldn't have been more than a handful of years older than Dilia's younger boy, was crouched nearby, playing with a marble. He glanced up at the sound of Sebastian's boot striking the wooden box, but it was the aromatic pastry that captured his attention.

The boy looked nothing like Sebastian, but he couldn't help seeing another, scrawnier version of himself in the skinny limbs. He'd been lucky enough to have not gone hungry for long—thanks entirely to the kindness of people who'd barely had enough for themselves.

"*Amiguito*, want an *empanada*?" The words popped out of Sebastian's mouth before his brain had much of a choice in the matter, and a second later the boy had snatched the *empanada* from his hand and scampered off with a hasty thanks.

Paulina was watching him, a small smile on the corner of her lips.

He shrugged, though she hadn't said anything. "I wasn't hungry anyway. I was just keeping you company."

Of course, his stomach chose that moment to growl, not just audibly but embarrassingly loudly.

"I'm not that hungry, either," she said.

Splitting her *empanada* in half, she handed him a piece, which he consumed in a single bite. It was still hot, but he had always been partial to the tender conch meat, and here in this former fishing village, the seafood was always fresh.

Paulina took the time to savor hers. At the first nibble, her eyelids drooped closed, and she let out a sound that made Sebastian grateful that they were half-hidden behind the hibiscus bush.

Her plump bottom lip was slick with grease. A gentleman would have offered her his handkerchief, but Sebastian's was limp with perspiration and, in any case, despite how hard Dilia had tried to turn him into one, Sebastian wasn't a gentleman.

He wiped his thumb firmly over her lower lip, and even though Sebastian wasn't given to impulsive gestures—and this most certainly counted as one—he raised his thumb to his own mouth and swept his tongue over the salty smear.

Her lips parted. Her gaze was trained on his mouth, as intently as he had been looking at hers.

"You can do it, you know," she said, in a voice so low he could hardly hear it over the sound of two men arguing as they walked down the street. "You can kiss me again. It wouldn't have to mean anything you don't want it to. It wouldn't…mean anything at all."

It wasn't the disarming vulnerability in her tone, or the frank desire in her eyes, that struck Sebastian—it was that once again, Paulina had proven herself damn courageous for giving voice to their desires.

More softly than before, he grazed her lip with his thumb, slowly rubbing it back and forth over skin as soft as a rose petal. "It would to me," he told her.

And then he kissed her anyway.

Sebastian had never been the sort of man who found pleasure in the forbidden. But as he plumbed the depths of her eager mouth, he couldn't begin to imagine why. He knew he shouldn't kiss his wife. He knew that every minute he spent with her, every time he had to avert his gaze from her curves or her distracting mouth, took him one step closer to plummeting over the edge.

He knew it all, and yet he couldn't stop.

Her warm hands slid under the lapels of his jacket and traveled up to his shoulders before twining behind his neck. She clung to him as if to a life raft, her body pressed tightly against his and soft moans escaping her salty mouth as he dug his fingers into the boning of her corset and pulled her even closer, wishing there was a handy tree he could press her against.

They were half-hidden from the street by the hibiscus bush, but anyone who came around it would see them. They should stop before that happened. His brain was screaming for him to stop, though his hands and mouth refused to heed it. For her sake, if not his own—he couldn't let her be seen like this, with her clothes in disarray and her mouth swollen from his kisses. San Pedro may have been turning into a cosmopolitan city, but its residents would not take kindly to a woman behaving wantonly in full view of them all.

"Well, well, what have we here?" said a cold, cruel voice behind them.

When Sebastian recognized the man the voice belonged to, his first instinct was not to spring away from Paulina but to draw her even closer into the protective circle of his arms.

"The devil do you want with us?" he snarled at Antonio Despradel.

Along with a gray-haired man, Despradel had come around the hibiscus bush and was contemplating Sebastian and Paulina with a smirk.

"Is that any way to greet your new brother-in-law?"

"I know a better one, and it doesn't involve any words," Sebastian ground out. Just looking at Despradel's face brought the sickening memories of the days he had spent in the cell bubbling to the surface of his mind.

"Always the brute," Despradel remarked, flicking a glance at his companion. "But then, can I really expect better from a man who thinks it perfectly fine to accost my sister in the public streets?"

"I'm not getting involved in this," the gray-haired man muttered and hurried away.

If Sebastian hadn't already been convinced of Paulina's innocence, the way she was recoiling from her brother would have more than done the trick.

"We don't have to stay here and listen to this," Sebastian told her in a low voice, ignoring Despradel. Her hand slid into his, and she nodded. "Let's go finish our errand."

Despradel stepped in their way. "Not so fast. I require something from you, Linares."

Sebastian gave Despradel a contemptuous glance. "There's nothing I would give you, save for the blow or two you deserve."

"Funny you should talk about deserving," Despradel replied, unruffled, "because I was just thinking that I deserve some compensation."

"Compensation?" Paulina echoed.

Despradel didn't so much as glance at her. "For the pain and suffering of having my sister abducted from my own home."

For a moment, Sebastian was too surprised to be outraged. He barked out a laugh. "Do you really think I'd give you *money* after everything you've done?"

"I should think you'd be willing to pay any price to keep the good residents of San Pedro from finding out about your villainous proclivities," Despradel shot back. "I want a hundred pesos." He scraped a glance over Paulina then, taking in her crisp shirtwaist and the blue skirt. "You can clearly afford it."

It was astonishing how quickly that man could provoke Sebastian into a blind rage. He took a step forward, his free hand clenched into a fist. From the corner of his eye, he could see a couple ambling down the street toward them, but he didn't care if the president of the republic himself was about to witness the violence Sebastian was about to unleash upon Despradel.

Paulina had other ideas.

"If you're here for *empanadas*, you really must try the *lambí*." She slipped her hand through the crook of Sebastian's elbow—mostly, he suspected, to keep him from doing anything unadvisable. "Sebastian, do you have the *dulces*? We don't want to be late for luncheon."

Inclining her head graciously, she bade her brother a good day and all but propelled Sebastian into the street.

Chapter Twelve

Well, that answered the question that had been plaguing Sebastian for days—like the leech that he was, Despradel was planning on using Paulina to extract enough money from Sebastian to pay for his lavish lifestyle.

Paulina was still holding on to his arm, though Despradel was long out of sight. Sebastian had been walking so quickly—stalking, almost—that he hadn't noticed the fine tremble running through her limbs.

He slowed down and looked at her more closely. "Are you all right?"

"I will be," she said. "He's a damn bully, but he can't force you to give him any money, can he?"

"He can try to blackmail me," Sebastian said. "Or have his henchmen throw me in prison again. I'd give him the damn money if I thought it would satisfy him. But men like him can never have enough."

"It's the only way he can find value in himself," she said contemptuously. "Owning things and having people under his thumb."

Sebastian grunted his agreement. "Did you happen to recognize the other man?"

"Yes," she said, and she bit her lip lightly before saying, "That was the magistrate."

Sebastian limited his response to a nod, though a great part of him wanted to rage. Not only were none of the lawyers in town willing to support his claim against Antonio, there was no authority to report him to, either. "I should thank you for your quick thinking. I don't know what he or I would have done were it not for your intervention. Get hauled into prison again, most likely, only this time for murder."

"Don't say that even in jest." She shuddered. "I never want to see you in that place again."

"Me, either," he said, giving her a crooked smile.

Instead of returning it, she nodded at the open doors below the sign reading, *Enrique Rijo, Gran Bazar de Novedades*. "It's almost noon. We should go in before they close for lunch."

He touched her shoulder. "Before we do, there's just one thing I have to tell you. I will *never* let him hurt you again."

"I wish I could promise you the same," Paulina said softly and went into the store.

Looking fairly grim, she picked out a tablecloth and several yards of ribbon. Then, lifting her chin in that determined way she had, she said both to Sebastian and the clerk, "I should like a pair of candlesticks as well."

His worry melted slightly into amusement as she selected two long tapers and the ugliest pair of pewter candleholders he had ever seen.

"You do know I can afford brass or silver," he said, coming up beside her and setting the basket on the counter.

"I didn't want to presume," she said primly.

"Presume away," he told her. "If it's finery you want for the new table, pewter just won't do."

"If you're looking for something elegant," the clerk said, turning with alacrity to produce two monstrous silver pieces the length and girth of Sebastian's arms, "I have just the thing for you."

Sebastian was stupefied into silence, and from the lack of a reaction beside him, he suspected Paulina was, too. The candlesticks weren't merely large—they were atrociously misshapen, towering pillars of silver infested with vines and squat, ugly little cherubs, each candlestick with five ungainly arms to thrust candles into the air. Here and there, the silver was dotted with red glass globes that Sebastian thought were meant to simulate grapes.

"Imported from Spain," the clerk said, surveying the horrid thing with an air of pride.

"What do you think, dear?" Sebastian asked Paulina, manfully containing his laughter.

Paulina's blink gave Sebastian the impression that she hadn't often been asked that before—with or without the endearment he had appended to the question, as if there was something humorous about the two of *them* posing as a real husband and wife.

"They certainly are grand," she said thoughtfully. "Wouldn't they look perfectly elegant on a table by the door, where anyone might see them the moment they step inside?"

Sebastian's smile faltered. "I…ah…"

"Surely that would justify the expense. Of course, we'd have to redo the entire parlor to make it suitable. Damask curtains, velvet sofas and perhaps a crystal chandelier or two? Marble and gilt tables, to be sure…"

Sebastian caught the wicked glint in her eyes and almost sagged with relief. "I'm not sure that's advisable at the moment, dear."

She shook her head with fake regret. "If you say so." She winked at the clerk, adding, sotto voce, "I'll convince him eventually. In the meantime, we should probably take a look at something a little less...elegant."

The clerk turned around, and Sebastian pressed against Paulina's side for a brief moment, feeling her body tremble with mirth.

In the end, they settled for a pair of blue ceramic ones with a white design wreathed around their bases that went nicely with the white tapers and the blue embroidered tablecloth made by Don Enrique's daughter. Sebastian put in an order for new sets of china, and silver, too, from the shipment that would arrive the following week.

It was a welcome distraction—not only that, but every step he took toward making Villa Consuelo a home kindled a glow inside Sebastian. Carlos and Dilia's generosity had never made Sebastian long any less for a home of his own; slowly, and ever so surely, the pile of bricks and stone that had been Villa Consuelo was becoming just that.

He didn't say as much to Paulina, though he couldn't help thinking about her habit of looking at houses in the newspaper. As wildly different as their respective upbringings had been, they shared a longing for a true home.

"Are we going to discuss what happened before we were interrupted?" he asked as they left the store.

She glanced up at him, and Sebastian felt his gaze skipping away to focus on the newly erected lamppost at the end of the street. "Must we? Something tells me you're going to be utterly impossible about it."

"If by impossible you mean sensible. We shouldn't

have…indulged. And you know that we can't let that happen again."

"We're married," she said heatedly. "It was one thing when you thought I was conspiring with Antonio and you couldn't stand the sight of me. But now—"

"If we were to consummate the relationship," he said, still avoiding her gaze, "we wouldn't be able to have the marriage annulled. And only parties over the age of twenty-five can request a divorce without the consent of a family member, so you would be tied to me for four years."

"I don't want an annulment," she snapped. Looking a little startled at the admission, she bit her lip. Then, with that defiant tilt of her chin that he found so appealing, she added, "Or a divorce."

"You might," he said softly, willing her to understand. "And I would be as much of a villain as your brother if I took that choice away from you. You said it yourself— you've never had the independence to make your own decisions. I refuse to bind you to a marriage you didn't choose." He took a deep breath. "I offered you friendship, and that's all I'm prepared to give you."

Sebastian couldn't have made it more clear. Paulina had been foisted upon him, and even though he was clearly as attracted to her as she was to him, he did not intend to…what was it he'd said? Indulge?

A most unladylike snort escaped her as she pulled at the tablecloth so that its edges hung evenly around the tabletop.

The worst part was that he wasn't altogether wrong. She was no longer bound by Antonio's strictures. She was a married woman, for as long as she chose to be, and as such she had something much more valuable than anything anyone had ever given her—freedom.

The notion made a little thrill of possibility leap in her stomach.

She was savoring the word when the housekeeper came onto the terrace to admire Paulina's handiwork. As well as fitting fresh candles into the new candlesticks, she had twisted long branches of greenery into wreaths that she wove around the serving platters, dotting them with small, fragrant white flowers she had found growing by the path to the mill.

Doña Josefa, who never hesitated to let her opinion be known, went into paroxysms of delight. Unused to such effusiveness, Paulina felt herself flushing at the praise.

"If I'd known a handful of cloth and ceramic would inspire such joy, I'd have stopped by the store more often," Sebastian observed from where he was leaning against the railing.

"Making another person happy isn't usually a complicated thing," Paulina said, going to join him as the housekeeper excused herself to return to her cooking. "You seem to manage it well enough."

He gave her a questioning glance, at which Paulina elaborated. "The *empanada* from earlier," she said. "You noticed I was hungry and were willing to stop for food even though I'm sure you had plenty of other things to do. It was small, as gestures go, but I can tell you that *lambí* made me quite happy indeed."

No need to mention everything else she had felt as a consequence of that *empanada*. Her knees were still quivering—though that may have been a product of spending the better part of an hour pressed against Sebastian's warm torso, her head pillowed on his shoulder and his arms around her in something that closely resembled an embrace.

"Well, if it's small things that please you, I have something for you. Only a token of friendship," he hastened to explain. "A small one."

"How small?" she asked.

"Minuscule." He held out a hand, long fingers unfurling to show the tiny things on his palm. "You were so busy looking at tablecloths that I thought I should get some finery for you. They aren't as elegant as the silver candlesticks, alas, but..."

"Nothing could compare to those," Paulina agreed, plucking one of the earrings and holding it up to the light. From a slender gold stem dangled a single bead of amber carved into the shape of a rose. It didn't so much catch the light as look as if it had been crafted from it—sunlight made solid. "These, however, are just small enough to be perfect."

Looking unaccountably pleased, Sebastian took gentle hold of her face and slid the earring he still held into place. She fought a shiver as his fingertips brushed the curve of her ear. It should have been entirely impossible for a touch to her earlobe to inspire such an intense sensation.

"I'll try for something even smaller next time—antlike."

Next time. The words hung in the air between them, heavy with a promise that Paulina knew he didn't mean to fulfill.

"I should go help Doña Josefa with the food," she said, touching the amber bead dangling from her lobe. "I... thank you, again."

Without waiting for a reply, she turned and headed for the kitchen, where the steam from the various pots and pans provided the perfect excuse for the heat flooding her face.

Doña Josefa had outdone herself. There was the guinea hen in a thick, red sauce scented with wine and spices. A mound of fluffy white rice sprinkled with bits of fried ripe plantain and flecks of parsley. A pineapple cut in half and hollowed out held the salad, which looked crisp and fresh despite the day's increasingly oppressive heat.

"It really is a feast," Leo remarked as he helped Doña Josefa carry the food to the table.

Paulina couldn't help but agree. The food was excellent, as everything prepared by Doña Josefa tended to be, but in Paulina's estimation, the best part of the feast came when they were enjoying small dishes of *dulce de coco* and Leo shyly asked Sebastian for a story.

From the way he worded his request, Paulina was given to understand that it used to be a regular occurrence, before Sebastian had acquired a wife and the sudden need to spend his days and evenings anywhere but home. It made Paulina sad to think that her presence had disrupted life at Villa Consuelo so drastically. If she had run anywhere else on the night of the storm, would they gather every evening to talk by the light of the lantern?

Paulina expected Sebastian to resist, or to insist that he had work to do, but he acquiesced easily enough to the boy's plea.

Sliding a spoonful of sweet coconut pudding into her mouth, Paulina watched Sebastian grow increasingly animated as he told the story of a farmer who had gone to water his *conuco* early one morning, only to realize that all his crops had begun to talk.

The story wasn't one Paulina had heard before. She almost forgot to listen to it, so absorbed was she in watching Sebastian's face grow mobile with humor. It only served to remind Paulina of just how short their acquaintance had been. She had thought him hopelessly serious when she'd first met him. Then he'd proved noble, and brooding, and responsible and desperate to protect everyone around him.

All that, and he was funny, too.

She wasn't sure she'd even heard Sebastian truly laugh before, and little wonder, what with everything that had happened. It was a bright, booming sound, underlaid with something like surprise, as if Sebastian himself had forgotten that he was capable of it.

Sebastian was in high spirits when he finished the story—the champagne they'd bought at Don Enrique's might have also had something to do with it—going so far as to tweak Doña Josefa's ear, which earned him a snap of her apron. He dodged it, still laughing, and fell to one knee in front of Paulina. "Will you join me in a dance?"

"But there's no music," she said.

Sebastian glanced at Leo, who obligingly began to drum on the table.

"There is now," Sebastian told Paulina, his hand still outstretched.

Sliding her palm into his, Paulina let herself be pulled from her seat. Sebastian seized her lightly by the waist and swung her into something that Paulina, inexperienced in such matters, thought might be a waltz.

"I don't think I'm very good at this," she said.

"It takes practice."

"And rhythm, of which I've got none. You do it wonderfully, though."

"I had a lot of practice in Havana. The secret is to look at your partner, not down at your feet. It also helps if you avoid treading on your partner's toes," he added with a grimace.

"I'm sorry!" she said, burning with mortification.

The problem with looking into his eyes instead of at her feet was that it felt like an extraordinarily intimate thing to do while his hand lay lightly on the small of her back and their palms pressed against each other's without the benefit of layers of fabric. The sensation did nothing to improve her coordination, and neither did the encouraging smile he was beaming down at her.

"No need to apologize. My toes were in want of a good stomping."

"How gracious. Is that what you told the debutantes in the ballrooms of Havana?"

A glint came into his eyes. "I didn't have to, actually. They were all good dancers."

Before she could laugh, the pressure of his fingertips on her waist heightened subtly, and she found herself being swept to the other side of the terrace, where a fluid twirl brought her up against the railing.

Paulina withdrew her hand from his and held it up in a silent plea for a moment's break, though she wasn't as out of breath as her panting indicated. After a moment's hesitation, Sebastian relinquished her waist.

"You seemed a bit quiet back there at the table," he said. "Are you all right? If you're troubled about what your brother said…"

"I'm not upset," she hastened to reassure him. "Just thinking."

"Oh?" Sebastian leaned against the railing, facing toward the house. "Anything you would like to share?"

There was no end of things she wanted to share with Sebastian, and that was part of the problem. "You may have been right, earlier. I hadn't really considered that now that I'm no longer under Antonio's control, I have the freedom to do whatever I want."

It might have been her imagination, but she thought she saw a flicker of pain in his eyes before he shifted his gaze to the sugarcane fields in the distance. "What *do* you want?"

"I want the *world*," she said, feeling as voracious as her words. She had always been reprimanded for wanting anything at all, so she saw no issue with wanting everything.

"You want to travel?"

"Oh, nothing as grand as that. I want to live, truly live in the world. I want to stroll down the streets on Sunday afternoons and sit on friends' balconies sipping juice and gossiping. I want to make a fool of myself flirting with handsome young men at balls and…and I want a home of my own. And a family to fill it with."

Her hands had clenched into fists. With some effort, she relaxed her fingers, placing them lightly on the railing, only inches away from Sebastian's back.

"Family," he said, and Paulina was taken aback by the intensity in his voice.

"Is that…not something you want for yourself?"

He shook his head. "I couldn't imagine wanting anything less."

"Not even children?"

Her heart in her mouth, Paulina watched him as he hesitated, then shook his head again.

Was that why he hadn't wanted a wife? Why he was refusing to share her bed? When he'd talked about giving her choices, did he mean himself? Of all the people she had ever met, she would have thought Sebastian was the least likely to desire the life of an unfettered bachelor—likely because he was so beholden to his responsibilities.

That only went to show how little she knew him.

Then he surprised her by adding fiercely, "I've seen too much misfortune in my life. I wouldn't be able to bear it if a child of mine had to go through even a fraction of what I went through as a child. Or you, for that matter."

She wrapped her arms around herself. "I was wondering, the other day, if you had any relations left behind in Havana. I take that to mean that you don't?"

"No," he said shortly. A furrow appeared between his brows, and he looked as though he was deciding whether or not to add something. "Josefa's my godmother."

Paulina's mouth fell open, even as she glanced at the table where the housekeeper still sat, chatting fondly with Leo. "I— She is?"

"She's my father's cousin. He was a cane cutter here in San Pedro. My mother was a washerwoman. She went from house to house helping with the laundry and the ironing, and I went with her, to perform small tasks for her and earn the occasional coin or two bearing messages for the mistress of the house." He looked at her, half defiantly and half expectantly.

Paulina's heart skipped a beat. "It was you, wasn't it? The washerwoman's son. You were the little boy I used to play with."

"I was."

The admission was hardly more than an exhalation, but it was still potent enough to wring a gasp out of her.

"Why did you never tell me?" she whispered. "The day of my birthday party, when I was talking about it…"

"Would you have treated me differently if you knew?"

She shook her head. "No, but…"

"I hardly knew you then. And I thought I had to hide the truth of where I had come from, because society wouldn't accept me otherwise, and I needed their help to make the mill a success. Business here relies so much on social connections—you can see it for yourself in how your brother operates." His voice sounded suddenly wry. "Although I didn't exactly go out of my way to secure their friendship. Maybe I'd have had an easier time of it if I'd done that instead of burying my head in my ledgers."

"I suppose that's true." Paulina bit her lip, then released it long enough to ask, "Why did you leave?"

"My father died, and my mother shortly after. Josefa did her best to look after me, but she had her own children and her own worries, and when an acquaintance of hers offered to take me along on her voyage to Cuba and later Spain, Josefa knew it might be my one chance at a better life. The acquaintance was a childless old lady, and I think Josefa was hoping that she would take me under her wing and provide enough schooling for me to make something of myself. But the old lady died on the ship, the night before it docked in Havana. And I arrived there alone." He made a small sound that under other circumstances might have been a laugh. "I wasn't penniless, not quite, because Josefa had taken up a collection among the cane cutters who had worked with my father, but I was swindled out of the money my first week there, and I was forced to live on the streets until Carlos's parents took me in."

Paulina felt a jolt as she recalled Antonio, in the coach home from town on the day of her birthday, saying something about how he suspected Sebastian of being of inferior birth. Her snob of a brother had been right about Sebastian not having come from a wealthy family, though not about the fact that he was concealing his identity.

Paulina hadn't been wrong, either—whatever his ancestry, Sebastian had proven to be far more noble than her brother.

"How old were you?"

"Eleven," he said.

Heartbreakingly young to have to fend for himself in an unfamiliar country.

"They all looked after me," he said. "The cane cutters, their wives, the washerwomen and the ones who worked as housemaids in the big houses in town. They all made their contributions so that I could have a better life. And I left them all to fend for themselves."

"You were a child," she tried to protest.

"When I first left, yes, I was. But I grew up. And as I was frittering my time away dancing and trying to flirt with fashionable young ladies, my people were going hungry. I don't know if I ever would have returned to San Pedro if it hadn't been for my own romantic failures and Carlos and his willingness to invest in the mill. He put in everything he had inherited from his parents—everything he might have saved for his sons' comfort and future. All of that is in the mill. In my hands.

"The mill was failing when I came back. Your brother had driven it to ruin, and everyone he employed was suffering for it. Their wages were so low as to be practically nonexistent, for backbreaking work, and Antonio kept threatening to lower them still more. And then there were the accidents, caused by your brother's neglect and his unwillingness to invest in better machinery. The foreman did the best he could, but your brother was no help at all. Did you know that Leo's father was killed in one of those accidents?"

"No," Paulina said, her voice quiet in contrast to his fierce tones. "I didn't know."

"They were my people, and they had been suffering while I danced my way through every ball in Havana."

"You're here now," Paulina said firmly, hoping Sebastian could take a measure of comfort in the fact. "You've done plenty for them—and for me."

"It's not enough." He scraped a hand over his face. "I don't know if it ever will be. I don't know if I—" Sebastian cut himself off before he could finish the sentence, but Paulina could fill in the blanks. He didn't know if *he* could be good enough.

If that was truly how he felt, it went a long way toward explaining why he claimed not to want a family. It wasn't bachelorhood he wanted, nor to be unfettered—what he wanted, Paulina thought, was to avoid feeling this way again.

Her heart broke for him. "You don't have to take care of everyone. Unfathomable though it may seem, you could even consider letting someone help *you*."

He stared at her.

"You have Josefa and Dilia and Leo," Paulina continued. "And, well, me. You could lean on me."

"I don't think anyone's ever said that to me before."

"Well, it was about time," she said firmly. She wanted to reach for his hand, but after all that had happened the day before, she wasn't sure it would be a good idea. Instead, she settled for lightly thumping the railing. "It isn't right for anyone to have to bear such burdens alone."

"I can shoulder them," he said with a twitch of his own broad shoulders, as if in illustration.

"I have no doubt that you can. That doesn't mean you should have to."

He was silent after that, his gaze distant as if he were looking far beyond the sunlit fields. Paulina knew she had given him a lot to think about. Falling into silence herself, she remained next to him long after the table had been cleared.

Chapter Thirteen

"It's not my place to say so, I'm sure, but it was nice seeing the both of you enjoy yourselves yesterday," Doña Josefa remarked the next morning as Paulina helped her clean the rice for the midday meal. "I thought the business with the table pure foolishness, though a pleasant enough diversion for you, but I can see that we were all in need of a little foolishness."

Like a candle being extinguished by a hurricane, Paulina had smothered the flicker of disappointment that had flared inside her when she'd tumbled out of her pallet from a dream of *empanadas* and horses and found that Sebastian had already left for the mill to make up the work he had missed the previous day.

"I remember your mother," the housekeeper added, holding a carrot and cutting it into perfectly even rounds without taking her gaze off Paulina.

"You do?" Eyeing her nervously, Paulina picked a piece of chaff from the white grains and flicked it into the bucket at her feet.

"A very elegant lady, with a laugh like silver bells and never too proper or too busy to help with a day's hard work. You resemble her, you know. And not only in looks."

Paulina's heart lifted. "It's wonderful of you to say so," she said softly. "I remember so little about her, sometimes I wonder if I made up the scraps of memories I do have."

She didn't have much of her mother's save the scant few items in the old trunk that Antonio had deemed not valuable enough to sell. There was the portrait, too, of course, though going to fetch it or asking Sebastian to do it seemed like a terrible idea at the moment.

Paulina's stomach clenched at the thought of her brother and his blatant attempt at extortion. Was there no limit to his dastardliness? It made her sick to think of all the people he had been winding around his web without her having noticed. Every fresh revelation made her wonder just how—or why—she hadn't noticed. It was true that she wasn't party to his life outside the house, but she had known, from the way he lorded over the *quinta*, that Antonio considered himself a man who was not to be crossed. He was a petty tyrant, and it stood to reason that he wouldn't limit his reach to just Paulina and the few people he employed.

She was stretching to rid herself of the kink in her lower back when the rumble of carriage wheels made her curiously head to the front of the house.

Even from a distance, the black-clad woman being handed down from her seat was instantly familiar to Paulina.

"I thought I would return your visit," Dilia said when she was within speaking distance, leaning to kiss Paulina on the cheek as if they had been acquainted for years. "I must say, I really should come out here more often. It's so peaceful—but then, any place is peaceful when there aren't twelve dozen little boys doing their best to use your finest linens as sails for their boats and generally tear your house apart for their amusement."

"I thought you had four sons," Paulina said.

"In theory. Sometimes I think they multiply when they're out of sight. They certainly eat enough for twelve dozen. In any case, I found myself in the mood for some companionship and remembered that I promised Sebastian I would call on you every once in a while."

It was on the tip of her tongue to ask why, but—somewhat belatedly—Paulina remembered her manners. "That's so kind of you. Won't you come sit down on the terrace?"

They went out to the kitchen first so that Dilia could greet Doña Josefa. Dilia was as inexorable as a cheerful cyclone, and Paulina found herself trailing in the older woman's wake, feeling slightly dazed.

As Dilia exclaimed over the new table—and the candlesticks that Paulina had lovingly dusted first thing that morning—Paulina set a chair next to the rocking chair overlooking the yard.

"He hasn't made a scrap of progress on the railing," Dilia said, running a hand over the stripped wood before taking the seat next to Paulina's. "I don't dare hope it's because he's actually taking the time to rest."

"He scrapes away at it sometimes," Paulina said. "I've helped where I could, but I'm not all that knowledgeable about woodworking."

"I'm sure the house will look infinitely better with your input. At the very least, I see that you've persuaded Sebastian to invest a little more in the way of creature comforts." Dilia drummed her fingers approvingly on the arm of the chair. "Are you settling in all right? I remember those early days of marriage—not a day would go by without me rushing home for advice or comfort or something I'd forgotten. I imagine you consider your-self equally fortunate to live so close to your childhood home."

Suspicion and defiance darted through Paulina's chest, and she found herself saying, with some heat, "If you're trying to ascertain whether I'm in contact with my brother, let me assure you I'm not."

Dilia gave a surprised laugh. "I wasn't terribly subtle, was I? If it's any consolation, Sebastian didn't send me to ferret out your secrets. He doesn't know I'm here, ac-tually. And I really did need to escape my house before it was fully overrun by children."

"I *have* no secrets," Paulina said firmly. "And while I can appreciate your desire to look after Sebastian, I can assure you, he's more than capable of determining by himself whether his wife is plotting against him."

"You're right," Dilia said after a moment. "He's more than capable. Or he would be, if he weren't so softhearted." To Paulina, there was something impatient about her sigh. "He's been swindled more than once by people pretending to need his help."

"I know," Paulina said, gratified that for once she ac-tually did know something about her own husband's past.

"Carlos was like that, too," Dilia said, a soft smile playing on her lips. "Generous to a fault, always ready to give whoever needed it the very shirt off his back." She rolled her eyes. "I can tell you, between Carlos and Sebastian, I had my hands full keeping them in shirts. And yet… I couldn't tell you how grateful I am that my boys have Sebastian to look up to. It may be selfish of me, but I'll do anything I can to keep the world from being tarnished for him and, by extension, for my boys."

"And for your memories of Carlos," Paulina said softly.

"For him above all. So, you see, I had to see for myself that you weren't taking advantage of Sebastian, particularly after the way the two of you hurried off yesterday."

"Nothing has happened between us," Paulina told her. "Nothing *will*."

"I wouldn't be so certain of that."

After that, the conversation turned to more prosaic subjects—the electric lines being put up in town, and whether nor not Dilia should make the switch from gas. The boys were fascinated by electricity, but was it really safe to have in the house?

It struck Paulina that perhaps Dilia was a little lonely, too, for all that she lived in town and had all those children to keep her occupied. She didn't have much time to dwell on the thought before they were interrupted by the sound of carriage wheels.

One unannounced visitor would have been odd enough. Frowning slightly, Paulina excused herself to go see who it was. The only other person with a coach she could think of was Antonio, and her heart started pounding at the thought that he might have come to finish what he had started the day before.

To her relief, it *wasn't* Antonio who was stepping down from the gleaming coach that had rolled to a stop next to Dilia's—it was Sebastian.

Paulina didn't do much but blink with surprise, but Dilia, who had followed her, brushed past her and regarded Sebastian with a hand on her hip. "Why, Sebas. Is that a coach?"

Sebastian jerked his head into a nod. "I've been meaning to get one."

"You only ever ride on horseback," Dilia pointed out, giving Paulina a conspiratorial look. "As a matter of fact, haven't you always said that riding inside a carriage feels as suffocating as being in a coffin?"

Paulina watched in delight as Sebastian's brows grew progressively thunderous under the onslaught of Dilia's ribbing.

"You should have gone into the law," Sebastian told her.

"Mothering my four mischievous little beasts has certainly prepared me for it. Five, if I count you, and I certainly should."

Paulina gave Dilia a curious glance. The other woman couldn't have been more than a handful of years older than Sebastian. There were faint lines on the corners of her eyes, it was true, and several strands of silver at her temples, but everything else about her was exceedingly youthful—particularly the way she was laughing at Sebastian.

"You didn't mother me so much as badger me until I had no choice but to relent to your endless commands." Sebastian glanced at Paulina, his lips curled into a grudging smile. "You're free to use the carriage whenever you wish," he told her a little gruffly. "I've employed a coachman, and he has instructions to take you wherever you want to go—so I'd be grateful if you avoided farmers' carts in the future."

Paulina received the news with something of a pang—while a carriage would be more comfortable, she hadn't exactly minded sharing a saddle with Sebastian. Feeling him nestle behind her had been almost as good as a true embrace.

Dilia's eyes were dancing with amusement, and Sebastian must have noticed them, too, because he added, with studied casualness, "Of course, it's mostly for Josefa. She's getting on in years, and with that new grandson of hers, she'll want to visit her daughter more often than ever. It isn't right that she should have to walk there or hitch rides in carts at her age."

"Of course it isn't," Dilia said in a voice brimming with laughter.

Sebastian gave her what for all intents and purposes ought to have been a furious glare, but it was spoiled by a sudden bark of laughter. "You rogue," he said, throwing an affectionate arm around Dilia and squeezing her to his side. He looked at Paulina over Dilia's head, and she softened when she saw the unvarnished affection in his eyes. "She never lets me get anything past her."

"It's my responsibility as your de facto older sister," she said, disentangling herself from his grip. "Now, I insist you take Paulina on a ride in the new coach."

A mixture of alarm and desire flashed through Paulina at the prospect of sitting in a small coach with Sebastian with their knees touching—or, worse, feeling the warmth of his body press all down her side.

"Oh, but don't you mean to join us?" Paulina asked Dilia.

"I couldn't possibly leave my little monsters alone for a minute longer—I'm sure to arrive home only to find the maid tied down and the cook tipped into her pot."

Before Paulina could point out that Dilia had just contradicted everything she'd told Paulina less than half an hour before, Dilia had bustled to her own coach in a flurry of blown kisses and twinkling promises to call on Paulina again.

Sebastian looked almost as dazed as Paulina felt when he turned to her with a quirked eyebrow, asking, "Shall we?"

Briefly, she considered telling him that they should take Doña Josefa with them. Then some tiny but insistent part of her gave a rebellious shake of its head. Paulina met Sebastian's gaze. "Let's go."

The memory of their last ride in a carriage was too recent for Sebastian to feel truly at ease as he climbed in next to Paulina, trying not to think of the raw anger and pain he had been filled with. That he had gone from that roiling mass of emotion to something so close to friendship was a testament to how hard Paulina had worked to make herself agreeable—not just to him, but to his entire household. He hadn't failed to notice the little kindnesses she did for Josefa, or the way Leo had started to turn to her with any problems.

Sitting almost diagonally to keep his long legs from tangling with hers, he had taken the seat that faced the rear so that she could look comfortably out the window.

The delicate lines of her face were outlined in sunlight. It gilded the curve of her cheekbones, lingering on the sweep of her brow and turning her plump bottom lip into something precious. It hardly seemed possible that just a day before he had kissed it with abandon.

Struck wordless, Sebastian was glad when she turned away from the landscape speeding past the window to abruptly ask him, "Do you regret having helped me on the night of the storm?"

He took a moment to consider the question. "I don't think there's much point in regret," he said finally. "Or dwelling on the past. I believe in looking forward and changing the things you *can* change."

"And when you feel like absolutely nothing is under your control? What then?" she asked with an intensity that would've been surprising to anyone who hadn't seen the steel beneath her placid demeanor.

Sebastian didn't have a chance to reply.

Against his better judgment, after the episode with Candida's goat, he had hired her grandson Alfonso as a coachman. The young man was only a few years older than Leo and something of a daredevil, judging from the speed with which he took the dirt road, still rutted deeply from the storm. To Sebastian, whose long limbs were cramped from how strenuously he was trying to avoid brushing up against Paulina, the rut felt more like a chasm.

The wheels bounced down, *hard*, and in the moment it took for the horses to pull the back wheels into and over the rut, Sebastian found himself with a bruise on his tailbone and a luminous beauty on his lap.

He had caught her reflexively as they were both jostled into the air by the seat's brand-new springs, shielding the top of her head even as his cracked smartly against the roof of the carriage. A swear escaped him, and he heard Paulina laugh breathlessly at the vulgar string of words that had left his lips.

He groaned. "I'd beg for your pardon, but I can't help but think that was justified."

"Unquestionably," she assured him.

Her fingertips grazed his forehead and continued in a gentle exploration of his scalp. Sebastian's eyes squeezed shut, and it wasn't only from the throbbing pain on his crown, or because her bottom and his thighs were once again renewing their acquaintance.

It had been a long time since anyone had touched him with such tenderness and care.

And even longer since he'd allowed himself to surrender to it.

Sebastian knew he'd done the right thing by telling Paulina that he wouldn't pursue a physical relationship with her. Unfortunately, his body was not as convinced.

He only had to turn his head a fraction of an inch before his lips were grazing the inside of her wrist, just above the healing scrape on her forearm. Even with the thunder of his pulse and the rhythmic pounding of hooves and wheels filling the carriage, he could hear her trembling exhale.

And then everything stilled, as if the world were holding its collective breath while Sebastian took on the superhuman task of pulling away from her and leaving her lips unkissed.

Her eyes were wide and a little grave when he looked up at her, still somewhat dazed from the blow and the gold on her gleaming brown skin. His gaze dropped to the tempting little hollow at the base of her throat, dipping lower to follow the shadow that deepened into another, much more dangerous chasm…

His tongue delved between them before he could think better of it. And when her nipples rose sharply to press against the fabric of her blouse, he circled one with his mouth, closing his teeth around her just hard enough to make her gasp.

"I shouldn't take liberties," he said roughly.

"You aren't." With excruciating slowness, Paulina undid the first several buttons of her blouse. "I'm giving them to you. I'm choosing to let you touch me. Isn't that what you told me? That I'm now free to do whatever I want?"

She brought his hand to her chest. "What I want is you."

He cupped her full, pliant breast, feeling it mold into his palm. The sound of her ragged breaths filled the carriage, and Sebastian's grew just as uneven when she ground herself against him, throwing her head back so that Sebastian had no choice but to follow the graceful column of her neck with his mouth, all the way to the warm lips waiting to receive him.

There was a bang on the outside of the carriage and Sebastian blinked, realizing that the world wasn't holding its breath—the carriage had stopped.

"Don, are you all right in there?" called Alfonso.

Sebastian swore again, under his breath this time, just loud enough for Paulina to hear. She dissolved into giggles.

"Fine," Sebastian snapped. "You can turn back now. And Alfonso?"

"Diga?"

"Go slower."

Inhaling deeply, Sebastian picked up Paulina and placed her back on her seat, from where she regarded him with mingled regret and mirth as she did up her buttons.

Sebastian ran a hand over the top of his head, wincing when his palm touched the rapidly swelling bump. "I suppose I can be grateful my head didn't split in half like an overripe *auyama*."

"That would be difficult, as it appears to be bone all the way through," she said teasingly.

He settled back against the upholstery, giving her a smile tinged with all the things he couldn't allow himself to say. "What makes you believe that?"

"Only an utter bonehead would purchase a coach without taking his own height into consideration—or his coachman's driving skills. I'd have that top padded if I were you," she said, laughing at him.

Sebastian had never wanted her more.

There wasn't a chance of his acting on that desire again. Fortunately—or unfortunately—the carriage came to an abrupt halt. A moment later, the door popped open, and Alfonso's anxious face appeared in the opening. Telling him to find Josefa for something to eat, Sebastian stepped down gingerly. Instead of firm ground, his feet sank to the ankles into something soft.

He didn't want to think about what would happen to the ache on his head if he looked down—fortunately, he could identify the pile underfoot from its vague scent of rotting vegetation.

"I've told Leo half a dozen times to burn those leaves before they molder," he said impatiently.

"I'd be surprised if he *had* heard you, with how he spends all day mooning over his books," Paulina said as he helped her down, lifting her by the waist to swing her clear of the rotting leaves. "Josefa told me that you're paying for him to go to school in town. That's awfully kind of you."

He waved the compliment away like he would a mosquito. "His mother has done more for me than I could ever repay. Even if she hadn't, I try to be good to the families around here. If only to make up for some of the indignities they've had to face."

"At my brother's hand?" she guessed.

"In part. He's not the only unscrupulous mill owner in the area, or alone in wanting to squeeze every drop of work from his workers without a shred of regard for their humanity." His voice had gone hard, as it tended to whenever Sebastian contemplated the injustice faced by cane workers.

"Is that what you're trying to do?" she asked interestedly. "Make up for how ill-used the people have been?"

"I don't think there's anything I *could* do to make up for some of the things they've been through. I just provide whatever little help I can."

"I'm not sure I would call all you do *little*," she said.

"I don't know how anyone around here would get along without you. Myself included."

The midday light filtering through the trees cast dappled shadows on her clear brow. Suddenly overcome with the desire to place a kiss just above her right eyebrow, Sebastian instead plucked off the tiny, elongated tamarind leaf that had fluttered down to catch among the curls haloing her face.

"I'm the one who couldn't get along without them." He cleared his throat. "Yourself included."

"I aim to be of service," she said lightly, turning toward the house. "In fact, if you've no objections, I think I'll ask Alfonso to take me into town to look at furniture tomorrow. I thought I would order some drapes for the windows, as well. Do you have time to walk through the house with me so I could explain how I'm thinking of arranging it all?"

When it came to her, he had all the time in the world. Experience told him that he ought to soak in every minute with her before she came to her senses and left, as everyone he'd ever loved had.

"Lead the way," he told her, trying not to let that thought show in his expression.

He hadn't quite realized it until then, but this was what he'd meant that day in town. Given the ability to make her own choices, and relieved of whatever misguided sense of gratefulness she felt she owed him, Paulina was sure to leave him. And when she did...

Sebastian was far too familiar with heartbreak, and with loss. Nothing, not even the promise of long, sultry nights with her in his arms—and in his bed—could persuade him to experience such grief again.

Chapter Fourteen

The *zafra* was finally underway.

All day, Paulina had heard the lowing of oxen as they pulled carts heavy with sugarcane through the dirt paths that bisected the fields. The mill must have been a hive of activity, with groups of men unloading the carts while others fed stalks of sugarcane through the machinery to be squeezed into pulp.

The familiar scent of burned sugar reached Villa Consuelo in clouds, as did the tiny vermin that raced to escape the fields that were now bristling with people. They took refuge in the rice barrel, inside the tin mugs that hung from nails by the kitchen table and, as they all realized when Paulina let out a bloodcurdling scream one morning, in the toes of her shoes when she discarded them before bed.

Doña Josefa had taken Sebastian up on his word and taken the carriage to visit her daughter and grandson, secure in the knowledge that Paulina would keep an eye on the house, and on Sebastian's unfortunate propensity for putting his work over meals.

The *zafra* having proven more interesting than food, however, Sebastian had spent all day at the mill or in the fields. Leo had gone home shortly before dinner, and after whiling away a few hours on the terrace, Paulina climbed into her bed.

It had taken a fairly short time for Paulina to grow attuned to the rhythms of her new household. In the mornings, she leaped from her bed the moment she heard its first stirrings, and she was more often than not lulled to sleep by the sound of Sebastian working on the railing each night.

Tonight, all was quiet on the terrace. Paulina turned on her mattress, straining to hear any indication that he had returned home.

Pushing her light blanket aside, she padded out to the terrace on bare feet.

The door to Sebastian's bedroom was ajar, and it swung open softly when she pressed her hand against the still-warm wood. "Sebastian?"

Silence answered her—Sebastian wasn't there.

The covered plate she'd left on top of his chest of drawers was untouched, except for a tiny brown lizard soaking up its residual warmth. Paulina felt her lips curl into a smile as she nudged its long tail aside with her fingertip. If Sebastian had not come to his dinner, then it would go to him.

She was closing the door behind her when a faint noise—the squeak of a floorboard, perhaps, or something just as innocuous—made her squint into the darkness. The hair at the back of her neck prickled with sudden alarm.

"Is someone there?" she asked sharply.

Her question was met by the usual nighttime noises— the soft whistling of a breeze making its way through the fields, the chorus of crickets and frogs, and the rustle of bats and other small creatures.

Once she had made sure that no one lurked in the deep shadows, Paulina dismissed the noise as having come from yet another creature seeking shelter from the cane cutters.

She placed the plate inside a basket and, with a glance back toward the quiet house, plunged into the sugarcane fields. Paulina would have been able to navigate the fields blindfolded, but fortunately a bright moon illuminated the way to the mill.

The night watchman, dozing on his chair by the door, didn't notice as she slipped into the mostly darkened building and followed the stream of light up a ramshackle set of wooden stairs that swayed slightly under her every step. At the very top was a small office with glass panes set into a window that overlooked the floor down below and a desk that faced the door. On a rickety chair that looked like it had been discarded from an old dining set was Sebastian, slumped over a snarl of papers and pots of ink.

He was sleeping.

Paulina leaned across the desk and touched his shoulder. "Sebastian?"

His lips parted in a smile of such uncomplicated tenderness and happiness it took her breath away. He must have still been dreaming.

"Sebastian," she said again, shaking him harder.

His eyes flew open.

His chair crashed to the floor as he flung himself backward. Leaping clear of it, he landed on slightly bent knees, looking frantically from side to side.

"It's just me."

He gave her a wild, uncomprehending look. "Paulina?"

"I brought you dinner," she said calmly, gathering his

papers and ledgers into a corner of the desk and not even flinching when she saw that at least two of the books were spread open to sections headed *Annulments* and *Divorces*. Sebastian was reading about how to dissolve their marriage.

Because he wanted to, or because he still persisted in the belief that she would?

She felt his gaze on hers but went on clearing the desktop, quickly and efficiently, until she had enough space on which to unpack the basket. "I thought you might be hungry."

Sebastian scrubbed a hand over his face. "I am. Thank you."

He righted his chair, then fetched her one from the pair under the window, which were holding still more books and his discarded jacket, slung over the back. The skin of his forearms looked dark against the crisp white of his rolled-up sleeves, and as he sat across from her, Paulina couldn't help but notice that he'd also unbuttoned his shirt at the neck.

The enamel plate Paulina set out was crowded with thick pieces of ham and boiled yuca topped with vine-gary onions. By now familiar with Sebastian's appetite, she had added two round crackers almost as big as her face and a bottle of the tamarind juice Leo had made in the afternoon, now gone lukewarm.

Sebastian reached for the juice first and grimaced at the first sip. "Leo made this, didn't he?"

Paulina laughed, nodding. "You'll want to mix in a little water if you have any. I swear, if you didn't make sugar for a living, that boy would be the ruin of you."

She perched on the edge of the chair he had brought her and looked with interest at the large map of Havana tacked up on the far wall.

"Do you miss it? Havana, I mean."

"Sometimes I do," he said, breaking off a piece of the cracker and offering it to her. "More so the people than the city."

"And the young ladies who danced so beautifully?" Paulina asked, nibbling on the cracker.

Somehow, he contrived to smile through the large piece of ham he had just wedged into his mouth. "Not as much anymore."

It was silly how such a little thing could make her want to squirm with pleasure.

Busy scooping rings of onion onto his fork, Sebastian hadn't noticed her reaction.

Paulina propped her chin up on her upturned palm, casting in her mind for a subject that would make him keep talking. He always looked so happy when he talked about his life in Havana. "How did you meet Dilia?"

"Her family had lived next door to the Gils for as long as anyone could remember. I would run errands for her grandmother, sometimes—mostly because she would sit me down afterward with a warm bowl of *arroz con leche* to fill out my skinny frame." Sebastian heaved a blissful sigh at the memory. "Dilia hadn't many siblings, either, only one much-older sister, and I suppose it was only natural that the three of us should fall in together. Though I can't imagine how Dilia found companionship in two rascals such as Carlos and me." Thoughtfully, he speared a piece of yuca with his fork. "Now that I think of it, I'm sure part of the appeal lay in having someone to boss around."

"She does seem a trifle…"

"Like she ought to have an entire fleet at her command?" He grinned. "Her mother was a schoolteacher, and I think Dilia would have liked to be one as well if she hadn't been otherwise occupied bearing those little scoundrels of hers."

"I can definitely see her heading up an entire school," Paulina said. "Do you think she would ever go back to Havana?"

And take you along, she added silently.

"We discussed it, once," Sebastian said. His lips compressed for a moment, then opened to admit another forkful of yuca. "Her grandmother moved in with Dilia's uncle, and with Carlos's parents gone and their house sold off, there didn't seem to be much of a reason to return."

"Not to mention the mill," Paulina added. "I don't see you parting from it anytime soon."

"Heaven willing." He poured a stream of water into the tamarind syrup—Paulina could hardly call it juice—and shook the jug. "Do you want some?"

Her teeth ached at the prospect. "No, thank you." She brushed a crumb off the edge of the desk, watching as Sebastian shoveled in the rest of his meal.

He *had* been hungry. Tired, too—she could see it in the faint shadows under his eyes. Paulina felt a pang of guilt. She'd been taking up an awful lot of his time lately, and he surely had to make up for it by working far into the night.

And here she was, distracting him again.

She knew she ought to leave, but she couldn't quite face returning to the darkened, lonely house. Not yet.

Turning away, Paulina gestured to the shadowy mill beyond the dusty panes of his window. Even up here, the musky, sweet scent of the sugarcane was underlaid with a heavy metallic smell and something she thought was engine grease. "Have you thought about having someone come in to read to your workers, like they do in tobacco factories?"

Sebastian shook his head. "The machinery's too loud for that, and everyone is too busy to take much notice."

"Not everywhere, surely. And certainly not at midday."

He raised an eyebrow. "Do you remember what you said the other day about not making a pest of yourself?"

Paulina made a brief assenting noise.

"You're failing miserably."

Paulina's laugh made his brow furrow even more fearsomely, but she wasn't worried. There was no heat behind his words, and he hadn't said no to her idea, either.

"I should think you'd enjoy being pestered every once in a while," she said cheerfully.

She went to the window and stood gazing past her reflection at the grimy machinery. "I feel like I'm inside a clock. If the clock were the size of a large house."

The great wheels did look like the cogs inside a pocket watch, only they were almost twice as tall as Sebastian.

His nod came with a brief laugh. "It's as beautiful as clockwork when the gears start turning."

He wiped his mouth with his handkerchief and came to stand beside her, his reflection a darker smudge beside hers. "She's a noisy beast, but she's damn beautiful."

For the first time that evening, Paulina was very conscious of the fact that she was still in a nightdress whose fabric was so thin she fancied she could feel his breath right through it. "I can just hear you describing your wife that same way," she said, forgetting momentarily that *she* was his wife.

All it took for her to remember was Sebastian's murmur. "My wife?" he said, and she could tell from his voice that he was striving to sound casual. "There's nothing beastly about her."

"Does that mean you think her beautiful?" she asked his reflection.

His head dipped a fraction of an inch—just enough for his voice to caress the curve of her ear. "Not just that. She's luminous."

Her breath caught, and even though she knew better than to read too much into it, she said, "I could say the same about my husband. You, Sebastian, shine with an inner light that touches everything around you."

"That's funny," he said, and Paulina turned to look at him properly, noticing for the first time that in spite of the deep shadows under them, his brilliant brown eyes were still warm. "That's what I think about you."

Turning away from Paulina, Sebastian busied himself returning the dinner things to the basket she'd brought them in. His pulse was racing so hard inside his ribs, his chest felt like it had been fed into the mill and spat out into pulp.

Unlike *bagazo*, however, there was nothing useful about the way he felt for Paulina—not when he couldn't act on it.

It was his own damn fault. He had been the one to start it, after all, this delicate, impossible dance, buying her earrings and devouring her lips with wanton recklessness, like someone who meant to do much more than touch.

Like someone who had the right to want her.

He swallowed, hard, and said as steadily as he could manage, "I do appreciate your bringing dinner—if nothing else, for helping me avoid Josefa's wrath."

Moonlight and lamplight dappled Paulina with silver and gold when he lifted the basket from the table and turned to face her.

"What are you doing?" she asked when she tried to reach for the basket and he answered with a shake of his head.

"Walking you back to Villa Consuelo. You shouldn't have walked through the fields by yourself—it's not safe."

"Nothing will happen. I've spent half my life wandering these fields, and I've never gotten lost or robbed or whatever it is you imagine will happen."

"The *zafra* has started. There are dozens of men with machetes roaming about." He sighed. "You're my responsibility now, like it or not, and I never shirk my duty."

Something wavered in her gaze. "I don't want to be anyone's responsibility."

"I can respect that," he replied. "I can even understand it. But it won't make me feel any less wretched if something were to happen to you after I sent you back on your own."

They went down together, past the quiet, hulking machinery, the mountains of cane stalks and the lightly snoring watchman. The moon was round and full, and out of the pool of light cast by the mill's lanterns, the shadows were deep enough to make stumbling a likely prospect.

Clouds of mosquitoes buzzed in the air between them, but neither they nor the dark seemed to trouble Paulina as she stepped unerringly into the narrow path. The cane was almost twice as tall as Sebastian. The long, slender stalks waved gently in the breeze, turning the path into a tunnel as they met overhead. It was hard to believe that within the next three months, this forest of stalks would be stripped away, the ground laid bare.

"Did you know that all this used to be grazing land?" Paulina asked suddenly.

"Was it?"

"My ancestors were cattle ranchers for over a hundred years. They had a horror of slavery, opposed it fiercely and vowed to have nothing to do with any industry that relied on it. So they raised cattle here and built the small but prosperous ranch where my father grew up. Now, *he* had no interest in cattle, and since his sisters had all married and moved away, he used my mother's dowry to plant the sugarcane and build the mill."

"I know," he said softly.

"Oh? I imagine Antonio told you all this when he sold you the mill. He's obsessed with the history of the Despradels and will prattle on and on about it to anyone who will listen. And here I am, doing the same."

He found her arm in the dark and touched it lightly. "It's only natural that you should want to talk about your parents. You must miss them terribly. Particularly after…" He trailed off, even though he felt no compunction about calling her brother all sorts of names.

"After my brother proved to be a villain?" she said archly but followed it with something that sounded like a laugh. "I think I missed them while they were still alive. They were always gone, or busy with their guests or planning their next frolic. They were wonderful to me when they thought to include me, but most of their amusements were unsuitable for children."

"And you hadn't any playmates," he recalled. "Save for me."

"I still have a hard time believing that was really you. That I've known you all my life." There was a slight movement in the shadows next to him, which he thought was a nod. "I consoled myself by thinking that when I was grown, I would have a whole lot of children—a dozen, at least—and I would plan frolics for *them*."

She gave a slight laugh, as if to indicate that she now found this idea ridiculous. As well she might, Sebastian reflected. After all, she was now wed to a man who wouldn't touch her or share her bed, never mind give her a dozen children.

The overwhelming loneliness of her life made his chest ache again.

"Paulina—" The sound of her name on his lips felt oddly intimate here in the dark.

He didn't know what he was about to say—probably something foolish like offering to give her any number of children she wanted—so it was probably a good thing that he was interrupted by a soft cry of pain.

"What happened?" he asked, stopping abruptly.

"I stepped on a rock, I think. It's nothing."

"Let me see."

Kneeling, Sebastian set down the basket and reached into the dark. His fingers brushed her bare ankle before encircling it and gently lifting it off the ground. Paulina made a small noise, and he felt her hand land on his shoulder for balance.

The scents of laundry soap and sunshine clung to the folds of her nightdress, which billowed softly over her calves in the slight breeze sweeping through the cane. Trying not to remember how transparent the thin fabric had looked in the lamplight, Sebastian held her ankle firmly in his left hand and used his right to explore the rest of her foot. Her sole was gritty with dirt. He brushed it clean with the back of his hand, in a gesture that could have seemed nonchalant to anyone watching but that made sweat bead on the back of his neck.

Her sharp intake of breath made him glance up. "Did I hurt you?"

"No," she said, though her voice came out soft and tremulous. "Just…keep touching me."

How could he help but to oblige? How could he help but to trace the long line of her calf, bare beneath the thin white fabric cascading past her hips? How could he help but press a kiss to the indentation at the back of her knee and touch his tongue to her salty skin until their breaths turned ragged?

His hand traveled higher, grazing the spot where the back of her thigh began to swell.

Her fingers dug into his scalp, and for a moment Sebastian wished he didn't keep his hair cropped short, so that she might lace her fingers through it and tug at his curls. He leaned into her touch, burning with need.

And then he pulled away.

"I can't give you what you want," he said in a low voice. "I can't be your husband."

I can't love you, he wanted to say, though he was starting to suspect that he already did. And to him, at that moment, there was not a prospect more terrifying than that of falling in love with his wife.

"Can't or won't?" There was something fierce in the way she said it, and in the gust of wind that swept suddenly through the field, rattling the cane as if it, too, demanded an answer from him.

Silently, he tugged his handkerchief out of his pocket and bound it around the pronounced arch of her foot, then lowered it gently to the ground.

"Sebastian."

He pulled a fold of her nightdress so that its hem tumbled down over her knee, covering her almost to her ankles.

"Will you be all right walking—"

"Sebastian," she said again, this time louder, her fingers digging urgently into his shoulder. "Did you hear that? It sounded like—"

"A scream," Sebastian said and pelted toward the house.

Chapter Fifteen

The kitchen yard was silent when Sebastian burst through the edge of the field. Half expecting to find the house engulfed in flames, he didn't see anything at first.

Then, aided by moonlight and the lantern they usually kept burning overnight dangling from its hook in the kitchen, he caught a glimpse of what looked like a quickly moving shadow slipping down the terrace steps.

Not sparing a moment for so much as a thought, he charged toward the dark figure.

Alerted by the sound of Sebastian's boots pounding on the hard-packed ground, the figure broke into a run. Sebastian put on a burst of speed. The other man was fast, but Sebastian was faster—he slammed into the man with his full strength, sending them both rolling to the ground.

They fetched up against the crumbling bricks that surrounded one of the yard's largest tamarind trees and Sebastian, moving with furious speed, seized the man by the back of the collar and pinned him down with a knee to his back.

The night was filled with grunts and breathless swears as Sebastian tried to keep hold of the frantically writhing man. Then the intruder bucked underneath him, hard enough to send Sebastian flying backward. Immediately surging to his feet, Sebastian lunged for the man.

This time, the pursuit was brief. It ended just as they cleared the next tamarind tree, the one closest to the kitchen, as Sebastian grabbed him once again by the collar and flung him against the trunk. He was breathing hard by then, and sweat was pouring into his eyes, and the intruder must have been tiring as well, because he didn't try to run away again.

It wasn't until Sebastian saw the metal of a blade catch the moonlight that he realized why.

The intruder wielded the knife as if he knew how to use it and, moreover, as if he was determined to inflict serious damage. The blade slashed through the night— Sebastian managed to block the thrust with his forearm, but he miscalculated the next one and felt the sting as the knife dug into his upper arm.

Sebastian leaned into the sharp bite, roaring out an expletive. It wasn't a sophisticated bit of maneuvering by any means, but it caught by intruder by surprise and made him lose his footing long enough for Sebastian to push him past the dark stone ring of the banked cook fire.

Holding the other man by the base of the neck, Sebastian slammed him against one of the sturdy wooden posts that kept the kitchen walls upright, so hard that the knife went flying in a silver arc, disappearing amid the grass and fallen leaves. Above their heads, the lantern swung wildly, tossing disorienting shadows on the two walls of the kitchen.

Desperate now, the man clawed at Sebastian's face, then changed tactics and began pummeling his midsection with short but powerful punches. The first blow knocked the breath out of Sebastian, but the second one skidded off his ribs as Sebastian twisted to the side.

Sebastian's right hook caught the intruder by the jaw. Sebastian had a moment to feel greasy bristles under his knuckles before the man's face jerked upward with the blow, suddenly visible as the lantern arced to the other side.

The guardsman.

The shorter, stockier one with the mean little eyes, who'd been so eager to gag Sebastian. Juan.

Taking advantage of Sebastian's momentary shock, he wrenched himself out of Sebastian's grasp and reached above his head for the burning lantern. His attempt to dash it over Sebastian's head failed when Sebastian ducked to the side, causing the lantern to crash to the ground instead.

It would have likely extinguished itself upon contact with the dirt floor, if it hadn't caught the edge of a can of peanut oil. The oil cascaded to the floor, igniting as it came into contact with the flames and roaring up into a blistering cloud.

Sebastian pulled back at the sudden stinging heat, throwing up an arm to shield his face. With a loud grunt, Juan shoved Sebastian toward the flames and made his escape.

For a fraction of a second, Sebastian hesitated, torn between giving chase and tending to the rapidly spreading fire.

The house was mostly stone and wouldn't burn, but it would be all too easy for the fire to spread to the piles of leaves and palm fronds that Leo had neglected to clear away, not to mention the trees in the kitchen yard—and from there, to the sugarcane fields.

They must be kept from burning at all costs.

It was that thought more than anything that stirred Sebastian into action—he emptied a sack of rice over the spilled oil, then snatched a rag from the table just before it was reached by the flames and began to snap it at the fire as it crackled up the wooden legs of the table and the boards of the wall behind it.

The guardsman must've had a horse waiting nearby, because a moment later, the clomping of hooves came from the front of the house.

All of a sudden, Paulina was there, wrenching the lid off the water barrel and dipping what looked like a bed-sheet into it. She tossed the sodden mass at Sebastian, and he used it to beat back the flames that had begun to crackle up the wooden wall.

"Stand aside!" Paulina cried, and she flung what must have been the entire contents of the cornmeal barrel at the flames.

The cornmeal smothered most of the flames, and Sebastian launched himself at the rest, raising his aching arm and bringing it down in swift, powerful arcs as he beat the wet cloth against the bright fingers rising from the wood, over and over again until a hand landed on his shoulder.

"It's over," Paulina said, panting. "The fire's out."

Sebastian's entire body was heaving with breaths. He staggered back, coughing, and wiped the sweat streaming off his forehead with the scorched cloth he was still holding.

Something tiny and blue caught his eye as he did and, belatedly, Sebastian glanced down at it.

It would have been unrecognizable if not for the remains of the embroidered band around one edge. Wishing it were a piece of paper he could crumple into oblivion, Sebastian cast the ruined tablecloth to the ashes and turned abruptly away.

There would be no more feasts at Villa Consuelo.

No feasts, no dancing and absolutely no more distractions.

"Who screamed?" Paulina asked hoarsely when they had caught their breath. "I thought no one was home."

"I asked Leo to stay here tonight so you wouldn't be left alone," Sebastian told her. "Have you seen him?

She shook her head, eyes wide.

Sebastian bolted toward the house, using his long legs to leap over the steps to the terrace. His heart leaped into his throat when he saw the young man crumpled in a corner, next to the overturned rocking chair.

"Leo!" cried Paulina, who'd followed on his heels.

The boy was already beginning to stir. Sebastian dropped to his knees beside him, calling over his shoulder for Paulina to light a lamp.

When it flared into life a moment later and the extent of Leo's injuries became visible, Sebastian sucked in his breath.

"He hit me from behind," the boy croaked. "And I fell against the railing. It's not as bad as it looks."

That wasn't exactly comforting.

Paulina, bearing a cloth and the basin of water from her room, nudged Sebastian aside and began to minister to the boy's cuts.

It occurred to Sebastian that he should go fetch the doctor, but the last thing he wanted was to leave them alone and unprotected in case the guardsman returned. Sebastian swore under his breath. Paulina had been right to call Villa Consuelo isolated. With no close neighbors to turn to, and no one to hear their screams if they were being murdered in their own beds.

It hadn't escaped him that with Josefa gone, Paulina

had been alone in the house all day. She could have easily been the one who was attacked.

Leo's fingers twitched.

"Don't try to talk," Sebastian said automatically, but the boy persisted. His fingers closed around the knee of Sebastian's trousers.

"I think he thought I was you."

It was an effort to keep still, his hand gripping the boy's in silent support, when all Sebastian wanted was to leap on his horse and gallop after the guardsman so that he could murder him with his own hands.

Paulina finished her ministrations, quietly winding another length of cloth around Leo's head. When she was finished, Sebastian carried the gangly young man to his own bed. At sixteen, almost seventeen, he was as tall as Sebastian and nearly as broad through the shoulders. No wonder the guardsman had confused them in the dark.

Paulina followed them inside, ostensibly to light the way with the lamp. Had Sebastian not grown to know her as well as he had, he wouldn't have noticed the tight grip she had on the lamp, or the way her eyes darted toward the deep shadows surrounding the house.

The fear in her eyes was like a knife digging into Sebastian's guts.

He helped Leo into a clean shirt, as his was rent and splattered with blood. Then, telling Paulina to give the boy some rum to drink from the decanter she had chosen to replace his cask, Sebastian slammed out onto the terrace, feeling choked by his own rage and fear.

Leo could have been killed, just because he'd been mistaken for Sebastian. Because Sebastian had once again put his compulsion to come to someone's aid above his own safety, and that of the people he was responsible for.

This was why Sebastian hadn't wanted a wife. This was why he couldn't let himself fall in love with Paulina even when his very limbs ached to twine around hers.

Loving someone—caring for them—only meant that it hurt that much more when that love was inevitably ripped away.

He didn't bother with a chair but slid down to the tiles and stretched out his legs, letting his spinning head fall back against the warm stone wall. His throat was raspy with the urge to cough out all the smoke he had inhaled, but he didn't want to leave his post, even for the few seconds it would take to fetch the water jug or the rum from his bedroom.

Presently, the door opened and Paulina slipped out, narrowly keeping herself from treading on Sebastian's stretched-out legs. Regaining her balance, she gracefully lowered herself to the spot next to him on the cool tiles, so close that he could have put his arm around her. He wanted to. He wanted to gather her against his chest and pull her long, silky legs over his lap and find comfort in the taste of her lips and the feel of her pliant body beneath his hands.

She wouldn't refuse him if he asked—and that was precisely why he couldn't.

Sebastian clenched his raw hands on his lap, but she didn't seem to notice.

"He's resting comfortably," she said.

"You should go to bed," he told her. "I'll stay out here until morning."

"I'm not tired," she said, drawing up her knees and clasping her arms around them. The thin white fabric covering her legs was scorched in places and had a long tear near the hem.

He started to ask if she was all right, but the words

stuck in his throat, and not just because of the lack of water.

Unaware of his inner turmoil, she continued. "I'm… confused. I couldn't get a good look at the man's face, but we both know he was no common thief. Am I mistaken in thinking you recognized him?"

Sebastian gave a brief nod. "It was one of the guardsmen from the municipal jail."

Also known as one of her brother's henchmen. He could tell when she registered the fact from the line that appeared between her delicately arching brows. He could also tell she was coming to the same conclusion as he had when Leo had said, *He thought I was you.*

"He was after me," Sebastian said bluntly.

"You think this may have been a warning? Because you didn't give Antonio the money when he asked for it?"

Sebastian shook his head. "No, not a warning. That blow to Leo's head…that was meant to inflict real damage."

Though left unsaid, Antonio's name hung between them. Paulina's brother might have been a lot of things, but it was clear that she had never thought him for a murderer and neither had Sebastian.

They'd both been wrong.

"He wants the mill back," Sebastian said.

Dawn was beginning to streak the sky with light, and though the terrace was still filled with shadows, Paulina couldn't fail to notice that the indentations under his eyes had grown even deeper. The skin above his eyebrow was split, grimy with blood and soot, and Paulina knew there must be bruises spreading across his ribs where the other man had pummeled him.

Paulina herself was tired, and hunger was beginning

to nibble at her stomach, but there was no question of making breakfast with the kitchen destroyed. And even though she knew she smelled strongly of smoke, she couldn't quite stomach the thought of lighting a fire to warm up water for a bath, either. Unobtrusively, she rubbed at a streak of grime on her arm.

"If Antonio has no money," Sebastian said, "and no way of acquiring enough to tempt me to sell, he must have realized that the only way was through you. That's why he went to extreme lengths to keep us from having the marriage annulled. Only it doesn't seem like he was planning to wait enough time for you to claim half my property in a divorce—not when he could kill me and have you inherit *all* of it."

"I'll divorce you," she said. "I'll do it tomorrow if that's what'll stop him."

"You can't. You need the consent of a relative if you're under twenty-five years of age, remember? Our best bet—our only bet—was an annulment. And your brother made that impossible by threatening or blackmailing or whatever he did to all the lawyers in town to discourage them from representing either of us."

"What will we do, then? If he tried it once, he'll try it again, and we can't sit around waiting for one of his attempts to succeed."

"I don't know," he said grimly.

Somewhere in the distance, a rooster began to announce the dawn. Paulina glanced at Sebastian, who was looking down at his clenched hands.

"I don't know how to tell Leo's mother that he was hurt while under my care," he admitted. "She's a widow, and Leo is all she has in the world. If anything worse had happened—if the guardsman had had a pistol…"

"It didn't," Paulina said firmly. "Leo told me that you

were putting them both up in town so that he could attend school later in the year. Why not send them now, ahead of time? I think you'll breathe easier if he's safely out of the way."

"That's a good idea."

"I've been known to have one, every now and then," Paulina said mildly. Sebastian didn't crack so much as a smile, which made Paulina frown. "Something else is troubling you."

He grunted his assent.

A sudden thought occurred to her. "You don't think I had anything to do with this, do you?"

"I don't blame you," he said, and she noticed that he hadn't said no. "I blame myself. I should have never left you all alone. I should have thought to hire someone to guard the house, or taken any number of precautions. I should have—"

"Been all knowing and all seeing? If you were to follow that line of reasoning, you should have known better than to take me in the night of the storm. You should have never walked me to Don Enrique's store, or even stopped to talk to me on the street. You couldn't have predicted that any of this would happen," she said, but she had the feeling that Sebastian wasn't listening.

She sighed. "Maybe you should leave town for a spell, at least until we can decide what to do about Antonio."

"*We* are not deciding anything. And in any case, I couldn't possibly leave the mill now, not as the *zafra's* beginning."

Making an impatient noise, he hauled himself to his feet and started to make his way to the railing. It wasn't until Paulina saw the slight stagger in his step that she realized that the guardsman hadn't only punched him.

"You're bleeding," she blurted out.

He glanced down and, catching sight of the red stain on his bicep, gave her a shrug. "Just a scratch, I expect."

"A scratch? It's soaking through half your shirt. Here, let me—"

He reared as she advanced toward him, for all the world like a shying horse. "I'm fine."

She gaped at him. "Do you really mean to play the hero right now?"

"I'm not a hero," he mumbled.

"No, you're just trying your damnedest to single-handedly save half the population of San Pedro."

"You don't understand—"

"How could I, when you don't tell me a thing? When you spend your days running yourself ragged trying to solve everybody else's problems and refusing to see all the people who are trying to help you? I am trying to help you, Sebastian. I could, if you'd only give me a chance."

"I can't give you a chance," he snapped. "I can't afford any more distractions."

"Is that all I am to you? A distraction?"

"If we hadn't stopped in the fields—" he began wretchedly.

"You think that if I hadn't distracted you with my foolish talk about cattle ranching and dozens of children, you would have come home in time to...what? Be clubbed to death in your own bed? You were asleep at your desk," she said, and her voice sounded ragged to her own ears. "If I hadn't woken you up, would you have come home at all?"

Paulina stopped, breathing hard.

The silence that fell between them, so tense that it surely had to snap, went unbroken—until Sebastian said, in a voice that was hoarse with smoke and emotion, "I'm meant to be the one protecting this household. Not bringing danger to the doorstep."

Paulina sank into one of the new dining chairs, suddenly and thoroughly drained. "But that's not right, is it? You're not the one bringing danger to it—I am."

She waited for Sebastian to deny it, or to say something reassuring, but he remained silent, looking out over the fields. Bowing her head, Paulina let out a quavering breath. "I can't be responsible for anyone else getting hurt. Maybe I should be the one to go away."

"No," Sebastian said after a moment. "Your going anywhere won't stop your brother."

Whatever scrap of reassurance Paulina might have scrounged from his telling her to stay vanished at the second half of his sentence.

"I'll find another solution. Antonio is not getting my mill and I sure as hell am not letting him get away with hurting my people." He turned to face Paulina. "If the magistrate is crooked, the only authority that can supersede his is that of the governor of the province. I'll find a way to plead our case to him."

Rage tensed every one of Sebastian's limbs. Standing against the blazing sunrise, he looked like some sort of avenging angel, burning with righteous strength.

This was the man who had taken her in during a storm, the one who had agreed to marry her rather than let her be mistreated.

This—this was the man she had fallen in love with.

Chapter Sixteen

The smoke might have cleared, but the air between Paulina and Sebastian was more charged than ever. Paulina's heart ached as she stood in her darkened bedroom, watching from behind the shutters as Sebastian clattered down the terrace steps.

No one had been badly hurt and only the kitchen had been damaged in the fire, but one wouldn't know it from looking at the grim expression Sebastian wore these days.

It wasn't only Sebastian who was on edge. More than once, Paulina had caught herself jumping at shadows, growing tense every time a tree branch swayed unexpectedly or a bird took sudden flight.

Leo had been dispatched into town ahead of schedule and set up with books and tutors until school started. Sebastian wasn't confiding much in Paulina these days, but she had learned from Dilia that he'd sent word to Doña Josefa to stay with her daughter for another few weeks.

It wouldn't have been so wretched if she had Sebastian's company, but he had begun going to the mill earlier than ever, hours before the sky began to lighten, leaving behind two burly men to look after Villa Consuelo…and Paulina.

Paulina had never found any use in tears and she wasn't inclined to indulge now, but neither could she ignore the desperate loneliness curling through her as soon as she opened her eyes, the birdsong uninterrupted by the bustle of Doña Josefa's cooking or Leo's quiet voice. The men Sebastian had hired were nice enough but not inclined toward conversation.

The furniture Paulina had ordered for the house had arrived, and while the pieces were as beautiful as she'd expected, arranging and rearranging them only took up so much of the day. It was a relief when, after a couple of days of solitude, the rumble of carriage wheels in the front yard announced a visitor.

Paulina was on the terrace. The homely rocking chair had been replaced by a handsome new set, with carved backs and flowered cushions on the seats. They were grouped around a round table, which Paulina had laid with a silver coffeepot and a delicate porcelain cup from the service she and Sebastian had purchased on one of their jaunts into town. Similarly arrayed in her sky-blue skirt and a white blouse bordered with eyelet lace, Paulina thought idly that she would trade it all for the tin mugs and the shabby yellow frock if it meant having people around her again.

The guards hired by Sebastian had been lounging in the shade of the tamarind trees; at the sound of the carriage, they rose from their spots with such alacrity that Paulina realized their lethargic poses had been nothing but an act.

"It's all right," she said when she spotted the familiar coach. "It's only Sebastian."

It wasn't like him to come home in the middle of the day. Not anymore. Paulina tensed as she watched him alight with a single bound of his long legs, her hands crumpling the newspaper she had been reading.

Sebastian's face was tight, and he spared neither a greeting nor a smile for Paulina when he stopped beside her.

"I couldn't get an audience with the governor," he said without preamble. "But I did secure an invitation for a ball he's hosting tonight. He leaves for Santiago in the morning on a health matter, so it's our only chance to approach him."

"A ball?" Paulina echoed. "But I haven't got a—"

"I went to Blanca's earlier. She still had your measurements, so it was only a matter of hours for her to alter a gown to fit you."

As if in illustration, Alfonso lugged a satin box into the terrace.

"I asked her to select shoes for you, too, and whatever accessories were necessary. It should all be in the box." Without further explanation, Sebastian started to turn around.

A sudden wild panic gripped Paulina at the thought of being left alone again, and she had the irrational urge to plant herself in his path and force him to acknowledge her. "Wait!" she exclaimed, her hand fluttering in his direction, though she stopped short of touching his retreating back, half-afraid that he would shrink from her touch.

Sebastian glanced at her, and it was as if a door that had previously been left ajar had been shut in her face. "Alfonso will take you to the governor's residence when you're ready."

"You're not coming with me?"

"I have some business to attend to, but I'll join you there later."

Paulina scowled. "Is that really all you have to say to me? 'Get dressed, we're going to a ball, meet you there'?"

His back stiffened. "What else do you want from me, Paulina?"

"The friendship that you offered me, for one," she snapped, her temper flaring. "And for you to stop treating me as though I was the one who clubbed Leo over the head. Stop pushing me away, Sebastian. I thought we were long past this."

He didn't reply, and her irritation at his silence made her say, "I'll go to the governor's ball with you, but there's something I want in exchange—when we are no longer married, I want you to book me passage on the first train out of San Pedro, and provide me with some funds to make the journey. I intend to get far away from here the very second I can."

She was horrified with herself the instant the words left her mouth—both because it made her sound uncomfortably like Antonio, but also because she hadn't realized how much it would hurt Sebastian until she saw his mouth clamp shut.

He gave her a hard nod. "Yes." The despair in his eyes hollowed out her chest. "I had a feeling you would."

She sighed. "Sebastian, I—"

"I'll give you anything you want, Paulina," he said tiredly, not letting her choke out an apology.

"And you won't even miss me, will you?"

He smiled at her then, finally, but it was a sad, regretful smile. "I think you know me better than to think that."

"I thought I did," she told him, and it was she who turned away, walking past the discarded newspaper and coffee and into her room.

The nights were much cooler in town than they were among the sugarcane fields. A pleasant breeze, tinged with the saltiness of the sea and the slight brackishness of the river water, swept through the open louvered doors at the far end of the governor's second-floor ballroom.

Paulina shivered as the breeze touched her bare shoulders. The evening gown that Blanca had hurriedly adapted to fit her had sleeves—cascading wings of topaz-colored chiffon that fell softly around her elbows, suspended from heavily beaded straps that left her shoulders uncovered. The gown was cinched tight around the waist with a taffeta sash that bore still more beading. Along with the low neckline, it made her aware of her own figure, and of the way her body slipped through the crowd as she went in search of Sebastian.

An ostentatious topaz necklace had been included in the box with the gown, but Paulina had worn instead the rose-shaped amber earrings Sebastian had given her. She raised a hand to touch them now, nerves fizzling in her stomach like the bubbles in the champagne flute a waiter had handed her earlier.

Trailed by the thrilling notes of music coming from the musicians on the dais, Paulina circled the crowd once again. There were dozens of people in the ballroom and a handful more on the balcony that stretched the entire width of the house and overlooked the lush gardens below. There had been still more people crowding the wooden staircase and spilling out into a wide street that was crammed with coaches.

Quite a number of them spoke in English or accented Spanish—Paulina remembered her brother bragging about being friends with all the foreign mill owners, though she'd had the impression that they did not exactly treat him as an equal, having little money and no mill of his own.

Having found no familiar faces among them, Paulina

was nearing the musicians' platform when she saw Sebastian through a gap in the crowd. He had paused near the tall arch of the entrance, framed between two columns as he scanned the room with that tense watchfulness he had developed since his fight with the intruder.

He turned his head as if to show off his strong profile and chiseled jaw, the noble lines of his head displayed to best advantage by his close-cropped hair. In response to the sight, the ever-present ache in her chest flared into life.

It had been mere hours since she'd last seen him, but she was struck by the solid breadth of his shoulders and the way his long, lean legs echoed the columns at either side of him. It was almost as if she were seeing him for the first time, but better, because now she was familiar with the callused roughness of his fingertips and the hardness of his arms and thighs.

He was hers. Nothing that had happened in the past several weeks would support that conclusion, but Paulina knew it with a fierce intensity. Whatever had happened, and whatever *would* happen. Even if she never saw him again after the governor granted their annulment, Sebastian Linares belonged to her.

The cool breeze was still making its way through the ballroom, but Paulina was suddenly filled with the urge to snap open her painted fan and wave it at her warm face.

Then a woman dressed in black and dripping with jewels moved in front of Paulina; by the time she and her mustachioed companion had strolled past, Sebastian had disappeared from where he had been standing.

For a moment, Paulina thought that he was going to avoid her until it was time to speak with the governor.

But as disappointment crashed over her, the crowd parted again and there he was, standing in front of her.

He looked even better up close. Paulina's lips parted, but every word she'd ever known had vanished from her mind.

Luckily, Sebastian wasn't paying her any attention.

"Linares?" said someone to their right. "It is you. Funny, I don't think I've ever seen you in one of these events. I was beginning to think you were some sort of sugarcane hermit."

The voice belonged to a pale-skinned man with a handlebar mustache and light green eyes. He spoke Spanish perfectly, though his accent, Paulina noticed, was tinged with a Cuban lilt.

"Bass." Sebastian gave the other man a hearty handshake. "May I present to you my wife, Paulina."

"Oh, yes, I did hear you married recently. Enchanted to meet you," he said, greeting her in the American fashion, with a brush of his hands over her gloved knuckles.

"Paulina, this is William L. Bass. He's the proprietor of one of the largest sugar estates in the province. And quite a cartoonist, from what I hear."

"Oh?" Paulina asked as the older man roared with laughter.

"Just trying to keep the powers that be in line," Don William said. "But I'd hate to talk about business on such a nice evening. Ah, here comes Vicini's widow. Doña Laura, you are acquainted with Sebastian Linares and his splendid wife, are you not?"

The flurry of introductions was, in fact, followed by business talk. As it turned out, Doña Laura also owned a sugar mill, and all three of them had plenty to say about…well, Paulina wasn't entirely paying attention. She was taking advantage of the conversation to watch

Sebastian. Though older by at least a couple of decades, Don William and Doña Laura listened seriously to what he had to say, making it clear that they truly valued his opinion. As for Sebastian himself, he looked as at home among these wealthy landowners with their diamond tiepins and blazing jewels as he had trying to solve a goat-related dispute in his shirtsleeves.

She was so absorbed in her examination of Sebastian's face that she didn't realize they were trying to include her in the conversation until Doña Laura had said her name two or three times.

"Oh, but we are taking too much of your time," she said when Paulina finally snapped to attention. "A young couple such as yourselves must be longing to dance. Come, William, let's stand aside and let them have their frolic."

Paulina licked her lips. To refuse would have been the height of rudeness. Surely Sebastian wouldn't…

"I believe my wife was just saying something about procuring refreshments—"

"Actually," Paulina said defiantly, "I would love to dance."

His gaze flicked toward her. Looking as if he was steeling himself, Sebastian bowed. "As you wish. Will you join me in a dance?"

Out of the corner of her eye, Paulina caught Doña Laura's beam. She could have hugged the older woman. Settling for a smile instead, Paulina took Sebastian's hand and allowed him to lead her to the dance floor as the first strains of a waltz began to play.

As he had when they'd danced on his terrace, Sebastian placed a hand at her waist and clasped her hand with the other. And as it had then, it felt extraordinarily intimate.

Or it would have, had Sebastian not looked furious.

"Your friends will wonder why the prospect of dancing with your own wife pains you so much," she remarked, though Sebastian's expression felt like it was scouring her from the inside out.

His shoulder flexed under her hand. "I don't give a damn what anyone thinks. I'm only here for the governor."

"I think he hasn't arrived yet," Paulina said. "So you might as well enjoy yourself. I may not be a Havana debutante, but I know how much you like dancing. Even with someone who treads on your toes."

For all that he was still in the grip of his foul mood, Sebastian was a pillar of grace and strength as he swept her along. He didn't seem to be troubled by her occasional misstep, and if she did injure his toes, he refrained from showing it, like a true gentleman.

"I didn't learn to dance in Havana," he said.

"Oh?"

"I learned by watching your mother's parties. I would climb up the mango tree outside the upstairs gallery and hide among the branches as I looked at the elegant couples swirling around."

"I was always watching, too," she said softly. "I hid under tables in my nightdress. Isn't it peculiar how we spent so much of our childhoods together, sometimes unknowingly? Only to end up here. Together, again."

"It was no coincidence that I ended up where I did," he told her. "Buying the mill from your brother, purchasing the only estate that neighbored your family's *quinta*... Those nights when I watched the parties from between the mangoes, I promised myself that I would have all of that someday—glittering friends, lavish tables bursting with flowers and all sorts of delicacies on silver platters, a laughing wife dripping with jewels."

He twirled her. "I dreamed about it when I was on the streets in Havana. A fine house, with great beds heaped with pillows and tables laden with everything I could eat. You want to know why I didn't tell you who I was at first? Because you only knew me as the little servant boy who came to play with you. You didn't know that when the games ended and the music stopped, I walked through the cane in the dark, to a wooden house with a cane-thatched roof that leaked and a floor made out of packed dirt that turned into mud at the slightest spill. I went home to an exhausted mother who had to rub lard on her hands to soothe the knuckles she had rubbed raw washing other people's clothes. We didn't spend our childhoods together, Paulina. We spent them near each other."

Her chest felt tight, even as she let him sweep her from one end of the ballroom to the other. He was right. Growing up, they had been separated by more than the cane fields. And yet. The achingly lonely little girl she'd once been still resided inside her, just as part of him was still a skinny boy with big eyes. Their pasts, and their losses, weren't something they had overcome, but what had made them into the people they were now.

People who were as irrevocably drawn to each other as if they'd spent their lives trying to find each other again.

The waltz was about to come to an end. Sebastian gave her one last twirl as the last strains of the song reverberated from the musicians' dais, and Paulina's gaze traveled around the room, over the matrons gathered in the sidelines.

When she returned to Sebastian's arms, it was with a pounding heart.

"He's here," she said. "Antonio's here."

* * *

In the deep ochre of her gown, sparkling in the oddly still electric lights, Paulina looked like she had been plucked from the midday sky. The fabric clung to her curves, glazing her in light.

It took a moment for Sebastian to register what she was saying, and still longer to respond. "I know," he said, "I saw him."

He'd given little thought to his own safety, because Despradel was a man who operated in the shadows—Sebastian couldn't fathom the man trying to cause him or anyone else any harm in this illustrious gathering.

Sebastian, on the other hand, was ready and willing to cause *him* grievous bodily harm, audience be damned.

His hand closed on Paulina's arm again, just above her elbow, but no matter how urgently he wanted to yank her out of the crowd and into safety, Sebastian knew that doing anything to attract the attention of the guests would draw her brother's as well, and he'd rather avoid that, at least until he had gotten Paulina safely out of the way.

Immediately grasping the situation, she raised a hand to his face and pulled him down as if to whisper something flirtatious. Sebastian couldn't hold back a shiver as her breath curled around his ear, even though her words were decidedly unromantic.

"Don't go after him. Please."

He was so tense, every single one of his muscles was screaming in protest. "I won't," he said. "Not until I get you out of here."

Her hand landed on his arm, squeezing with urgency. "We shouldn't leave until we've spoken with the governor. He hasn't arrived yet." Anticipating Sebastian's answer, she added, "It'll be better if we're both here to present our case."

"Fine. We'll wait on the balcony." Sebastian straightened and, telling himself it was mostly for the benefit of the people around them, offered her his arm.

She relaxed, but only fractionally, her hand light on his arm, as if she expected him to yank it away at any moment. Fair enough. He wasn't at ease touching her, either, or walking so close to her that the scent of her perfume overpowered all others.

Just outside the balcony, so close he was sure he'd be able to touch it if he stretched, was one of the new electric streetlamps. The unwavering light inside its glass globe was bright, dimming even the full moon that peeked out from behind the trees across the street. Two other streetlamps farther down the street shone like smaller, lesser moons.

Paulina, in that golden dress that shimmered with beads, was as resplendent as the sun.

Settling in an out-of-the way spot where they wouldn't easily be spotted, Sebastian turned away from her so as not to be dazzled.

With his back to the streetlamps, he would be able to see anyone who wandered onto the balcony before they had a chance to spot him. Paulina was also watchful. He knew it without having to look at her, the same way he knew that she was nervous about seeing her brother—and not only because of what Sebastian might do.

Whatever instinct he had developed where Paulina was concerned, it didn't extend to the other member of her family. Before either of them could break the silence growing between them, Despradel strode out onto the balcony, deep in conversation with another man.

Acting in unison, they shrank into the shadows of a potted palm. Sebastian turned to Paulina, leaning a hand against the wall behind her to obscure her face. He lowered his own in a gesture that might have looked amorous from the outside, with his expression concealed.

Paulina was tense in the circle of his arms. He couldn't stop himself from touching the sliver of bare skin at her shoulder with his free hand, meaning to be comforting but feeling as though sparks should be coming off the beaded band attached to her diaphanous sleeves.

Maybe it was himself he meant to comfort—regardless, all he'd done was make himself feel so unsteady on his feet, he was glad for the sturdiness of the wall under his right hand.

"It will take some time," Despradel was saying. He had lowered his voice somewhat but seemed to be trusting that his casual tone would dissuade potential eavesdroppers. "It's a delicate matter, after all, and one that needs to be handled with certain discretion. But it *will* get done."

Both men came to a stop in front of the wooden railing, less than a meter away from the dark corner where Sebastian and Paulina stood.

Despradel's companion made a low sound that Sebastian didn't know how to interpret. "And you're sure you can keep your hands clean?"

"It's easy enough to arrange all manner of accidents. I've a man who can do it quite inconspicuously. Don't you worry—I'll get rid of both of them by the end of month, and then we'll be free to toast our new venture."

Both of them. Sebastian's blood ran cold.

It wasn't just Sebastian that Antonio meant to have killed. It was Paulina, too.

Exploding into violence, Sebastian pushed off the wall and lunged for Despradel, grabbing him by the shoulder and hauling him around. Caught unaware, Despradel stumbled and didn't struggle as Sebastian wrenched a fistful of his shirt and used it to lift the shorter man to his face.

"You murderous little bastard," he hissed, pressing Despradel to the wooden railing that was now behind him.

Despradel's eyes, wide with surprise, narrowed into calculation. And then, with disconcerting ease, he rearranged his expression, affecting concern that looked so genuine it would have fooled Sebastian himself. "Sebastian Linares?" Despradel said, blinking. "Whatever's the matter?"

In response, Sebastian slammed him against the railing again, enjoying the flash of panic on Despradel's face when the wood shook beneath him. He was dimly aware of Paulina behind him, talking in an urgent voice, and of the fact that Despradel's companion had melted into the crowd that was beginning to gather in the balcony.

Despradel was much more cogent of his surroundings—and of the fact that he had a captive audience. "You may want to release me, Linares. This is the second time you have accosted me in public—completely unprovoked, I might add. If you're not careful, the good people of San Pedro will think you've something against me." Still smiling pleasantly, Despradel added softly, "And they won't be surprised if I find myself having to do something drastic to defend my life against your violent attacks."

His smile broadened when he saw the hesitation flickering in Sebastian's eyes. A rise in volume in the murmurs around them told Sebastian that this was indeed the case—anyone who was here tonight was a witness to the fact that Sebastian Linares had just tried to assault Antonio Despradel.

"You can't win against me, Linares," Antonio said,

just loud enough for Sebastian to hear the gloating in his voice. "It's pitiful that you even think you can try."

The truth of it slammed into Sebastian like a punch to the chest. He had just provided Despradel with an excuse for whatever the hell he was planning to do to him and Paulina.

So he did what he'd been wanting to do for weeks—he slammed his fist into Despradel's sneering face.

The other man's head snapped back violently, spraying blood. Sebastian felt it splattering the front of his starched shirt before two men seized him by the arms and hauled him back, away from Despradel, who was pressing a handkerchief to his streaming nose. Sebastian didn't bother to struggle but contented himself to look at Despradel's bloody face with satisfaction.

It was short-lived, vanishing the moment he saw Paulina's stricken expression. Then his gaze shifted over her shoulder, toward the man making his way through a gap in the crowd. No, not a gap. The people who had gathered to watch the altercation with eyes greedy for gossip were stepping aside to let him through.

He was glowering at them, eyes narrowed above his thick, dark mustache and beard. The medals pinned to the sleek black lapels of his jacket caught the light as he strode toward Sebastian, bristling with authority.

"What is the meaning of this?" he asked furiously. At a single stroke of his arm, the musicians stopped playing.

Sebastian didn't need an introduction to recognize him—it was the governor.

Chapter Seventeen

Antonio had wasted no time in ingratiating himself with the governor. He didn't simper or act injured—all he had to do was nobly absolve Sebastian of guilt while allowing the others guests to clamor on his behalf. Before Paulina could quite catch her breath—or meet Tío Ramon's troubled gaze—she and Sebastian had been summarily ejected from the governor's house.

As they left, escorted by one of the governor's man-servants, Paulina heard Antonio express what sounded like sincere concern over "the blackguard my sister saw fit to marry." The impulse to wheel around and tell the onlookers the truth about him was almost as strong as the sense of betrayal coursing through her.

It would have been useless.

Paulina wasn't quite sure how she managed it, but she held off the tears until Sebastian had helped her into his carriage. Only when they were speeding through the night in the direction of Villa Consuelo did her short, tremulous breaths dissolve into sobs.

She had never been close with her brother, nor particularly friendly. Shocking though it was to overhear him contemplating his own sister's murder—and to see how nonchalant he'd looked about it—it shouldn't have been so painful. And yet, her chest felt so tight with it, she was sure it would burst.

She'd always known he was despotic and petty and occasionally cruel, but capable of murdering her? For money, property and influence? She didn't want to believe it.

Her sobs echoed inside the small coach, and after a moment, she found herself being presented with a crisp white handkerchief. "Are you all right?"

"Would you be?" she snapped.

"No." Under her hand, his arm had been hard as steel—a marked contrast to the gentleness in his tone. "I don't suppose so."

"How could he? His own sister? His only one, for that matter. I know I've never been more than a pawn to him, but you'd think he'd have *some* consideration for my life."

Sebastian let out a slow breath, as though steeling himself to do something. Stooping to keep the top of his head from striking the bouncing carriage roof, he switched seats so that he was next to her rather than across and close enough to put an arm around her. "I haven't words foul enough to express what I feel about that *lacra*, so I won't even try. What I will tell you is that you have my word that I won't let anything happen to you," he said fiercely.

Her head fit perfectly against his shoulder. "What are we going to do?" Her voice, though still ragged with sobs, was starting to reflect the fury kindling in her chest. Her fingers clenched around Sebastian's handkerchief. "Would it be any help at all if I were to leave town— or even the country? Do you think he would continue to pursue you if he couldn't get the mill through me?"

"I wouldn't put anything past him. And I damn well

am not letting you go anywhere on your own. We'll go together."

Paulina twisted to look up at his face, though it was pitch black inside the coach. "But what about Dilia and Doña Josefa and the mill? You would leave them?"

"If it means ensuring their safety... I have to, don't I?" His voice sounded so bleak, it made Paulina put an impulsive hand on his.

Half expecting him to shake it off, Paulina was surprised when Sebastian turned his hand so that their palms touched. His fingers, strong and long and slightly rough with calluses, threaded through hers.

"I'm sorry," she said. "I know how fond you are of them, and how much you'll miss and worry for them."

She could hear his breathing above the rattle of the wheels. From experience, she knew that even if he felt them, he would never say the things she wanted him to say—*I'm fond of you, too. I would miss you if we were parted. I worry for you every day.*

He disengaged his hand from hers, as if he could hear her thoughts. But when he drew in another deep breath, what he said was, "Carlos didn't make me promise to look after his family. He said so to me, just before he died—that he didn't have to because he knew I would. And Josefa—I vowed to myself that I would look after her in her old age. Instead, all she's done is look after me. And now I'm just going to leave her, again."

Over the time they had shared, she had learned to read his expression, which she had once found inscrutable. She had come to understand the tones shading his words, too, enough to know that it was despair, not anger, that was making his voice rough.

"You feel like you're letting them all down," she murmured. "Just like you felt you failed everyone who looked after you when you stayed in Havana so long. And I think," she continued, too struck by her sudden insight into Sebastian's feelings to realize that he probably didn't appreciate her laying him bare, "though you haven't admitted it to yourself, that you feel that way because when Carlos died, he let *you* down."

The quality of his breathing next to her told her she had struck a nerve.

"You had so many plans together. With his help, you were going to put everything to rights. Then he left and left you shouldering all the burdens. And you've been so braced, waiting for everyone else to leave you, too, that—"

"Stop," Sebastian commanded, breathing harshly. Then, almost whispering, he echoed, "Stop."

Paulina gripped his arm. Under his jacket, his muscles were so tense it was like holding on to a tree branch. "They will be all right, even if you have to go away again. You've made every provision to ensure that."

Sebastian was silent for a long while. It wasn't until the carriage turned into the dirt road leading to Villa Consuelo that he spoke again, so low she almost missed it. "Everyone leaves. I was meant to be the one who stayed."

"We'll leave at first light." The front room, with its elegantly draped curtains and gleaming new furniture, came into view as Sebastian finished lighting the brass lamp on the table. Its paltry glow was no match to the abundance of light in the governor's ballroom, but Paulina still glimmered like a streak of gold in a dark mine as she hovered near the louvered door, which he'd pulled firmly closed behind them.

He should have sent her to her own bed, but even with

his hired guards stationed outside, Sebastian didn't want to risk leaving her alone. Grimly, he poured a glass of rum and handed it to her.

"I wouldn't leave if it were just myself in danger. But I'll be damned if I let that brother of yours harm a single hair on your head." He accepted the battered tin mug from her, pouring more rum into it before taking a deep sip and reaching up one-handed to undo the white bow tie at his throat. "We'll leave the country, both of us. I'll go at once to buy us passage on whatever steamer is sailing today—first I have to stop by the mill, though, to leave instructions for my foreman and take some money out of my safe. I need to make sure Dilia has enough for her family, and there's Leo and Josefa…"

"Will we stop in town to say our goodbyes to Dilia?"

Sebastian gave a hard shake of his head. "It's not safe. We have no way of knowing what your brother will do, or when he will strike. It's best for everyone if we leave as soon as possible."

"And after that?" One of the beads on her dress had come loose, and she plucked at it with her eyes lowered, her long eyelashes casting lacy shadows on her cheekbones.

"I suppose it's only sensible to make our way to Havana—I know plenty of people there, so it won't be too difficult to get ourselves situated."

From there, he would be able to hire a lawyer. He didn't know if putting the mill in Dilia's name would stop Antonio's pursuit of it, but the possibility certainly had to be explored. And, he thought reluctantly, he would also be able to hire someone to start annulment or even divorce proceedings. He wasn't familiar with the Cuban laws regarding such things, but surely it wasn't impossible.

Even if that were to happen immediately, though, they would probably have to remain in Havana for at least a year or two, until they could be damn sure that Despradel knew how futile it would be to go through with his plan—and that he wouldn't decide to carry it out anyway, out of sheer spite at having it thwarted.

He was startled to discover that it didn't feel like a terrible prospect. Not because he wouldn't miss his people, or because he was eager to escape his responsibilities, but because of the glow that ignited in his chest at the prospect of spending two years or more with Paulina.

The guardsman's violent intrusion into Villa Consuelo and Leo's resulting injury had shaken him, badly, when he realized just how close Paulina had come to being hurt herself. The strength of his reaction had led him to discover that his feelings for her went so far beyond friendship, or even mere attraction, that the notion that anything could have happened to her had made him put as much distance between them as he could.

He loved her.

And he wanted to keep her safe. And if that meant staying married to her instead of rushing to separate…

It was probably best not to mention any of that to Paulina, who looked troubled enough already. He touched her arm, briefly, and gestured toward the bed. "You might want to get some rest. It's only a few hours until we have to leave. I'll stay on guard, in the chair."

She nodded, but didn't move. "I hate that it's come to this. I can't help but feel that I should have said something—"

"It's my own damn fault, for losing my temper." And for not paying attention to the snakelike cunning in Despradel's eyes.

Swirling some water around the mug, he emptied it

into his shaving basin before filling it up with clean water and giving it to her to drink.

She shook her head, her brown fingers clasped tight around the dented tin. "I didn't mean only tonight. I've had years to do something about his cruelty. If I'd stood up to him…"

"You have stood up to him. I've seen you."

"Tiny, inconsequential acts of rebellion that in the end amounted to nothing."

"I'm sure—"

"Don't," she said. "I don't need to hear whatever placating thing you were about to say. All of this might have been avoided if I'd just stood up to my brother once or twice."

Sebastian leaned forward, seizing her hand from the handful of silk she was clutching. "This is not your fault," he said distinctly. "Whatever your brother does or fails to do is not on you. He and he alone is responsible for his actions and his decisions and his murderous intentions."

Despite the conviction in his tone, he could tell that his reassurance rang as hollow as hers had earlier. He touched a fingertip to the teardrop glistening in the corner of her eye like another bead. "Go lie down. Tomorrow will be a long day, and you'll need your strength."

She must have been tired, because she consented without much argument, following him through the inner door of his bedroom, where a straight-backed chair awaited him like a sentinel.

Turning away from the sight of her in his bed, he heard the soft thud of the glass being placed on the table, then the rustle of silk as she settled into the mattress.

Sebastian jerked off his bow tie, leaving it crumpled on the marble surface of his washstand, and headed for the chair. The sound of her voice followed him to the other side of the room.

"You can't stay in the chair all night." He glanced back, and damn if he shouldn't have been turned into a pillar of salt on the spot. She was propped up on one elbow, the folds of her dress spread out over the bedcovers. "You'll be terribly sore in the morning, and if anyone will need strength tomorrow…"

She had a point, but Sebastian shrugged it off. "I'll lie on the floor. I don't exactly mean to sleep tonight." He'd told Alfonso, the coachman, to watch the house along with the guards, but he'd feel much better if he remained alert himself.

"The bed is more than big enough for both of us." She sat all the way up and drew up her legs, wrapping her arms around the silk covering them. From across the room, she looked very small and very dark against the vastness of his bed. "I know you won't kiss me, and I won't ask you again. But will you…will you hold me?"

It would have taken a far better man than he to deny such an entreaty. It was her eyes, though, that broke his resolution. The exact color of the rum blazing a trail down his chest, they were filled with so much heartache that nothing could have stopped him from trying to ease it.

She watched him remove his polished shoes and dark socks. He had cast off his jacket inside the coach, and now he made quick work of his white waistcoat and the stiff white collar at his throat. He remained in his shirtsleeves and trousers, but the small act of partly undressing in front of her unwavering gaze felt breathtakingly intimate.

The mattress dipped beneath his knee, and the slight movement made the beads on her dress tremble and shimmer as if in welcome. When he gathered her to him, it was with the impression that he had taken a handful of candlelight into his hands—warm and necessary and potentially scorching.

Ignoring the danger, he tucked her against his side. He would burn, if he must.

"Sleep," he said against the curve of her neck. "You'll be safe here. I'll keep you safe."

"I know." She turned in the circle of his arms and regarded him seriously. "I should have recognized you as the little boy I used to know."

"Oh?"

"By your eyes if nothing else." Her fingers explored the ridge beneath his right eyebrow, which was now bisected with a thin line where the skin had split open during his fight with the guardsman. It was no longer painful, but his breath hitched regardless. "You've always made me feel safe. Even that young."

The back of her hand followed the contours of his face, not stopping when it reached his neck and the crest of his shoulder. The knife wound on his arm had broken open again earlier that day as he'd helped unload a cart at the mill, and he'd bound it quickly so that it wouldn't ruin his good shirt. She ran a hand over the thick bulk of the bandage and continued down his arm.

The marks the manacles had left around his wrist had mostly faded, but she touched those as well, looking grave. "You made me feel braver, too," she said.

Asking for his permission with a flicker of her eyes, she waited until he nodded before reaching for the buttons on his shirt. One by one, she eased them from their tight buttonholes. His shirt gaped, then parted, aided by her questing hand, and she swept it aside to reveal the discoloration over his ribs.

Her solemn accounting over, it was his turn to touch her.

He hardly knew where to begin.

The air was thick with humidity, and her face was surrounded by a crown of ringlets. Paulina looked on with solemn eyes ringed by long lashes as Sebastian wound a single curl around his forefinger. Under the weight of her gaze, he felt himself become unmade.

She was the one who guided his face down to hers. He felt her breath first, sweeping over his lower lip in much the same way he had once swept his thumb over hers. They breathed in unison for the space of a heartbeat, then another—and then they closed the remaining distance between them and Sebastian was hard-pressed to keep from gasping out loud at the heat of her mouth. Her mouth opened beneath his, as pliant and warm as her body.

He'd been right. Sparks came off her when he touched her, sending an electric current rippling up and down his spine.

The bodice of her dress cradled the lush curves of her bosom, skimming over the tantalizing crevice between them. He traced the edge of the beaded band around the neckline, right where it met her amber-colored skin. When he lowered his lips to the spot his fingers had just vacated, he was rewarded by a soft, shuddering moan.

No—it wasn't sparks. It was lightning.

Rucking up her dress, Paulina caught his hand and pressed it to the heat between her legs. Their gazes locked, and the frayed remains of his resistance snapped.

And he gave in. To his desire, to Paulina's pleasure and to their future, whatever it held.

Paulina arched against Sebastian and was rewarded by something that sounded gratifyingly like a growl as he dragged his lips just below her jaw. Then his merciless mouth found the hollow of her throat.

She had seen enough glimpses of Sebastian's raw desire to know how much it must have cost him every time he chose restraint over indulging in passion. Selfishly, she wanted to see him lose every shred of self-discipline—and she wanted to be the one to drive him over the edge.

She reached for the waistband of his trousers and undid the first few buttons, using her thumb to explore the deep ridge pressing against them.

He hissed in a breath, and before either of them had time to take another, he had seized her wrist and was pinning it just above her head.

Hooking a finger into her bodice and dragging it down until he had exposed her nipple to the cool air, he nipped at the tight bud. She gasped at the sharp sensation, hardly able to draw breath enough to say, "Touch me, Sebastian. I want your hands all over my body."

He *had* promised to give her everything she wanted.

Each caress of his fingers on the sensitive skin of her thighs felt like raking coals. Like she should be bursting into flames—or fireworks.

His thumb traced gentle circles on the inside of her thighs, moving higher and higher until—

She bucked against his hand, biting her lip to hold in a gasp. The throbbing pleasure of his touch was more than she'd dared to dream of. It was almost more than she could bear.

She wrapped her legs around him, trapping his hand against her, and all of a sudden, he was the one gasping.

"I've wanted you from the moment I first met you," she told him, dragging his trousers down. "I want you, and I mean to have you. All of you."

"You already have me, Paulina." He sought her mouth again, exhaling kiss after kiss into it. Kisses that tasted of rum and sugar and the sweetest satisfaction. "You always have."

In the haze of her spiraling pleasure, she was barely aware that she was chanting, over and over again, "You're mine. You're mine. You're mine."

And all the while, her heart was thudding to the same rhythm, *I'm yours. I'm yours. I'm yours.*

Chapter Eighteen

Darkness still pressed against the louvered doors when Paulina heard a voice close to her ear. "It's time to go."

She hadn't slept much, but she had slept deeply. Even so, she didn't feel the least bit disoriented when her eyelashes fluttered open and she saw Sebastian sitting on the edge of the bed. The pillow under her cheek smelled faintly of him, just as she'd imagined it would. The scent was as comforting as the pleasant soreness between her legs—she hadn't imagined last night, nor had she dreamed it.

Sitting up, she reached for him, stroking the back of his neck as she brushed her lips against his.

The bristles on his jaw scraped against her skin, reigniting the glow of desire that pooled low in her belly as surely as if he had lit a lamp. Paulina would have liked to nuzzle against the delicious roughness, but he pulled away almost immediately.

"I fetched your clothes from your bedroom," he said, handing her the faded yellow dress. With a slight pang, Paulina thought of all the clothes they had ordered from Blanca—hopefully Dilia would be able to stop the dressmaker in time. "There's soap and tooth powder by the basin. We'll leave as soon as you're dressed."

Was it her imagination, or was he avoiding her gaze?

He certainly wasn't watching her as she slipped into her clothes, though his eyes had hungrily consumed every inch of exposed skin as she stepped out of her dress the night before.

Quickly, Paulina twisted her hair into a slightly hap- hazard knot at the back of her head, securing it with the pins he had placed on his bedside table after easing them from her hair. She didn't ask if anything was wrong—if he was having second thoughts about what they'd done, she didn't want to hear it. It had meant too much for her to hear it be called a mistake.

"I'm ready," she said past the lump in her throat. She hadn't any luggage—she would leave Villa Consuelo the way she had arrived, with empty hands and an ach- ing heart. The only pang she felt was at the thought of her mother's portrait, secured within the plain locket that she had hid among her meager possessions in her family's *quinta*. It was the only thing she was sorry to leave behind.

They stepped out into the hush of very early morn- ing. The frogs and crickets and other small creatures that came alive in the night were all quiet, and it was too early for birdsong. It was too early for sunlight, too. The car- riage was a hulking shape in the gloom, the two horses at its head softly whickering shadows.

Paulina climbed inside without waiting for Sebastian's help; he remained outside for a moment to give instruc- tions to the coachman, then followed her in and sat across from her, shifting so that his legs didn't touch hers.

The distance between their two seats could have been

kilometers. It welled up inside her chest until it felt tight enough to burst.

"Did you mean what you said last night?" she asked.

"You should know by now that I don't say things I don't mean."

"Then you've changed your mind. I don't regret it, you know," she told him, feeling infinitely tired. "Even if you do."

Those hours in bed with Sebastian had been more than stolen momentary happiness. Paulina knew it all the way down to her bones—the same way she knew that their coming together, as impossible as it had felt, had been inevitable.

"You're so willing to put your body on the line for the people you love," she said softly. "But not your heart. Is that how you truly want to live your life?"

He didn't answer. Out of the corner of her eye, she saw as Sebastian knocked a fist against the roof of the carriage, calling for the coachman to go faster.

The rattle of the wheels turned into a roar. Paulina's breath caught in her throat—not from the increased speed, but because there was something subtly wrong in the movement of the carriage, a certain reckless wobble. She met Sebastian's gaze, as wide as her own.

He had no time to shout a warning to the coachman.

There was a sickening sound of grinding metal, and the carriage swung suddenly to one side, as if it had been sideswiped by an unseen force. Paulina crashed into Sebastian with bone-jarring force.

One of the wheels must have caught on something, because the carriage came to a jarring stop and hung suspended for the longest second Paulina had ever experienced.

Then, slowly yet inexorably, it began to overturn.

* * *

Clouds were gathering.

It had smelled like rain all night. Lying next to Paulina, Sebastian had spent the hours between her drifting off to sleep and her eyes fluttering open feeling the humidity mount alongside something that felt like guilt.

It had taken him a long time to disentangle the snarl of thoughts and feelings that had taken residence in his chest. He had ruined their chances at an annulment, of course, but there was always divorce if she still wanted to head down that path.

Sometime in the very early hours of the morning, when the world outside his bedroom was still dark and quiet, it had come to him. Sebastian had always prided himself on being a protector of the innocent. He didn't take advantage of anyone in a precarious position—and he certainly didn't bed them.

If they hadn't done what they had the night before, she could have gotten her annulment and sailed straight into another marriage without having to provide any explanations or tell anyone about her misadventure at the hands of her brother.

She could have pretended that none of this had ever happened.

Would she have, given the opportunity? Sebastian didn't see why not. It didn't matter if there truly was love between them—ultimately, everyone left, whether on purpose or not. His parents had, and Carlos, and even her own parents. Why not Paulina as well?

He had opened his eyes to see the glint of the decanter Paulina had purchased for him, the new washstand topped with marble, with its shelf for his shaving implements that had replaced the mirror hanging from a single nail. She had put her imprint all over the house,

and all over Sebastian's soul. If she did choose to leave…
would he survive it?

The distant rumble of thunder made Sebastian wrench
his eyes open. He was next to Paulina, but not in bed—
they were jumbled up inside the carriage, like a brace of
plantain that had been tossed into a sack and shaken. His
temples were throbbing, and the stinging sensation on
his upper arm told him the knife wound had reopened.
Paulina groaned, and all of a sudden Sebastian jolted
into awareness.

She lay on her back with one arm pinned beneath her.
Crouching to avoid bumping his head on the padded seat
above their heads, Sebastian helped her sit up.

"Are you hurt?" he demanded.

"My arm." Her face was creased with pain. "I
wrenched it, I think—it hurts terribly."

Sebastian probed at it, his lips tightening at her wince.
"I'll have to fashion a sling out of my jacket," he said,
slipping out of the black garment and tying the sleeves
around her neck. "We shouldn't linger here."

With his help, she managed to crawl out of the overturned coach. Her attention went immediately to the
coachman.

"Alfonso!" she cried, lurching forward.

The young man had managed to jump out of his seat
and was sitting in the brush several meters back, looking
dazed. Blood streamed freely from a cut on his forehead.
He blinked it away, looking up at Paulina and Sebastian.
"The axle broke," he said, though neither of them had
asked. With a shaking finger, Alfonso pointed at the
wheel that hung at an improbable angle above the carriage, like a wounded limb. "It just…snapped."

"Cut, more likely," Sebastian muttered. His horses

looked fine, already scrambling to their feet. "We'll have to walk the rest of the way. Alfonso, can you stand?"

"I think my leg's broken, Don," Alfonso said with a grimace toward the stretched-out leg in front of him. "I don't think I can move."

Sebastian cast a glance up at the sky, which was growing pink with the incipient dawn above the storm clouds gathered on the horizon. "Stay with the horses, then. I'll send someone for you when we get to the mill. We haven't much time to waste."

Paulina made a small sound of protest.

"He'll be fine," Sebastian told her. "He's not the one your brother wants."

He started marching in the direction of the mill. A moment later, he heard Paulina scramble to catch up with him. "What in the world is *wrong* with you today?" she asked breathlessly.

"Nothing that wasn't wrong with me yesterday," he said without turning around.

"I'll have to agree—you've been out of sorts for days. I've had enough of your dark moods."

"Well, forgive me if I'm getting a little tired of fighting for my life. I wasn't bargaining on any of this—it's not like I had any choice in the matter."

"And I did?"

"No!" he exclaimed, whirling around to face her. "You hadn't a choice! That's precisely the problem! Neither of us had one, but if I'd held out long enough to get the annulment, we both would have. And then you'd have been free to seek out any sort of life you want."

"Oh?" she asked acidly. "And what sort of life am I supposed to want? I suppose you have it all figured out."

He spread his hands, sighing. "I don't know anything."

"She's good for you," Dilia had told him the day before in town, when he'd gone to fetch the invitation and Paulina's gown. "I know you're not in the mood to listen to what I've got to say, but I *have* to say it—I promised Carlos I would do my best to keep you from being too bullheaded, though we both know that's a losing proposition." Her lips had curled up with humor—not that Sebastian was inclined to admit there was any in the situation.

"Say it, then," he'd told her, taking pains to make his disinterest obvious.

"Paulina Despradel is good for you," Dilia had said with her usual bluntness. "The way you act around her… I haven't seen you this happy in years. I can't understand why, but you seem to be bent on ruining your chances with her. Whatever penance you think you need to pay, it's not worth it if it means you have to go through life alone."

"Are you finished?" he'd demanded, putting a foot on his carriage's mounting step to communicate his intent to be done with the conversation.

"No," she'd told him. "But I can see you're going to insist on being a fool." She gave a dramatic shake of her head. "Heaven spare me from stubborn men!"

The mill came into sight, the main building dark against the gray clouds that were beginning to cover the sunrise. By all rights, the mill should have been humming with activity—most planters kept their mills running day and night during cane season. Sebastian, however, had flatly refused to countenance such a thing, preferring to give his workers a decent night's rest even if it meant diminished profits. Beyond the mill, the wooden warehouse where the sacks of sugar destined for the refinery would be stacked also lay dark and empty.

It was as comforting as coming home, but Sebastian didn't dare draw a sigh of relief—not yet.

"Why are you trying to push me away?" Paulina asked as Sebastian dug into the pockets of his trousers for the key. "Why are you so afraid to let me in?"

Instead of answering, he unlocked the door and headed upstairs to his office. Over the sound of their footsteps on the rickety wooden steps, he could hear her snort of exasperation.

"You don't trust me, do you? You don't trust me to know my own mind."

"I have some rum around here," he said. He rummaged in one of his drawers until he had produced a bottle and a cup. "Have a drink while I get the money."

His safe was in a cupboard, shielded from prying eyes by towering piles of ledgers. Sebastian was in the process of clearing them away when she stepped into his path. "Is that it, then? Is that all you're going to say? Some nonsense about choices—after all we've been through? It's not enough to let me make my own decisions, Sebastian. You've got to respect them, too."

He tried to turn his face away, but she grasped it with her free hand.

"Even if I had a choice, I wouldn't want a different husband," she said fiercely. "Nothing has changed for me, Sebastian. I want you."

His breath rasped out into the warm room.

"I want a life with you," she said, digging her nails into his jaw to impress upon him the urgency of her words. "Even if it means…" Her voice wavered for a second, but she rallied. "Even if it means not having children."

"I would never ask that of you."

He kissed her. Not gently, like he had the night before, when he'd caressed her lips with his. This kiss was hard, and hot, and full of need. It made no promises and offered no peace.

Paulina pressed against him, pushing him against the edge of his desk. He sat, heedless of the papers and ledgers on its messy surface, and pulled her between his open legs to kiss her, again and again until they were both breathless.

Her fingers trailed down his neck to clench in the fabric of his shirt. "I want everything you can give me, Sebastian Linares—and so much more."

He could have gotten lost in the fire in her eyes. "Paulina, I…"

She pulled him down to her again, offering him as much as she took. Her lips were scorching on his, her little pants and gasps kindling. She scraped her teeth along his lower lip, then soothed the sting with the tip of her tongue, and if Sebastian had been undone the night before, now he was remade.

The door slammed open behind them.

"Well done, little sister," said a voice that sent chills of foreboding down Sebastian's spine. He pried himself away from Paulina to see Despradel lounging in the doorway, his cruel mouth twisted into a smirk. "I didn't think you had it in you to carry out orders, but you've played your part to perfection. Tell me, Linares, did you enjoy the line about her feeling safe with you? I thought it was a bit much, myself, but if it worked for you…"

"You unspeakably filthy liar," Sebastian said hoarsely. With a raw, animal roar, he launched himself over the desk, intent on wringing Despradel's sorry neck.

He didn't get within a meter of the doorway.

Calmly stepping aside, Paulina's brother raised the hand that had been concealed at the side of his leg. In it was a pistol, and its muzzle was pointed directly at Paulina.

Chapter Nineteen

It wasn't hesitation that made Sebastian draw to a sudden halt, but the certainty that Antonio Despradel wouldn't think twice about shooting his sister in cold blood.

"I didn't think you were the kind of man to do your own dirty work," Sebastian remarked in what he hoped was a sufficiently casual tone, leaning back against the wall with his arms loosely at his side to show Despradel that he meant to stay put.

It was a lie, of course, and seeing as there was nothing Sebastian wanted more than to slam his fists into the scoundrel, it was so damned difficult he could feel his muscles bunching with the effort of remaining motionless.

Despradel gave a nonchalant shrug. "Every great man has had to get his hands dirty now and then."

After their encounter with the guardsman, Sebastian was confident that Paulina would keep her cool, even as Antonio cautiously edged into the room and went around the desk to shove the pistol toward her head.

"Do you really mean to shoot us?" Paulina asked in a voice that was remarkably steady. "I thought you were going to try to make it look like an accident."

"Thanks to your beloved husband, I no longer have to—it didn't take much to convince the governor's guests that I was worried for my sister's life after her marriage to such a violent man." Despradel's eyes flashed with glee. "And it took even less to hint that they should be concerned for their own daughters, were he to require a new wife once he did away with my sister. I was so worried, in fact, that I went to see her as soon as it was light. Imagine my surprise when I walked in to find her husband standing over her with a loaded pistol."

It was chilling, the way Despradel spun his little narrative with the smug confidence of someone who thought he could alter reality. "Everyone in town will think me a hero."

"Everyone in town will know you for what you are," Paulina bit out. "A murderer."

Despradel laughed. "Dramatics don't suit you a bit," he told his sister. "You have done nothing to restore our family to its former glory. This is the very least you could do."

"Give you my life? That's unreasonable, even for you." There was genuine grief in her eyes, but there was nothing Sebastian could do for her but watch it grow. "Did it ever occur to you to work for it, like our ancestors did? They didn't sit around waiting to inherit the land, or kill anyone for it—they worked for it, and for everything they had. That, Antonio, is what made them worth admiring. Not the gold and silver they stuffed into their bank vaults."

"Still naive, I see. I had thought marriage would cure you of it, but I can see I was mistaken. I have no need to explain myself to you, but I will tell you this—no one who had any money worth remarking of ever got it by *working*." The disdainful emphasis on the last word was accompanied by a curl of his lip. "Anyone who's ever made a fortune has done it by seizing opportunities, and that's exactly what I'm doing. You can go ahead and call me a murderer if it will make you feel better, but everyone will know me for what I really am—a man of brilliance. A man of power. And, thanks to your husband over there, a man of extensive means. I'll buy their good opinion of me if I have to."

Sebastian let him talk. He felt himself go quiet as he tracked the other man's movements with the careful watchfulness of a hunter. His silence clearly unnerved Despradel, who had no way of knowing that Sebastian had never had a taste for pursuing innocent animals— and that Sebastian's limbs were burning with panic.

"Not that this conversation isn't terribly stimulating, but do hurry up and open the safe," Despradel commanded, carelessly knocking the barrel of his pistol against Paulina's head. "As long as I have you here, I might as well help myself."

She was very still, but only Sebastian recognized it for what it was—not the stillness of prey, but that of someone waiting for the perfect time to strike.

Paulina Despradel was no one's prey.

Sebastian let her see the admiration filling his own expression. Noticing that Sebastian was looking at his sister rather than the safe, Despradel glanced down at her. It was the barest distraction, but it was enough— Sebastian shouted at her, and she reared back, pushing Despradel away.

At the same instant, Sebastian vaulted over the desk and crashed into the other man's torso. The pistol went off, and Sebastian had only the sound of shattering glass and the absence of Paulina's scream to know that the shot had gone wide before he was grappling with the other man.

He managed to knock the pistol out of Despradel's hand before grabbing him by the collar and, much like he had done the night before, rushing him through the door and slamming him into the spindly wooden railing.

Wrenching himself out of Sebastian's arms, Despradel managed to shove Sebastian halfway down the stairs. Sebastian started to pick himself up, but a well-placed kick to his shoulder sent him rolling down to the main floor of the mill.

"Don't let him get the pistol!" he shouted up at Paulina, who had taken a heavy ledger from his desk. Despradel whirled around, but before he could touch Paulina, she struck out at him with the ledger. He took a step back to avoid it, clearly forgetting he was on the top step, and lost his footing.

Sebastian was waiting for him at the bottom of the stairs, battered and bruised but still standing.

With more agility than Sebastian would have given him credit for, Despradel flung himself over the side of the railing, landing in a crouch.

"Don't you understand by now?" he told Sebastian with a taunting smile as he walked backward into the shadows of the mill. "You will never get the best of me— either of you. You aren't clever enough, or strong enough. Your lives are mine to do as I see fit. Your so-called friends are mine to bribe and manipulate. I'd wager my family's entire fortune that you had no idea your coachman was in my employ—and all it took was a promise of twenty pesos for that scraggly goat of his grandmother's."

Alfonso? Sebastian's eyes narrowed. Damn the little bastard.

"Everywhere you go," Despradel continued, melting

farther into the shadows so that Sebastian was forced to rely only on the sound of his voice as he stalked after him, "everyone you think you trust…"

There was a sudden roar, like that of a great, metallic beast. The sudden scent of smoke and oil filled Sebastian's nostrils and he glanced back to see the milling machine coming to life.

Pistons churning and wheels turning, it was a sight to behold even while not in the middle of a fight with a murderous madman. To Sebastian, at the moment, they spelled out relief.

His foreman had arrived.

Heartened by the thought, though aware they wouldn't hear him call out over the machinery's noise, Sebastian started to turn.

Despradel took advantage of Sebastian's momentary distraction to charge him—the momentum of his running charge sent Sebastian falling backward, right toward the grinders used to crush sugarcane stalks into pulp. Sebastian thrust himself forward, but Despradel drove him back with a punch calculated to land on the cut above his eye. It hurt more than it should have, and it wasn't until Despradel wound his hand back that Sebastian caught the faint gleam of metal on his knuckles.

Clouds of steam were billowing from the machinery, clouding Sebastian's sight.

A second punch landed on his eye, and blood joined the sweat streaming from his face. Dazed, Sebastian struck out at the space in front of him, but Despradel dodged him nimbly, laughing.

The disembodied sound guided Sebastian's own fist.

He landed a glancing blow on Despradel, who answered it with an almost casual backhanded slap against the side of Sebastian's face. The brass knuckles cracked against his throbbing head, sending Sebastian reeling.

Suddenly, Despradel loomed out of the steam, his face contorted with concentration. He pushed Sebastian back, far enough that the backs of his thighs pressed against the iron railing around the rolling grinder. Sebastian struggled, but Antonio had the front of his shirt in a viselike grip and was reaching for Sebastian's arm with the other hand.

Most parts of the running machinery were dangerous in their own right—any number of accidents could befall the reckless and the unwary, which was why Sebastian had had the railings installed in the first place. The pistons could break a man's legs, the metal canisters where the sugarcane juice was boiled could get so hot they could sear a person's skin right down to the bone…

The grinder, with two metal rollers relentlessly crushing cane into pulp—it was singularly the most dangerous part of the entire mill.

And Despradel seemed determined to feed Sebastian's arm right into it.

Sebastian strained to break free, or at least pull his hand away, to no avail. Despradel was just too strong.

"Give up!" Despradel was shouting into Sebastian's face, spittle flying. "You will never win against me!"

It was the least tempting offer Sebastian had ever received, but he could feel his strength waning with each passing second. How much longer would he have to hold on? Any minute now, the rest of the men would arrive to start feeding cane into the grinder. They would surely come to his aid.

Any minute now…

His fingertips were so close to the grinder, he could

feel the whoosh of wind as the rollers reached their normal speed.

Out of the corner of his eye, he saw Paulina picking up one of the stalks of cane with her good hand. The length of a sword, and the general circumference of three broom handles tied together, it must have been heavy to wield. But wield it she did, hefting it in her arms.

Sebastian looked straight into Despradel's eyes. "Go straight to hell," he said and ducked.

The cane in Paulina's hand connected with the back of Antonio's head.

Despradel turned to her, screaming with rage. The blow he delivered to her sent her flying back—Antonio went after her, the hand with the brass knuckles raised to strike her again.

Summoning up the last of his strength, Sebastian dived for Antonio. He ripped him away from Paulina, noticing the long, angry scratch she had left on the side of her brother's face. Grabbing Despradel by his midsection, almost lifting him bodily off the floor, he hauled him away from Paulina and collapsed to his knees.

There was a scream behind him—a high, desperate, keening sound that sliced even through the powerful roar of the machinery. It was cut off abruptly. By the time Sebastian found the strength to turn around, Despradel was utterly silent.

A sudden flood of people rushed past Sebastian—the rest of the mill workers had arrived at last.

Paulina helped him up, and he turned, then wished he hadn't when he saw the mangled body they were laying on the floor.

"Call for the doctor," he croaked, but the grim look on the men's faces told him it would be no use.

Antonio was dead.

* * *

The skies had broken open and rain was gusting into the dirt clearing in front of the mill when Paulina stumbled out, followed by Sebastian. The mud had been churned by dozens of feet as the cane cutters and mill workers gathered for the start of their day, and Paulina felt equally churned up.

Someone helped her to a stool, and Paulina didn't so much as sit as crumple down onto its scarred wooden surface. The overhang of the roof prevented her from getting soaked, but the breeze blew welcome droplets into her overheated face.

Antonio was dead. Her brother, who had tried to murder her and Sebastian, who had pointed a pistol at her head with as little care as he would have pointed it at a sack full of beans…

He was dead. And this whole sorry business was finally over.

It wasn't relief that filled her, but an odd sense of numbness, as if the thunderclouds had taken residence inside her mind.

A handful of horses came galloping through the heavy rain, coming to a stop in front of Paulina's stool. Someone must have alerted Sebastian to their approach, because he was suddenly there at the entrance to the mill, a group of men in a semicircle around him.

Paulina got to her feet and slipped her hand into Sebastian's as two of the new arrivals came up to them. Their faces were mostly obscured by their hats and the relative darkness of the morning. It wasn't until she realized that one of the men was in uniform that she recognized them as the magistrate and one of the guardsmen from the prison.

Paulina could feel Sebastian drawing up stiffly, and

she realized that the rest of the men were also in uniform. She squeezed Sebastian's hand—and he responded by pulling his out of her grasp. It reminded Paulina that he hadn't said anything earlier when she'd told him she wanted a life with him.

Had it been due to Antonio's interruption, or had he never meant to say anything at all?

Was he reconsidering everything he had ever said now that he no longer had to contend with Antonio?

There was no time to worry about it just then.

"Are you Sebastian Linares?" the magistrate asked, pushing back his dripping hat with an air of distaste, looking annoyed to have been called out into the rain.

Sebastian nodded.

"We were summoned by your coachman," the magistrate said. "Something about his fearing for your wife's life. What seems to be the trouble?"

"Alfonso?" Paulina interrupted. The magistrate flicked a glance at her, noticing the arm that was still bound in Sebastian's jacket. "He was injured in a carriage accident—as were we. He was waiting by the side of the road until we could send for help."

"We came across the carriage on our way here, Doña," one of the guardsmen said. "There was no one there."

"Because he was in town, reporting the altercation." The magistrate shot the guardsman a quelling look before turning back to Sebastian. "Well?"

"As you can see," Sebastian said, with surprising equanimity given what he had just endured, "my wife is unharmed, save for the injury she sustained in the accident. As am I."

That was not altogether true—blood was coming down in ribbons from a cut on his temple, staining the shoulder of his shirt. Under the blood, his brown skin was ashen.

"My wife's brother, however, is not," Sebastian continued.

Paulina, who had been watching the guardsman's face, noticed the way his eyes bulged.

"Where is he?" the magistrate demanded grimly.

The crowd behind Paulina and Sebastian parted, and Paulina caught a spare glimpse of the sacks the cane workers had used to cover Antonio's figure. The magistrate ordered the guardsman to uncover Antonio, and Paulina turned her face away as the uniformed man twitched away the sacks.

The machinery must have been turned off. Over the clatter of rain, she heard the magistrate demand, "What the devil happened?"

A different voice, one Paulina hadn't heard before. "He fell into the grinders."

She glanced up at Sebastian, who looked briefly surprised.

"Linares?" The magistrate again. "Is that true?"

Sebastian was silent. He may have been too honorable to lie, but Paulina had no compunction in doing it for him.

"It's true," Paulina said, stepping forward and looking at the magistrate straight in the eye. "My brother fell."

Clearly unwilling to take the word of a woman, the magistrate turned furiously to the men gathered in clusters on the mill floor, his frown deepening when they all gazed impassively back. They all meant to stand by Sebastian, just as he had stood by them when it would have been easier, and far more profitable, to do what all other mill owners did. What Paulina's own brother had done.

The guardsman, she noticed, was giving Sebastian

a thoughtful look. Without Antonio to appease, or to defend himself against, he must have felt there was no need to pursue Sebastian any longer, because he came to a swift conclusion. "Señor Magistrado," he said, "I believe these people are speaking the truth. A most unfortunate matter, no doubt, but it does appear to have been no more than an accident. Is that not so, Don Sebastian?"

Sebastian jerked his head into a nod.

The magistrate threw up his hands, though Paulina noticed that he, too, looked relieved at being done with the whole business. "Death by misadventure it is, then," he pronounced. "I trust the deceased's family will see to the remains?"

He barely waited for Paulina's nod before stalking outside.

It was too bad that the stool wasn't nearby, because Paulina felt like crumpling again, only this time it was with relief. She reached for Sebastian, but he had turned away as someone called out for him.

Injured as he was, and likely shaken after such a close brush with dismemberment, he was still holding himself together in front of his staff as he answered their questions and issued commands. Tall and straight-backed, Sebastian moved through his people, patting a shoulder here and making a remark there, providing reassurance as well as instructions for how to proceed. It was clear, to Paulina and to the other people assembled inside the mill, that Sebastian was born to lead.

As for his marital responsibilities… It felt like centuries had passed, though it was surely no more than a handful of hours, since he had stood in the dirt of the road and talked about choices. Had he meant more by it than she'd understood in the moment? He had made no secret of the fact that he regretted being intimate the night before, after all.

Everyone's generosity had limits, and maybe she had come to the end of Sebastian's. With no threats to bind them together anymore, and no Antonio to put his family in danger, Paulina had to wonder if Sebastian wouldn't prefer to be done with her entirely.

She had told him she wanted to have a life with him. And he had said nothing in response.

Chapter Twenty

Villa Consuelo was dark by the time they got home, much later that day. It was silent, too, and still—for the first time since Sebastian had moved in, there was no one there to greet them when they arrived.

It made him feel a little hollow, but on its heels followed the realization that he needn't leave after all. He needn't leave the island, nor his home nor his people. He was free to do anything he wished—including getting the damn annulment.

A look at Paulina told him that she was, as usual, one step ahead of him. By unspoken but mutual agreement, they remained quiet as they gave their thanks to the cane cutter who had borne them home in his cart, through a half-denuded field dripping with the last of the day's rain.

Her hand in his, they strode through his property on their way to his bedroom, and Sebastian felt a tightening in his chest as he saw the marks of what they had been through. The blackened walls of the kitchen. The table with its matching chairs at one end of the terrace. The louvered doors to her bedroom with the new hinges that made them open without so much as a whisper. He wasn't the only one to bear scars—or to have been remade.

There was no question of Paulina sharing his bed.

First, however, they cast off their filthy clothes. Sebastian dipped a clean handkerchief in the few inches of water left in his bedroom jug.

"Come here," he said softly. Grasping Paulina's chin, he cleaned grime and tears and rainwater off her face. She tilted her head up, eyes closed, as he swept the rag over her collarbone and shoulders, outlining first one arm and then the other, and turning her to follow the long, elegant line of her spine.

Paulina leaned back against him, letting out a sigh when he encircled her with his arms. "I'm so tired," she said.

"Let's go to bed," he said against her neck. They still had plenty to talk about, and even more to decide, but that could wait for morning.

The sheets billowed above them like the sail of a ship they no longer needed to take. Before the thin cotton had settled over their bodies, they were both asleep.

Sebastian didn't fall so much as crash into unconsciousness. For the first time in weeks—months, really—he slept so hard, he was utterly unaware of the world beyond his bed. When he finally awoke, it was to the stifling heat of midday. He had given the workers the rest of the previous day off, but they must have already been at work for hours, and he would have to join them soon.

But first…

He kicked the light blanket aside, shifting to his side to slide an arm around Paulina—but there was no one on the crumpled sheets. Sitting up, he saw an envelope on her pillow.

His pulse was roaring in his ears, drowning out the birdsong and the sound of the breeze whistling through the trees. Ripping out the contents of the envelope, he skimmed the long letter that had been folded inside. Paulina wrote in a fair, neat hand, her letters looping into elegant twists that did not betray whatever it was she'd been thinking as she wrote. The letter itself wasn't addressed to Sebastian, but to Governor de los Santos. In it, she explained everything that had happened from the day of her birthday—avoiding, of course, the details of her brother's death—and ended with a plea to grant Sebastian the annulment he had sought.

His jaw was clenched so tightly, it was as painful as if someone had smashed it with a fist. But what was one more ache to Sebastian?

He lowered the letter and noticed a scrap of paper that must have fallen out of the envelope.

There is always a choice, it said in Paulina's hand.

He threw himself out of bed and into his trousers, heart pounding.

She couldn't have—she *wouldn't* have.

Slamming open the louvered doors, he burst out into the terrace, where he was arrested by the slight creaking of the rocking chair.

"Oh," he said, when he recognized its occupant, his heart in his mouth. "Dilia."

"Do try to contain your enthusiasm," she said wryly, then gestured at the large wicker basket sitting on the table. "I heard what happened yesterday and thought I had better bring food."

He glanced at the basket and gave it a dismissive wave. "Have you seen Paulina?"

She looked startled. "I thought she'd be with you."

"She was."

The patter of raindrops, which had slowed down considerably since the day before, started up again. Sebastian went to the railing, to the unfinished section he had been working on for months, and braced himself against the stripped wood.

"Should I take the disconsolate droop of your shoulders to mean you think she won't be coming back?" Dilia asked behind him.

"I don't know." The rain had gone on so long that it had saturated the ground of the kitchen yard, forming puddles that quivered as they were struck by raindrops.

"Will you go after her, then?"

"I don't know," he said again.

"I don't know whether to scold you or comfort you." Dilia let out a sigh. "After everything the two of you have been through, will you really let your pride get in the way of everything you could have together?"

"It's not pride." With a flex of his forearms, Sebastian pushed himself upright and turned to face Dilia. "I'm not sure how much you know about Paulina's life. Her parents died when she was young, and she was raised—if you could call it that—by her brother. He never allowed her to have a say in her own life. She wasn't allowed to make any decisions."

Dilia nodded as she grasped his meaning. "And with her brother gone, now she can."

"She wrote a letter detailing her brother's plot against us. She means for me to take it to the governor and annul the marriage. The first thing she did after gaining her freedom, Dilia, was seek to be separated from me."

Dilia cocked her head. "Does she know that you love her?"

"It wouldn't make any difference."

"Wouldn't it?" Dilia shook her head. "How can you not see it, Sebastian? Paulina is so obviously in love with you, I would be surprised if she meant anything by that letter other than to give you a way out. The only reason she left is because you can't seem to let her in."

"Let her in?" he asked indignantly. "I brought her into my home!"

"Let her into your heart, you absolute dolt," Dilia said, with an exasperated roll of her eyes. "You've kept her at arm's length far past the time when you realized she wasn't guilty of trying to trap you. And you have made every excuse you can think of to continue doing so even though anyone can see that you would die for her—and almost did."

Sebastian stared at Dilia, wanting to deny her assertions even as the truth of them tumbled over him. "I... But..."

"Quite," Dilia said dryly. "It's natural to be scared. She's your first love, isn't she?"

"My only love," Sebastian replied.

Dilia nodded. "Well, what are you going to do about it?"

The first thing Paulina did upon arriving at her family's *quinta* was go directly into her bedroom, where she found the locket with her mother's portrait. She flicked the catch with her fingernail, easing the enamel face open to reveal her mother's image in miniature.

She was laughing in the photograph, as she was in Paulina's memories. Life had been easy for her in a way it hadn't been for Paulina. And yet, Paulina didn't harbor any resentment for her.

Her mother had had the world. She'd lived her life, and she'd enjoyed it. It was up to Paulina to find a way to do the same.

The trembling in her hands made it difficult to clasp it around her neck, but she managed it.

It felt unnerving to be in the house—not only because she half expected Antonio to come stomping in and demand what she was doing, but because she felt so far removed from the person who had once lived within these walls. In a fearsomely short time, Villa Consuelo had become more of a home than the *quinta* ever had.

And Sebastian...

He was more than home to her. Her protector, her heart, the man who had given her things she never knew she could want. She'd awoken with his muscular arm around her waist, his long-limbed body tucked protectively around her, like she had longed to the first night she'd arrived at Villa Consuelo.

So much had happened since the night she had arranged her hair on her pillow in the hopes that Sebastian would visit her in the night. And yet, how much had really changed?

He had refused to believe her when she told him that he was what she wanted. That given every choice in the world, she would choose him, over and over again.

But that only went so far. At some point, he had to choose her, too.

If Paulina was certain of anything, it was that she wasn't willing to settle for anything less than true, unreserved love. Sebastian could keep his doubts and his mistrust. He could push everyone away if it made him feel safer.

Paulina touched the locket resting against her chest, feeling comforted by its solid weight. And then she fashioned a sling for her arm out of an old shawl and began to pack up the house.

Chapter Twenty-One

Sebastian was soaked to the skin before he made it out onto the road that stretched between Villa Consuelo and the Despradels' *quinta*. His horse had never minded the rain, and neither did he—in fact, it felt fitting that the same kind of weather that had delivered Paulina to his doorstep would accompany him to hers.

The lantern by the front door was lit, though it was blowing in the wind, the flame hissing at the raindrops that managed to evade its protective cover. Sebastian struck the old iron knocker against the wood of the door, once, twice, and was about to lift it for a third time when the door opened.

She was in the yellow dress, her hair bound back with a kerchief and a long streak of dust on the prominent curve of her cheekbone. She looked, momentarily, as if she'd had the wind knocked out of her. Then she straightened her back, lifted her chin and said as gracefully as a society matron, "How nice it is to see you here. I'm afraid the house is not fit for company at the moment—"

He let out a bark of laughter, though what he wanted was to howl.

"You needn't let me in if you don't want to," he told her. "I only came to tell you something."

The glimmer of curiosity was obvious even through her polite, "Oh?"

"I do trust you. The one I haven't been able to trust is myself. Not because I didn't love you, but because I knew what would happen if I did. I…" Sebastian rubbed a hand over the back of his head. "If you had asked me as much as a day ago, I would have told you that I'm not a man who has ever lived in fear. And yet, that's what I've been doing for years."

"Fear?" she asked softly.

"Of losing more than I already had. Of being left by yet another loved one. I realize now how selfish that was—keeping you at arm's length so that I wouldn't have to risk the pain of your leaving me. But if you have the courage to choose me, of all people, I should have the courage to love you regardless of what may happen." He let out a breath. "Of course, if you've changed your mind and you really do want to be done with all this, I will take your letter to the governor."

"Sebastian," she said, in an altogether different tone than she had used earlier. She reached up, her fingertips featherlight on his dripping jaw. "I didn't want to leave you. I thought it was what *you* wanted."

A sharp, bright ray of hope lanced through him.

"In that case…" His aching fingers released the door frame. "I never gave you a wedding present."

She frowned at the sudden change in subject. "That hardly…"

Sebastian didn't mean to let her finish. Thrusting his hand into his pocket, he held out a small box. It wasn't covered in velvet, nor bound with a silk ribbon, but its contents were no less precious for that. "Please. Just look at it."

Her frown didn't budge even as she unwound the twine holding the box closed—in fact, it only grew deeper when she plucked out what Sebastian had laid inside. "A scrap of newspaper?"

"A promise," Sebastian said softly. The square he had neatly clipped out of that day's paper contained a listing of all the houses for sale in town. "And a question. I can't give you the world, but I can give you a family. Paulina Despradel, would you like to make a home with me?"

The frown faltered. "Sebastian, I…"

"You're the light of my life. And it wouldn't be much of one if I couldn't spend it beside you. I should have told you so weeks ago, the moment I realized I had fallen in love with you. I want you," he said in a ragged whisper. "And the opportunity to give you the world. All of it. A house in town, and a dozen children to fill it up and to have frolics with. All the dresses and candlesticks and tablecloths your heart could wish for. Everything you have longed for, and everything you deserve."

Her hand drifted to his shoulder, which she used as leverage as she rose on her tiptoes and sought the side of his neck with her lips. "I do love you, you know."

Her mouth found his, and she melted against him, as if her body no longer had the will or the reason to offer any resistance to their melding into one. Sebastian pressed her against the ancient wooden door, feeling her dress absorb the rainwater from his clothes until she was as soaked as he was. Beyond the wooden porch, the rain continued to pour down, faster now, and the thunder rumbling in the distance was as loud as Sebastian's pounding heart.

"I could curse at the fates for the way they brought us

together," he told her, spanning his hands over her narrow, uncorseted waist and letting them trail down the swell of her hips. He laid a delicate kiss on the corner of her lips, smiling when she tilted her face up for another. "But I will never regret the fact that they did."

Chapter Twenty-Two

Two years later

The pale yellow house at the end of Calle de la Restauración was fairly ringing with noise on the day of Paulina's twenty-third birthday.

Paulina had sold the Despradel *quinta* to Sebastian's foreman, but they still owned Villa Consuelo. The handsome old house welcomed them and their friends on the occasional weekend jaunt to the country. Most of their time, however, was spent in town, in the house they had built on San Pedro's busiest street.

With its balcony that overlooked the plaza where the town's residents promenaded on the weekends, and two long galleries shaded by cascades of white bougainvillea that Paulina used as a ballroom whenever the occasion arose, it was everything Paulina had imagined it would be when she saw the land being advertised for sale in the newspaper.

The parlor was as large and airy as she had once dreamed, its tall windows hung with delicate lace drapery that filtered the light and cast intricate shadows on the plush upholstered armchairs and shapely tables. Brass electric lamps with shades like miniature moons were dotted around the room—all the better, Sebastian said laughingly, to complement Paulina's luminosity.

Best of all, the house was equipped with modern plumbing and a great claw-footed bathtub next to which Sebastian kept a stool, so that he could keep her company while she bathed…and kiss the droplets that trailed down her back when she rose out of the water.

Her good taste in furnishings had been a source of intense conversation among all the friends she had made in town, who flocked to her for help in decorating their own homes. Devouring many a book on the subject, she had smugly informed Sebastian that the blue-and-white candlesticks she had chosen at Don Enrique's store were actually jasperware, and likely designed by Mr. Wedgwood himself.

Her favorite part of the house, however, was the wall where the portrait of her parents hung next to a daguerreotype of Carlos that Dilia had given them and a framed painting of Villa Consuelo that Sebastian had commissioned. In a prominent place beside them was a photograph of what Paulina called their *true* wedding—the one they'd held in Villa Consuelo, four months after the one that had been forced on them by Antonio.

Once the thunderclouds left behind by his death had receded, Paulina had allowed herself to mourn. Not so much his person, but what could have been. The brother she could've had if he had cared for her half as much as he'd cared about maintaining his wealth and influence. The scars he had left behind would take a long time to heal, but she was well on her way.

Paulina was up on a stool, nailing a garland of greenery above the frames, when the mouthwatering scent of *lambí empanadas* preceded Sebastian into the room. He almost dropped the platter he was holding when he saw her aloft. Setting it hastily on a side table, he hurried to her side, arms outstretched.

"I won't fall, you know," she said with amusement, staying on her perch as he wrapped his arms around her hips. "I fixed this stool myself."

"I know," he said, looking up at her. "But you won't deny me the pleasure of helping you down, will you?"

She held the back of his head, stroking his close-cropped hair as he laid a kiss on the barely perceptible swell beneath the waistband of her skirt. "I can't seem to deny you much of anything these days."

"Isn't that the truth!" Doña Josefa bustled in from the hallway, a vase full of flowers in one hand. She frowned when she saw the precariously placed platter of *empanadas* and went immediately to its rescue, nudging it farther onto the table. "You're getting to be quite spoiled these days, my boy. Along with someone I won't name."

That someone toddled in at her heels, managing to grab an *empanada* and shove it into his mouth before any of the adults could react.

Paulina felt Sebastian's laugh vibrating against her stomach. "All right," she told her husband, "get me down from here so I can help Josefa defend the *empanadas* from ravishment."

"Oh, let Carlitos eat," Sebastian said comfortably. "I can always go and get more."

"You're not going anywhere," Paulina told him. "There's a lot to do before the party tonight. And like my mother used to say, the preparations are half the fun."

"Before we get started on the fun," Sebastian said, helping Paulina down and extracting a small velvet box from his pocket. "Carlitos, will you help me give Mama her birthday present?"

Obligingly, their son toddled away from the *empanadas* on his chubby little legs. Paulina and Sebastian both crouched to receive him, and he nestled comfortably into Sebastian's arms as Paulina opened the velvet box.

Inside lay a length of red ribbon. Paulina misted over, more touched than if the box had contained a handful of diamonds and pearls. She unwound the ribbon, meaning to tie it immediately into her hair even though it clashed with her leaf-green skirt…and gasped out loud when she caught a glimpse of the bracelet nestled beneath it. Caught between twining bands of gold were diamonds, pearls and tiny beads of amber that looked as if they had been carved into roses to match the earrings he'd given her almost two years before.

"Do you like it?" Sebastian perched his chin on Carlitos's curls and regarded her with his intense brown eyes. Paulina knew he meant more than the ribbon, or even the bracelet.

"It's all I ever wanted," she said and kissed him.

* * * * *

If you enjoyed this story, be sure to look out for more great books from Lydia San Andres, coming soon!